BLURB

They said we were lucky to survive.
But they didn't see what came after.

Seventeen-year-old Isadora was supposed to die that night—on a quiet road, in a twisted wreck, with nothing but memories in her hands. Instead, she woke up underground, trapped in a stranger's basement with no way out... and no one coming.

Her captor calls it a second chance.
He says they're a family now.

But family doesn't chain you to the bed.
Family doesn't watch you beg.
And family doesn't bring home a little girl and call her your sister.

As days turn into years, Isadora learns to hide her pain behind a smile, and Selecia learns to survive by becoming what he wants. But freedom comes at a price. And in a place where every choice is controlled, the hardest part isn't escaping...

It's deciding who you'll become when you do.

A chilling and emotional psychological thriller about trauma, sisterhood, and the fight to reclaim freedom—even when your past refuses to let you go.
Perfect for fans of *Still Missing*, *Room*, and *Verity*.

Registered with the U.S. Copyright Office.
Cover design and formatting by Gabrielle Bosch.
First Edition: 2025
ISBN: 9798293408221

Printed in the United States of America
Published by Amazon Kindle Direct Publishing
www.amazon.com

For inquiries or permissions, contact:
gabriellebosch2015@gmail.com

Dedication

To my mom,

Thank you for believing in me through every chapter—especially the hardest ones.
Your unwavering support, love, and encouragement gave me the strength to write this story and the courage to share it. This book would not exist without you.

And to every survivor—every silent voice and every soul still healing—this story is for you.

The Fatal Crash is a work of fiction, but the pain, fear, and longing for freedom it explores are very real for many. If you've lived through trauma, loss, or abuse, please know this: you are not alone. You are not what happened to you. You are strong, you are worthy, and you deserve peace.

This story does not aim to glorify pain—it aims to give it voice.

If you are struggling, please reach out. Help exists. Hope exists. Healing is possible.

You are not alone.

Resources for Support (U.S.)

RAINN (Rape, Abuse & Incest National Network)
- 1-800-656-HOPE (4673) — 24/7 free & confidential
- www.rainn.org

National Domestic Violence Hotline
- 1-800-799-SAFE (7233) — 24/7 with translation available
- www.thehotline.org

National Suicide & Crisis Lifeline
- Dial 988 — Free, confidential mental health support
- 988lifeline.org

⚠ TRIGGER WARNING LIST FOR THE FATAL CRASH

This novel contains sensitive and potentially distressing content. Please review the following list before reading:

- Abuse & Trauma

Child abduction and long-term captivity

Psychological manipulation, gaslighting, and grooming

Physical abuse (e.g., slapping, confinement, hair-pulling)

Emotional and verbal abuse

Sexual assault (non-graphic, with lasting consequences including pregnancy)

Forced isolation and deprivation (food, sleep, hygiene)

Use of restraints and locked rooms

Coercion under threat and delusional "family" roles

Power imbalances between adult and minor

Complex trauma endured over multiple years

☐ Violence & Suicide

Suicide (both successful and attempted, including a minor character)

Threats of violence and physical intimidation

Off-page murder and suicide (including the abuser)

Graphic emotional breakdowns

- Mental Health Struggles

PTSD symptoms, panic attacks, and dissociation

Depression, anxiety, and hopelessness

Survivor's guilt and internalized shame

Suicide ideation and mental health crises

⬜ Family & Sexual Trauma

Incestuous undertones and past sexual abuse by a parent (non-graphic)

Toxic family relationships and abandonment

Discovery of abuse by a parent post-captivity

Pregnancy resulting from assault and subsequent abortion

Adoption/foster care instability

- Medical & Bodily Themes

Physical deterioration from abuse

Pregnancy and medical trauma

Menstrual trauma due to hygiene denial

Discomfort with bodily changes after assault

- Other Sensitive Content

Law enforcement involvement and relocation via witness protection

Trauma-related memory loss and identity changes (name, records)

Death of an abuser without justice

Depictions of survivors rebuilding life post-captivity

Reader's Discretion Advised: This novel explores the psych

PROLOGUE

I could feel the weight of every second as the clock ticked and time crawled forward. My mind constantly replaying the trauma, searching for an explanation- one I would probably never find, searching for meaning in the madness. Each sound echoed with a deeper menace than the last, every word from him twisted into a reminder of what he had taken.

When I was little, all I wanted was to grow up and be like my parents. They were successful people who never seemed to struggle. But that was only what they showed the rest of the world. Behind closed doors, they were on the brink of divorce and never paid any attention to me, at least not the kind I needed. My father's praise was rare and fleeting, and my mother's concern always filtered through the lens of her career.

Ever since I could remember, I was taught to keep my problems confined to my bedroom. "Don't cause a scene," they'd say. "You're lucky to live the life you do," they'd say. But luck didn't keep my bedroom door locked at night. And it didn't stop my father's hand from wandering into places it never should have.

I found it ironic that the bedroom that should have been a safe place became my prison. Though that prison seemed like nothing in comparison to the hell I was in now. It wasn't uncommon for my bedroom door to creak open in the dead of night, and the shadows that spilled in weren't comforting. They were haunting. As exhausting as hiding my truth had been during high school, I would've preferred that torment over this. I had traded one hell for another, and my situation hadn't improved. If anything, it had escalated. I used to dream of freedom, of escape, of walking across a graduation stage and boarding a plane to anywhere outside of Hadleigh, Arizona. But now? Now I just wanted to survive another day.

Growing up, my parents always told me I had to work hard and make something of myself. They believed money could insulate me from pain—that success would spare me the struggles they had faced. And so, they pushed. My mother, Juniper Callista Rose, was a top cardiothoracic surgeon. My father, James Carter Rose, was a well-known anesthesiologist. Together, they were a power couple, and yes, they had heard every joke about their matching names.

They had met in the sterile halls of the hospital, fallen in love under fluorescent lights, and never looked back. Or at least that's how the story went. To the world, they were brilliant, compassionate, picture-perfect. But to me, they were absent, emotionally unavailable, and eventually dangerous. Their careers kept them away most nights, and I vividly remember sitting at the table, crying as I waited for dinner, wishing my parents would come home and eat with me.

As I got older, I stopped hoping they'd walk through the door and instead began to welcome my father's absence. I learned to cook for myself and take care of my own needs. The days when it was just my mom at home were my favorite. I loved her deeply, and even though her career demanded a great deal from her, I always knew she cared for me. I would have traded every dollar they earned for a family dinner, a bedtime story, or a heartfelt conversation.

Hadleigh was a small town where secrets had short life spans. With a population of just over 7 thousand people, everybody knew everybody. Or at least they thought they did. That made survival in the town even harder. Reputation was currency here, and whispers behind cupped hands forged mine.

Getting a summer job wasn't just about independence; it was about rewriting my story. I needed people to see I wasn't just the pampered daughter of the town's doctors. I was also hardworking; I knew struggle, and I had dreams. And if I could prove that, maybe just maybe- they'd stop looking at me like I was the enemy. Like I was this fragile, spoiled child, made of glass.

All of that led to this moment. To this mattress. This chain. This basement.

The door above slammed open, and footsteps thudded on the stairs like thunder. My heart raced with primal terror.

I couldn't breathe. I scanned the dim, mold-stained room. The frayed mattress I lay on reeked of mildew. Chains bit into my ankle, heavy and cold. This wasn't a nightmare. This was real. And I had no idea if anyone was coming to save me.

CHAPTER 1: THE BEGINNING

One year earlier

"Hey, Mom! I got the job!" I shouted as I burst through the front door, the words tumbling out of me like they were on fire. "I'm going to be waitressing at the Cheesecake Factory downtown. They just called. My first shift starts at eight—well, I have to be there at seven for my uniform and training." I didn't wait for a reply. Not that I expected one. I bolted up the stairs two at a time, heart pounding, fueled by a rare surge of excitement.

I threw open my closet, dug out my best pair of navy jeans and a fitted T-shirt, and then stood in front of the mirror —just a little gloss, a bit of mascara, and some eyeliner— Tara's trademark tutorial. I smirked, hearing her voice in my head, coaching me like she always did. Tara wasn't just my best friend; she was the closest thing I had to another sister. We'd survived private school drama together at Rosetta Stone High—a polished place full of privilege and whispered secrets. Having her in my corner made the world feel less sharp.

By 6:50, I was in my car, adjusting the AC and smoothing my shirt for the fifth time. The 2019 Tesla—my parents' idea of a "practical gift"—was all sleek surfaces and cold luxury. It didn't say "I love you," not really. But I knew better than to expect warmth from them. I would've traded every feature for one honest conversation. Then again, maybe that was part of why I was doing this—to prove something. To them, to my classmates, to myself. That I wasn't just the daughter of Juniper and James Rose. That I had something of my own.

Charlotte would've been proud of me. She was only five, but she was my shadow. I tucked her in most nights, packed her lunches, and protected her in ways no one ever protected me. I did for her what I had always wished someone would do for me. If I could build a better future, it would be for both of us. The Cheesecake Factory smelled like butter and ambition. I met Samantha, the manager, who was brisk but not unkind. She handed me my uniform and ran through the basics like she'd done it a thousand times before. I didn't mind. I learned fast. I wanted to learn. By the time I hit my third table, I'd found a rhythm. Smile. Seat. Take orders. Deliver plates. Smile again. It wasn't hard, and weirdly, it felt good to be needed. To be seen.

That was the night I met him.

He was slouched in a booth near the window, shoulders hunched, eyes rimmed red like he hadn't slept in days. Shaggy brown hair fell across his forehead. He looked... broken. At the time, I told myself that's why I approached him with such care. I placed my hand lightly on the edge of his table. "Hey. Would you like me to bring you something?" He flinched at the sound of my voice. Then slowly, he looked up.

"My name's Isadora. I'm your server tonight. Are you okay?"

There was a long pause, then a sigh. "Found out my fiancée's been cheating on me. Today."

My chest tightened. "I'm sorry. That's awful."

"Yeah. It is."

I offered a soft smile. "Well, it's her loss. Can I get you

something to eat?"

He nodded. "Fettuccini Alfredo. Black coffee."

"You got it."

I walked away, thinking that would be the end of it. Another table. Another tip. But I felt his eyes on me the entire night. That was the first time Blake entered my world. And I had no idea how far he'd go to stay in it.

CHAPTER 2: THE REPEAT CUSTOMER

He came back the next night. And the night after that. Always in my section. Always ordering the same thing —Fettuccini Alfredo and black coffee. I learned his name was Blake. He was polite, almost overly so. He spoke softly, always with this careful calm that made my skin crawl. But it wasn't anything he did at first; it was more what I felt. A tension under my skin I couldn't explain. At first, I told myself he was just lonely. Many people came in for the company more than for the food. But Blake never talked to the other servers, never smiled at anyone else. Just me. He asked me things—harmless things at first: What school do I go to? Do I like working here? What are my plans after graduation?

I gave polite, vague answers. I'd had customers take an interest before. It didn't mean anything. But he never broke eye contact. Tara noticed him one night and leaned in as we passed each other between tables. "You've got a fan."

I rolled my eyes. "He's just being friendly."

"Friendly is a smile and a tip. This guy's one stare away from writing poetry on napkins." I laughed, but deep down, I wasn't sure she was wrong.

That night after closing, I walked out to my car in the back lot. The sun had long since gone down, and the air was thick with heat and quiet. As I unlocked the door, I noticed a car a few spaces away, engine running. Someone sat inside. Watching. When I turned to look directly, the headlights flashed on, and the car pulled away slowly. I told myself I was being paranoid. That it wasn't him. The next shift, he showed up with a bouquet of green roses. I wouldn't learn until later that roses symbolized fresh starts and a new beginning.

"For you," he said, placing them on the table before I even opened my mouth. "I thought you might need cheering up."

I forced a smile. "That's very thoughtful, but I'm not allowed to accept gifts from customers."

His smile didn't budge. "It's just flowers. Not exactly contraband."

"I know, but company policy. I could get in trouble."

His face tightened, just for a second. "Right. Of course." He ordered his usual, but barely touched it. And he didn't talk much after that—just watched me. Eyes too focused, too still. Later, after we'd closed, I found him waiting outside the side door—the one the staff used.

"Isadora."

I flinched at the sound of my name. "Blake? You scared me."

He stepped toward me. Not threatening—just... close. "Sorry. I didn't mean to. I just thought, maybe, you'd like to grab a drink or something? Off the clock. You've been kind to me. I thought we had a connection." My heart dropped into my shoes.

"I'm seventeen," I said quickly, trying to keep my voice even.

He blinked. "So?"

"I'm still in high school."

He looked confused, as if he were trying to do the math. "Age doesn't matter when people connect."

"No," I said firmly. "It does. And I'm not interested. I hope you understand."

His jaw clenched, and for a second, I saw something flicker across his face, disappointment maybe. Or something darker. But then he nodded, slowly. "Of course," he said. "Just thought… never mind."

I got into my car and locked the door before he could say anything else. He didn't follow me. Just stood there, watching. The next night, he didn't come in. I thought maybe that was it. But the night after that, he returned. He didn't sit in my section this time. Didn't order food. Just sat at the bar, watching. Every move I made, every laugh I shared with a table, every plate I carried—his eyes followed me. Tara noticed. "Okay, no. This is not normal anymore."

"He hasn't said anything."

"Exactly. Creepy silence is worse than awkward flirting." I told her I'd be fine, that I'd park closer to the entrance. That I'd text her when I got home.

The following Friday, she offered to drive me. My car had been acting up, and I was almost tempted to say yes. But I didn't want to inconvenience her. "I'll be fine," I told her again—famous last words. I took my usual route home—Route 68, past the stretch of nothingness where the trees pressed too close to the road and the streetlights barely worked. My headlights were the only thing slicing through the dark. That's when I saw them—another pair of headlights. Behind me. Getting closer. Too close. I changed lanes. The car followed.

I sped up. So did they. My chest tightened. I gripped the wheel and kept my eyes on the road. Then the car behind me swerved left, shot forward, and slammed in front of me.

I slammed on the brakes. The screech of tires. The shattering crash. Metal twisted. The airbag exploded into my chest. Pain erupted across my ribs. The world spun sideways.

I coughed, disoriented, trying to move—but the seatbelt was locked tight. Smoke curled around my head. A door opened. Footsteps. My door was yanked open. Blake. No expression. No hesitation.

He reached in, unbuckled me, and dragged me from the wreck. I kicked weakly, shouted something, but he shoved something damp over my face—a rag. The world faded fast. The last thing I heard was his voice, calm and chilling: "I told you we had a connection."

CHAPTER 3: THE BASEMENT

I woke up to darkness and pain. My head throbbed, my mouth was dry, and for a moment, I didn't know where I was or what had happened. I tried to sit up, but something heavy tugged at my leg. A sharp, cold weight. A chain. My pulse spiked. I scrambled to sit up right, gasping as the room tilted around me. My temple was sore, and I could feel the dried, crusted blood down the side of my face.

My hands trembled as I pressed my fingers lightly to the side of my head. I blinked, trying to clear the haze from my eyes. I wasn't in a hospital. I was on a stained mattress in what I assumed was a basement—concrete walls, no windows, one flickering bulb overhead. A bucket sat in the corner. A tray of food, a turkey sandwich, and a bottle of water sat on the floor a few feet away. The chain around my ankle was bolted to the wall. It only took a few seconds for me to take in my surroundings fully. Panic consumed me. I screamed till my voice was raw. Praying that someone would hear me, someone would come for me. I didn't even consciously decide to scream; it just erupted out of me—a raw, broken sound. I screamed again and again, until my throat ached and I collapsed against the mattress, fighting to bring air into my lungs.

The door at the top of the stairs creaked open—footsteps on the stairs. I scrambled backwards. I pressed myself as close to the wall as I could get. Then I saw him. Blake. He came down slowly, carrying another tray, this one with a bowl of what looked like soup and a spoon. He looked at me like I was a sick animal he had rescued.

"You're awake," he said, like it was good news. "I was starting to worry."

"What is this?" My voice cracked. "Where am I?"

He set the tray on the floor and crouched near the mattress. "You're safe."

"Safe?" I spat the word. "You crashed into me! I should be in a hospital!"

"I saved you," he said. "You were hurt. I couldn't just leave you there."

"You Kidnapped me!"

His jaw clenched, making his anger even more apparent. "No. I brought you here because you needed someone to care for you. You don't know it yet, but this is the best thing that could have happened to you."

I couldn't breathe. The walls were pressing into me on all sides. "You're insane!"

His eyes flickered. "Don't say that. I know how this looks. But I've seen you, Isadora. Isadora Amber Rose, I've seen you. At work, at school. You're drowning in that perfect life of yours. No one sees you. No one listens." He wasn't entirely wrong, but that didn't mean he was right. Nothing could make this ok. He wasn't making anything better.

He stood up and gestured to the soup. "You need to eat something. Your body's been through a lot."

" I'm not eating anything you give me."

His expression hardened, then softened again like he was forcing it. "That's your choice. But I want you to be strong. We are going to build a life here, a family. You and me." A life? My stomach turned. I wasn't sure I wanted to know what he meant.

He walked back towards the stairs. "Rest. We'll talk more tomorrow."

"Please," I called after him. "Let me go." He paused, one hand on the railing.

"No one's looking yet," he said quietly. "And by the time they do, I'll make sure there's nothing to find." Then he disappeared upstairs. The lock clicked, and I was alone. I sank back into the mattress, the chain rattling with my movement. The silence was too loud. I could hear each of my breaths. My heartbeat rang like a drum in my ears. This couldn't be real. But it was. And no one even knew I was gone.

CHAPTER 4:
THE RULES

I had lost all sense of time. There were no windows to show the sun rising and setting. No sunlight to break up the endless gray. No clocks. Just the flickering overhead bulb, the hum of old pipes, and the sound of my breath echoing off the concrete walls. The chain gave me maybe six feet of movement. Just enough to reach the stained mattress, the bucket in the corner, and the tray Blake left with food that tasted like cardboard and metal. It didn't matter. I ate it anyway. My hunger was louder than my pride.

It must have been days. Even though I said I wouldn't eat anything he gave me, I gave in. My stomach cramped with the force of my hunger. He had been gone for days. The two trays he had left were long gone. The silence pressed down on me like a weight I couldn't lift. I had resorted to talking to myself to break up the quiet. I pretended I was talking to Tara or Charlotte. They had to be looking for me by now.

The cold seeped in through the floor and settled in my bones. I paced in circles until my legs gave out. I curled up on the mattress until my muscles ached. I counted cracks in the wall. I screamed until my throat burned. No one answered. Eventually, I stopped crying. I wouldn't do that again, as my dehydration had become unbearable. My throat felt like fire.

When the door opened again, I was ready, almost relieved. He hadn't left me to die. Blake came down the stairs holding another tray, along with a plastic bag. "Hey," he said, like this was normal. "I brought you something." I couldn't answer. He pulled out a pair of leggings and a sweatshirt and tossed them onto the mattress. "I thought you might want to change. It gets cold down here." It did get cold down there. I had spent days shivering on this mattress, starving, walking in circles so I wouldn't freeze. I didn't move. I didn't speak. I just stared at him.

He set the tray down carefully, as if I were an unpredictable animal. " Soup again. I added some apple slices this time. I thought it might be nice." I kept staring. Blake sat on the old wooden crate across the room, resting his elbows on his knees. I slowly reached for the tray. Shoveling food in my mouth, I watched him warily.

"I know this isn't what you wanted. But I need you to understand I didn't do this to hurt you," he said.

"Then why did you?" My voice came out broken and raspy. "Why did you take me?"

He looked at me for a long moment. "Because you were disappearing. Every time I saw you at work, I could tell. You smiled, but it never really reached your eyes. You were always so polite, so good, but it was like you weren't really there."

I felt bile rise in my throat at the thought of him watching me. "That's not your decision to make."

He nodded like he understood, but I knew he didn't. "You're right. But I couldn't just let it go. Not again." Again? I didn't ask. I didn't care. I didn't want to know more about him. I wanted to go home. He reached into his pocket and pulled out a folded paper. "I think it's important we have some ground rules."

I blinked at him. "Ground rules?"

"I know this is a lot, but if we both know what to expect, it'll be easier. Safer. More... comfortable." He laid the paper on the floor and smoothed it out with his hand. "Here's what I came up with."

He began to read:

1. You will eat everything I bring you to eat.
2. You will not scream or try to leave
3. You will not lie
4. You will be polite and respectful
5. If you disobey, you will be punished
6. If you are good, you earn privileges. But you can also lose them

My eyes burned with tears I refused to shed. "I'm not your pet."

He shook his head. "No. You're more than that. You're someone I care about. You are mine. And if you let me, I can help you feel whole again." He stood up and looked down at me with a calm expression that heightened my terror more than his anger ever could. "You'll see—one day. You'll thank me," he said as he turned and climbed the stairs.

"Wait!" I shouted. "Blake, please, at least tell me how long I've been here!"

He stopped and looked down at me. "A few days. Maybe a week." He said it like it didn't matter. He didn't even know. And then he was gone again. The lock clicked. I curled into myself and pulled the sweatshirt to my chest. It smelled like detergent and dust. I didn't cry this time. Instead, I started to think. Blake wanted me to be compliant. Sweet and polite. To be quiet. To earn "Privileges." Fine. I could play along. I wasn't giving up, because I was going to survive. And when I got out of here, I'd make damn sure he didn't.

CHAPTER 5: THE GIRL

I woke to the sound of the lock turning. It caught my attention because every day had been the same for so long. I don't know how long I've been here, but nothing ever changes. I sat cross-legged on the mattress, pretending to read one of the eight tattered books Blake had brought me. I had no idea what time it was or even what day it was. I'd stopped trying to count. My body felt sluggish, like it had forgotten how to measure time altogether. But the second I heard the footsteps, I sat up straighter. Something was different. They didn't sound right.

They weren't Blake's usual slow, heavy steps. These were lighter. Uneven. Hesitant. And then I heard a voice. A girl's voice. Soft. Confused.

"Where are we?"

I froze. There was a pause, and then Blake's calm response: "This is your new home." No. No. No. No. No. No, my thoughts screamed.

I scrambled to my feet, the chain tugging hard at my ankle. I stumbled forward, reaching the edge of my space just as the basement door creaked open. Blake appeared holding a small duffel bag. Behind him, partially hidden by his frame, was a girl, maybe eleven or twelve years old. Light skin, long blonde braids, oversized hoodie, and blue eyes so wide they barely blinked. He walked down slowly, gently guiding her as if he were bringing a shy animal into a new enclosure.

"Isadora," Blake said with a soft smile, "I want you to meet someone very special." The girl looked at me warily, then at the chain on my ankle. I wanted to tell her to run, but I was frozen in place. "This is Selecia," he continued. "She's going to stay with us now," He turned to her. "Say hi." Selecia didn't move. I stared at her, stunned. My mouth opened, but no words came out. Who knows how long I have been in this basement? She was the first person I had seen since I arrived, other than Blake.

"She's like you," he said, voice full of pride. "She was lonely. Abandoned. She needs someone, too."

I backed away slowly, my chest tightening with his every word. I finally found my voice. " You... you brought a child here?"

"She's twelve," he said, as if that made it better. "Barely had anyone, her foster family didn't care. I found her walking home from school. Alone. Again." He said it in that way; he used to justify everything.

"You kidnapped her," I whispered.

"I saved her," he said, eyes narrowing. "Just like I saved you." Selecia stayed by the stairs, arms crossed over her chest. She didn't cry. She didn't speak. But I could see it in her eyes: confusion and Fear.

"Where are we?" she asked again, voice barely audible.

Blake didn't answer. He just sat down the bag and reached into it, pulling out a McDonald's bag. He began to place the food where he usually left the trays. "I know you're tired and hungry. This is your room now. You and Isadora can get to know each other," he stated. My heart broke. He was creating a family. Twisted, fake, and built on control—but in his mind, it was real.

"She can't be here," I said quietly, stepping closer. "You can't do this to her."

"She needs you," he said, cutting me off. "She needs

someone like you. You understand what it's like to be forgotten, neglected."

My hands shook. I haven't talked back in a long time. I know the consequences now. My voice shook with rage. "She's a child!"

Blake turned, facing Selecia. "Why don't you sit with Isadora? She's very kind. She will help you." He didn't give her much of a choice as he grabbed the duffel once more and brought out another chain, thicker than mine, newer. I saw it and felt sick. Selecia looked at me, then at the chain on my ankle.

"No," Selecia said quickly, her eyes narrowing. "I'm not doing that."

Blake crouched in front of her, a smile still painted on like a mask. "It's for your safety. Just until you settle in."

"No," she said louder this time, stepping back. "I'm not staying here. I want to leave!" I held my breath. I wanted to grab her and shield her, but I couldn't move fast enough. I wasn't strong enough. The chain around my own ankle reminded me how powerless I really was.

Blake's smile didn't waver. "It's not safe out there. You were walking alone. Remember?"

"I wasn't alone!" she screamed, backing into the wall, her fists clenched. "I don't want this! I'm not like her!"

The words stung, but I didn't blame her. "Blake, we don't need her in our family. Let her go." I yelled at him desperately. Praying that he would change his mind.

"I know what we need, Isadora," Blake growled. Selecia lunged toward the stairs, but Blake caught her easily. She kicked and twisted, shrieking as she fought him. I saw a flash of her sneaker collide with his shin. He grunted but didn't yell. He never yelled anymore; now his rage came in silence.

"Let me go! Get off of me!" she screamed, tears streaming down her face now. Her voice cracked with raw terror, and something inside of me shattered. Blake wrestled her toward the pipe, locking her wrists together in his grasp. Her foot caught his knee, but it was too late. He pulled the cuff closed around her ankle with one hard tug. She collapsed, panting, curled in on herself, sobbing.

He didn't say a word, just stood there for a second. He was breathing heavily; his eyes glazed over with something cold. Then he turned and walked up the stairs like our entire lives hadn't just shifted.

"I'll come back later," He tossed over his shoulder as he closed and locked the door.

Selecia didn't look at me. Her shoulders were shaking. Her hands were red from where she'd clawed at him, at the chain, at anything she could grasp. I crawled closer, slow and careful, and sat beside her without saying a word. Tears silently streaming down my cheeks. For a long time, neither of us moved.

Finally, she whispered, "I hate him."

I nodded. "Me too." We sat there in silence, both of us chained to the same pipe. She was still trembling. I wanted to promise I'd protect her. But I'd made that promise to myself once, too. And I was still here.

CHAPTER 6: RUN

Selecia didn't speak much for the first few days. She stayed curled up on the opposite side of the mattress, arms wrapped tightly around her knees, eyes staring at nothing. She slept with one eye open, at least it seemed that way, and flinched anytime there was a noise from upstairs. Her wrist was still raw from where she'd clawed at Blake. Her ankle was red and swollen from her tugging at the chain when she thought I wasn't looking, as if sheer will might break it loose. I didn't blame her. I had been right; Blake didn't need to yell. His punishment was silence. Withdrawal. It had been at least two days since we had seen him. He hadn't brought food or water or even come down to taunt us. This was his version of anger. He used starvation and neglect as a quiet, calculated reminder that we were at his mercy.

We didn't talk much at first. Just exchanged a few short answers here and there, mostly practical stuff.

"It's your turn to use the bucket."

"He still hasn't brought water."

"How long do you think it's been?"

Awkward, mechanical routines that didn't feel like bonding. I wasn't used to anyone being around anymore. I'm not sure I even remember how to have an everyday conversation. But slowly, she started talking to me more. Quiet things. Careful things. She asked about the chain. About how long I'd been there. About what he was capable of.

Blake finally returned like nothing had happened — sat

down a tray of food, smiled like he was dropping off groceries in a typical house, and walked away. Then the next day, he brought more: a small box of crayons, two blankets, and a radio that only worked sometimes. The day after that, he brought books and a shelf, as if he were furnishing a life like he was building a home.

Selecia didn't speak to him, not unless he demanded it, but she started talking more to me. I learned that her birthday was in November, she liked drawing animals, and that her favorite color was sky blue. That she hated raisins and had been in four different foster homes before Blake took her. He parents had died in a fire when she was 7 years old.

She never used the word 'kidnapped,' and neither did I —not out loud. We both knew but didn't want to acknowledge it. One night when the lightbulb overhead had dimmed to its usual flicker, I turned to her and asked, "What's the first thing you'll do when you get out of here?"

She didn't even hesitate. "Run. I want to feel the ground beneath my feet. The wind in my hair."

I smiled a little. "Yeah. Me too. I used to hate running, too."

She looked over at me then. Really looked at me. Do you think anyone's looking for you?"

The question hit me like a slap. I wanted to say yes. I wanted to believe that Charlotte missed me, that Tara had called the cops, that someone noticed I was gone. That my mother cared despite her distance. But I didn't know anymore. "I hope so," I said.

Selecia was quiet for a while. Then she said, " I didn't really have a home before this, but I don't want to stay here. Blake tells me I'm important. Like I matter, he tells me I'm part of something now. I know he's crazy, but sometimes I pretend he's right. So, I don't go crazy." I couldn't find a way to respond/

"I do push-ups," she added. "Sit-ups, jumping jacks, until my body hurts too much to think."

I nodded slowly. "Selecia, you are special. Just not for the reasons he says. And that's smart, you are staying strong."

"Not strong," she said. "Just tired." I reached for her hand, and this time she didn't pull away.

CHAPTER 7:
TICKING CLOCK

I woke up with the image of a clock in my head. The ticking second hand, circling endlessly, never stopping, until the moment my eyes opened and I realized there was still no clock. No window. No sun or moon. Just the bulb, flickering. Still watching me.

Selecia stirred beside me, shifting beneath the blanket. She's started sleeping closer to me most nights, rather than curled at the foot of the bed. I waited quietly until I saw her eyes open.

"Selecia," I whispered. "Do you know what day it is?"

She blinked. "What?"

"I need to know what day it is. The date." I pleaded.

She rubbed her eyes. "The day Blake took me was Tuesday... I think. September twenty-ninth."

My stomach dropped. "What year?"

She gave me a weird look. "Two-thousand twenty-one."

I stared up at the ceiling, unable to draw a full breath. "I was taken in May," I whispered, more to myself than to her. May of 2020."

There was silence. Then: "You didn't know?"

"No," I said, shaking my head. "I thought it was still the same year. My voice broke. "I've been down here for 16 months.

Over a year..."

Selecia sat up slowly, legs crossed. I looked at her. "Where were you? When he took you?"

"Phoenix. I was walking home from school. He said my foster mom was arrested and that he was with Child Protective Services. He knew my name." She wiped her eyes as a tear leaked out.

I reached over and took her hand. "You didn't do anything wrong."

"I know," she said quietly. We didn't talk for a long time after that. Then Selecia said, " I hope somebody remembers my birthday. That somebody is looking for us."

My throat tightened. "When is it?"

"November 11th," she replied.

"I'll remember," I said. "We'll celebrate. Even if it's just the two of us."

CHAPTER 8: PLAN

(Blake's POV)

I watched them settle in. Selecia had started asking for paper. She was actually initiating a conversation. Isadora stopped flinching when I walked in. The silence was less tense now, less like fear, more like... acceptance. When Selecia smiled, just once, when I brought her a new set of markers, I felt something settle in my chest. This time it was working. Maybe they were finally starting to see what I had built for them.

Isadora? She was slower to trust. Careful, always guarded. Her eyes were sharp even when her mouth stayed quiet. I didn't mind. She was strong and resilient. She needed time to understand I wasn't the enemy. And if it came down to it, I would make her believe me.

I walked upstairs to prepare their dinner trays. I took pride in this part; I was taking care of them. This wasn't chaos, this was healing. This was routine, structure, family. I had planned this for so long. I was going to create my family. It wasn't just a delusion; it was a detailed plan. And it was almost real.

CHAPTER 9: BIRD IN A CAGE

Selecia drew a bird in a cage. The lines were messy, rushed— but the wings were stretched wide, as if the bird didn't know it was trapped. Below it, in blocky black letters, she wrote:

"STILL"

I taped it to the wall with the roll of Scotch tape that Blake had brought down not too long ago. Our prison had a picture now—one square roll of hope.

"What does it mean?" I asked.

Selecia shrugged. "It means I'm still me. Even in here."

I sat down beside her. "He's watching us," I whispered. I could tell by the blue light on the camera in the corner. The light changed when he was online.

"I know," she said. She looked over at me a couple of minutes later. "I don't want to forget who I am."

"You won't," I promised.

"But you did, right?" she asked softly. "You forgot how long you'd been here. You couldn't remember the date or the year."

That hit like a slap. I opened my mouth, but nothing came out at first. "You aren't me. And it's different for you. You are not alone."

CHAPTER 10: DINNER

He brought down a table. A white plastic fold-out table. With three cheap plastic chairs. In the middle, he placed a bunch of daisies in a chipped glass vase. He set it up in the middle of the basement, as if he were getting ready to host Sunday brunch. Selecia went stiff beside me as we watched him set up. I squeezed her hand.

"I thought we could all eat together tonight," Blake said, his voice cheery. "Families should share meals." He laid out plates—Instant mashed potatoes, dry chicken, and green beans. I didn't look at the food. I looked at him. This was different. And with Blake, it was different and scary.

He pulled out a chair for me. I sat. Selecia hovered behind me. He turned to her and smiled. "Please," he said. She sat. "This is nice, right?" he said, slicing into the chicken. "I always wanted a family like this. Peaceful. Real. I grew up with shouting. Broken things, but this—this is different," he stated as he smiled at us. I bit my tongue until I tasted blood and shot Selecia with a look and an encouraging smile.

He kept talking. He talked about the meal prep, the music playing softly from the speaker he'd brought down. He asked us how our day had been. Like this was normal. Selecia didn't answer. I lightly kicked her foot under the table, and she forced a response. I forced a smile. I played the part. It was the only weapon I had left. After dinner, he packed everything up. He took the table, the plates, and the flowers like it had never happened.

Selecia crawled under the blanket and turned her face

towards the wall, quietly. I sat staring at the space where the vase had been. He wasn't just delusional. He was rehearsing. And I didn't know how long I could keep acting. The longer I bit my tongue and acted polite, the more pissed off I got. Eventually, I was going to explode.

CHAPTER 11: PETALS

The silence after dinner hung heavy in the air, like a blanket soaked in something thick and wrong. Blake had dropped a single daisy on the floor—a fake one, fabric petals faded and crinkled. It sat between the door and the mattress like a forgotten offering. Selecia was still curled under her blanket. I couldn't sleep. My head throbbed. And the fake flower—it reminded me. It reminded me of the first time he brought me real ones in the basement. It was the second time he had given me flowers. The first time he had given me flowers was at the restaurant, and they were green.

It had only felt like a few weeks since the crash. I hadn't eaten in a while. I hadn't bathed in even longer. I was too weak to cry anymore. He came down with a single rose in his hand and a paper towel wrapped around a small chunk of banana bread.

"I want us to have a fresh start," he said softly. "No more fighting. No more hunger." I had barely looked at him. I didn't have the energy. "Here," he said, placing the flower next to me. "For my girl." Then he knelt, pulled my hair back from my face, and pressed his lips against my forehead. His breath was hot. His fingers lingered on my neck for too long. "I could give you so much," he whispered. "But you have to let me."

And I... I didn't move. I didn't flinch. I didn't speak. That was the night I learned the fastest way to avoid punishment was to stay still. The next day, he brought me a full meal.

Now, staring at this fake flower, I felt that same pressure behind my ribs. My lungs were tight. My chest felt empty. He hadn't changed. He was pacing himself.

CHAPTER 12: STEAM

"Do you ever get to take real showers?" Selecia asked. The question made me flinch harder than I expected. And she noticed. "What?" She questioned.

"Nothing." I lied. "Sometimes." She twisted the cap off a water bottle and poured some into her hands, trying to smooth her tangled hair.

"My hair's going to turn into a nest." She complained. I forced a chuckle, but my mind had already gone back to the first time Blake brought up bathing. He had said I needed to earn it. I'd gone, what he said was, three weeks without bathing. My skin crawled with its own stench, my hair heavy with grease. I'd begged and whispered at first, then louder, then through tears. He finally brought a plastic tub and used a bucket to fill it with cold water. He'd told me to say thank you as he handed me a towel. I'd obeyed, trembling. He'd told me not to be afraid that he wouldn't hurt me.

Then his hand grazed my back—too slow. Too firm. He claimed he was helping rinse the soap off, and he'd let me bathe in my T-shirt, which was more than I'd expected. He'd said, "See? I take care of you. This is Love." I hadn't asked for a bath since I was too scared of what he might do.

Selecia nudged me. "You, Okay?"

"Yeah," I whispered. "Just tired." She didn't press. We both had memories we didn't want to describe out loud.

CHAPTER 13:
THE BLANKET

Blake brought us a new blanket today. Selecia smiled when she saw it—it was soft and warm, made of thick, light gray fleece. A stupid part of me wanted to smile, too. But all I could think about was that first winter. He hadn't given me anything. I slept on the mattress without any sheets or covers. He said it was "temporary".

The cold was so bad that I used my socks as mittens. I ran in circles rather than slept because I was afraid I wouldn't wake up. One night I broke. I told him I was freezing. I told him I needed him to take care of me. I was shivering so hard my teeth hurt. My body felt sluggish. He walked down the steps with a single wool blanket in his arms. He draped it over my shoulders, gently, then knelt and took my face in his hands.

"You're finally learning," he whispered. "Good girls get comfort. Bad girls get punished. I needed to see you beg." His thumb brushed my lip. I didn't move, and that night I cried silently into the blanket he had given me. Now, as I tucked the new one over Selecia's legs, I smiled. She didn't have to ever know the price of warmth. And I'd keep it that way for as long as I could.

CHAPTER 14: SISTER

By now, the novelty of Selecia's presence had worn off. I'd grown used to her constant presence. The novelty for Blake hadn't worn off, though. He still insisted on treating every interaction like a staged performance, his delusion of a perfect family unfolding in slow, suffocating scenes. Tonight, he brought a bowl of popcorn, M&M's, and a stack of old DVDs, along with a laptop. He set them down on the small coffee table he had brought down the previous day. He was slowly adding more furniture to the basement. We now had a box spring, a wooden nightstand, and a coffee table.

He set the items on the coffee table with a flourish, as if it were some grand offering. I couldn't remember the last time I had watched a movie. I didn't move from the mattress. Selecia sat cross-legged by the radio, sketching something with one of the dull pencils he'd given us. Blake looked between us, like a proud father. Flashing us with an excited smile.

"You two really are becoming something special," he said. "This... this is what I always wanted." Selecia didn't look up, but I forced myself to give him a timid smile. Blake walked over and crouched beside me. "Isadora," he said, voice low, "I hope you see it now. Everything I've done... it was so you wouldn't be alone."

I couldn't contain my anger and clenched my jaw. "I was never alone."

He frowned but only for a second. "You were. You just didn't know it." He stood and brushed his hands off. "We're all each other has now." Then he opened the laptop and inserted one of the DVDs. A movie began to play, an old Disney one, the kind that would've felt comforting anywhere else. He didn't ask what we wanted to watch. He just made the choice, like always, and stepped back with a smile like he'd done us a favor.

Selecia finally looked at me, and I could see in her eyes how tired she was of hearing this. How weary we both were. "We already know what you want," I said quietly. "You don't have to keep explaining."

Blake smiled, a twisted thing. "It's not about explaining. It's about reminding." And then he stood, packed up the stuff, and walked out. When the door clicked shut, I let out a breath I hadn't realized I was holding.

Selecia set down her pencil. "Does he really think this is what a family looks like? He really believes we are happy?"

"Yeah," I sighed. "He does."

She shook her head. "Then he's more broken than we are." I didn't respond. I just leaned back and stared at the ceiling. Because Broken things... don't always look like they're falling apart. And as much as I hated Blake, I hated even more that she was here. Selecia wasn't supposed to live like this.

I'd learned to survive in the dark, but I'd never be okay with her being trapped in it beside me.

CHAPTER 15: COMPROMISE

The laptop sat on the coffee table once more, playing some scratched-up DVD. It was one of the only DVDs that would actually play. I tried to focus on the screen, on the colors and music, on the way Selecia smiled at every scene with Pascal. But I couldn't enjoy it.

Bake was sitting behind me, too close, his arm draped across the back of the mattress like it belonged there. I could feel the tension in Selecia's body beside mine, even as she tried to watch the movie. I hated this. I hated *him*. But most of all, I hated that U was getting good at pretending.

When the movie ended, he stayed where he was. He didn't move his arm from around me. He didn't speak; he just watched me. "You're getting more comfortable," he said eventually, a quiet triumph in his voice.

"The movie was nice," I said instead of responding.

"Yes, it was." He responded. He had barely watched it. Then he leaned in and pressed a kiss to my cheek. Just one. Soft. Measured. Like he was testing me. My stomach revolted, but I didn't pull away. He noticed.

"I knew you'd come around," he whispered. Selene said nothing. She turned off the laptop and began winding up the charger with trembling fingers. When he finally left, she didn't look at me right away.

"You let him kiss you."

I swallowed hard. "I had to."

"No, you don't. You don't have to let it happen," she retorted back.

"I have to make him believe I am his," I said. "It's the only way we'll ever leave. We can't keep waiting for them to find us. What if they aren't even looking? I'm not staying here forever. I can't do it. This is the only way we have power. I have to get him to bring me upstairs. So, we can escape."

She nodded slowly, lips pressed into a line. "I know. I just... I hate it. I don't want him to hurt you."

"I know. I do too." We sat in silence. The movie was over. Packed up and gone, but the performance had never ended. And every act left a crack that I wasn't sure could ever be undone.

CHAPTER 16: CRACKS IN THE WALL

I hadn't asked Selecia what day it was since that night. I didn't want to confirm how long I'd been here. But I couldn't stop thinking about it for at least a year and a half. And if I was right, it had been a couple of months since Selecia had been brought to the basement. Time bled together, but my memories of him didn't fade; they sharpened. I couldn't picture the faces of my family as clearly. I missed Charlotte with everything I had in me. But I knew she would be about seven now. She might not even really remember me. And Tara, I missed her warmth and friendship so severely that my chest ached.

Blake was getting bolder. That morning, he'd brushed his knuckles along my cheek. Just brushed his fingers lightly over my skin while I lay half-asleep. He said I looked peaceful, like a wife waking from a pleasant dream. I wanted to scream. But instead, I smiled because survival meant pretending.

Selecia was already awake, sketching, and watched it all from the corner of the room. She said nothing. Not when he lingered for too long or stared too hard. Not when he mentioned a "wedding someday." Not when he said she could be our flower girl. But later, when he left, she said, "He thinks this is real."

I nodded. "That's the danger."

"What if he tried to—."

"He won't," I interrupted. "Not yet."

I looked her in the eye. "I said I'd get us out. And I will. But to do that, I have to let him believe he already has me."

She shivered. "How do you pretend so well?" Because I stopped being a child the moment my father first sneaked into my room. I stopped the minute Blake sat in my section, because pretending was safer than fighting. Because Lies were the only thing Blake believed, and he would never listen to the truth. The truth is that I hated him. But I didn't say that.

I just said, "I've had practice."

CHAPTER 17: FAVORITE

"He said you're the heart of the family." Selecia's voice broke the silence as she drew slow, looping lines in the corner of her sketchbook. Her back was against the wall, knees pulled up, and her eyes were locked on the paper. Like if she didn't look at me, it wouldn't hurt to say it.

"What?" I asked, though I already knew. She was here because of me.

"He told me yesterday," she continued. "That you're the one holding us together. That you're the reason he brought me here. 'To give Isadora the sister she always deserved. "I bit the inside of my cheek. "He calls me his little girl now," she added, her voice quieter. "Like it's supposed to make me feel safe." I didn't know how to respond.

"He doesn't... touch me. Not like that," she clarified quickly. "But he watches. Like he's studying me. Testing how well I fit the part."

"That's what he does," I said finally. "He builds a script and expects us to perform it."

Selecia looked up. "And if we don't?"

I met her eyes. "He rewrites the scene. With punishment."

She nodded, eyes glistening. "Is this how you've lived this entire time?"

"Yes." I didn't sugarcoat it. It wouldn't help her. "And I've made peace with surviving, even if it means pretending."

She hesitated at my words. "You pretend... with him?"

I felt my stomach twist. "When I have to."

There was a pause before she asked, "Does it help?"

"No," I whispered. "But it stops him from hurting you."

Her shoulders dropped, and she wiped at her eyes with the sleeve of her shirt. "I hate that you have to do that for me."

"I hate that you are down here at all. I'm sorry." That part always burned the most. I'd found a rhythm in this prison —a strategy. But Blake throwing Selecia into the mix shattered every fragile piece of my routine. No amount of pretending could make this right. She deserved sunlight. Laughter. Freedom. And I would never be okay with her being down here. Ever.

She looked at me carefully, her voice barely a whisper. "Then why do you smile when he touches you?"

My chest ached. "Because if I flinch, he punishes both of us. He doesn't like it when the story doesn't go his way."

She blinked at that. "What did he do to you before I came?"

I sat very still. I wasn't sure I wanted to answer her. "A lot. I've been locked in the dark. I denied food for days. Had my hair yanked until I bled. I've been kissed by a man I wanted to kill. I slept without warmth. I've bled into my pants because he wouldn't bring tampons. I've begged." Her face didn't move, but her eyes welled.

"He said we're a family," she whispered.

"He says a lot of things," I replied. I could tell she didn't understand how anyone could do that. I hope she never has to experience it firsthand. And as long as I was here, she wouldn't.

CHAPTER 18: PRESENT

He brought me a dress. It was a pale blue, knee-length dress with white lace on the sleeves and trim. It was innocent. Like something a child might wear to church. But I knew what it meant to him. Fantasy. He held it out like a peace offering. "I thought we could have dinner tonight. Just the three of us."

I took the dress with careful hands. "Thank you," I whispered.

His face lit up. "You're starting to get it."

When he left, Selecia practically spat, "You're not wearing that."

"I have to."

"No, you really don't." I turned to her. "Yes, I do. You haven't been here for as long as I have. You have to trust me. You don't understand what happens when he feels rejected."

Selecia folded her arms, defiant. "Let him feel rejected."

"He doesn't get sad. He gets dangerous." She opened her mouth, but I cut her off. "I'll wear it. I'll smile. And I'll survive."

Her eyes softened. "You shouldn't have to."

"I know," I whispered. But I would.

CHAPTER 19:
THE DINNER

He set up the white folding table in the corner of the basement, as if it were a picnic. Three paper plates. A battery-powered lantern. Three cups of orange juice. A napkin was folded neatly beside each plant, like we were in a restaurant and not this hellhole he had trapped us in.

I walked slowly in the dress. The fabric itched at my sides. It was too tight around the ribs.

"You look stunning," Blake complimented.

"Thank you," I murmured back obediently as I sat down. Selecia sat down quietly as well, but Blake didn't acknowledge her. He served the food himself, reheated pasta, and garlic bread.

"To new beginnings," he said, lifting his cup.

I mirrored him. "To family." Revulsion littered my stomach as I spoke the words. His hand reached across the table and rested lightly on top of mine. Not demanding. Just possessive. His thumb stroked my skin slowly, like he owned it. Goosebumps rose on my arms from apprehension.

"I used to dream of this," he whispered.

"It's not just a dream anymore, Blake," I gave him a dreamy smile.

I ate silently as I thought about all the ways I would live my life once we got out. Blake's voice interrupted my thoughts.

"You're quiet," he notes.

"I'm just taking it all in." He smiled widely, pleased with himself. And I wanted to vomit.

CHAPTER 20:
THE PLAN

When he left, Selecia hissed, "I thought you were going to throw the cup at his head."

"I thought about it. But not yet."

"I don't know how you stomach letting him touch you like that?!"

"I needed him to believe it. And when I am done, he will never touch either of us again."

Her voice cracked. "You are playing a dangerous game. What if he realizes what you are trying to do?"

"Everything is a dangerous game here. And doing nothing might be worse."

She stepped towards me. "What's the next move?"

"I ask him to take off the chain."

Her eyes widened. "He'll never—"

"If he thinks I love him, he will."

"And then?"

I looked at her. "Then we wait for the right moment. He trusts routine. That's his weakness."

Selecia shook her head. "I don't see how we will ever get out.

"We don't have to see it yet. We just have to survive long

enough for the door to open."

"And if it never does?"

I swallowed hard. "Then we make our own door."

CHAPTER 21: I CARE ABOUT YOU

I waited until the timing was perfect, after dinner, when he was in a good mood and humming to himself as he cleared the plates to take upstairs. He had taken to leaving the table and chairs in the basement, and now ate with us every night. His eyes flicked to me and lingered, and I smiled at him shyly.

"Blake?" I asked gently. I lightly pressed my fingers to his upper arm and stepped closer.

He perked up. "Yes, sweetheart?'

My stomach turned at the word, but I kept my voice smooth. "I've been thinking…" I could see Selecia at the small table pretending to sketch while she listened intently. He sat beside me, eyes alert, almost hopeful. "I know the chain keeps me safe. I know it's not about control now. But… I think I've earned some trust, don't you?" His brow furrowed, and I saw it, hesitation. The part of him that wanted to believe I was his. The man who built a world of lies and desperately needed it to feel real.

"I never try to run," I added. "I talk to you. I wear what you give me. I… I care about you, Blake."

His face softened. "I know."

"Then maybe… just for a little while. A trial?"

He reached out and ran his thumb across my cheek.

"You'd stay close?"

I nodded, forcing my lips into a soft smile. "Always."

He studied me for a long time. Then he said, "Let me think about it."

CHAPTER 22:
DISTANCE

"He's considering it," I whispered to Selecia after the door clicked shut.

She looked at me, her eyes wide. "I can't believe he didn't just say no. This could change everything."

"Once the chain is off, I start learning the layout. Upstairs. Check if there are locks, alarms, or weapons. Anything I can use."

"You aren't a spy, Isadora. How will you even know what to look for?"

"No," I said, voice harder. "I'm a survivor and I'll know." We both fell silent.

Selecia sat with her knees to her chest, hugging them tightly. She always did this when she was unsure of something or needed comfort. "You're braver than me," she whispered.

"Not braver, just older. You would've done the same thing if you were me."

She shook her head. "I used to think being alone was the worst thing. If I had been alone, I would have given in a long time ago. "

My heart cracked. "You are so much stronger than you think. And you won't have to be alone."

CHAPTER 23: DISTANCE

He brought a key the next night. "I'm trusting you," he said as he unlatched the chain from around my ankle. "Don't make me regret it."

"I won't," I whispered, rubbing the skin where the shackle had bitten into me for so long. I had forgotten what it felt like to move without its restricting weight. The sound of the chain dragging on the floor. I glanced at Selecia and could see the tears welling in her own eyes as well. She knew how much of a victory this was for us. And I swear she wouldn't be wearing her own chain for much longer. I would free us both.

Blake held out his hand. "Come see your new life." He whispered in my ear as he helped me stand. I followed him up the stairs, my legs shaking not only from fear, but from lack of strength. They hadn't walked this far in so long.

The house was quiet, clean, and neat. Not what I expected. Family photos lined the hall, none of which contained me or Selecia, of course. Just Blake. As a child. A teen. His eyes were empty in all the ones where he was older. But he seemed like a happy child. How did he get here?

He led me to the Kitchen. "You can help cook tomorrow." I nodded slowly. "Bathroom's that way. But only with permission. No locking the door."

I smiled faintly. "Of course."

He reached out and ran a hand through my hair, fingers

catching in the tangles. It had been at least a week since our last "bath" in the bucket downstairs. "You're perfect," he whispered.

Inside, I screamed. Outside, I smiled.

60

CHAPTER 24: A FLASH TOO SHARP

That night, I couldn't sleep. Not because of noise. Not because of the cold. Because of him. His touch from earlier still burned on my skin, like a bruise that hadn't surfaced yet. It brought everything back. Not just moments. But sensations, smells, and sounds. Things I had worked so hard to bury.

Like I was a prize on a shelf, and he was waiting to unwrap me. It made my skin itch. My thoughts spiral.

It triggered something old. A memory I hadn't touched in a while: I felt him gripping my wrists until I cried. Forcing food into my mouth while I gagged. Staring too long while I changed. Kissing my forehead like it meant something. Whispering that I should be grateful he wasn't like "other men". That he was patient. That he was building a life for us. He hadn't touched me sexually, and I had been lucky so far. But I knew he would.

But the way he circled, the way he claimed parts of me with words and touches and silence, it was enough to make me want to disappear. I turned around and saw Selecia curled up on the mattress, one arm flung over her eyes. She deserved so much better than this. We both did.

"I asked him to unchain you too," I said suddenly, my voice barely above a whisper.

She blinked. "What? You don't think it was too soon to ask?"

"I told him you are important to me. I trust you. That it wasn't fair to keep you like that."

She stared at me like I'd done something impossible. "Did he say yes?"

"Not yet," I said. "But I'm going to keep asking."

She sat up, eyes wide. "Why risk pissing him off?"

"Because if I'm free and you're not... that's not freedom." She didn't say anything, just reached for my hand under the blanket and squeezed. But her touch couldn't stop the dread pulsing in my chest because freedom felt close now. But so did something else. Something dangerous.

CHAPTER 25: NO CHAINS, NO FREEDOM

Blake came downstairs with keys in his hand and a smile that made my stomach turn. "I've decided," he said, looking at Selecia. "You've earned it." She froze where she was sitting, back against the wall, one knee pulled to her chest, blonde hair falling lightly over her shoulder.

"Earned what?" she asked carefully. He knelt beside her and slid the key into the lock around her ankle. The shackle clicked open. Her foot recoiled like it didn't believe it was free.

"No more chains," Blake said brightly. "We're a family. I want you to feel that." He looked at me, waiting for praise and waiting for some acknowledgement, some reward. I stood up and wrapped my arms around him, forcing a smile as I leaned in and pressed a kiss to his cheek. "Thank you," I whispered, hoping the gratitude in my voice sounded real. Blake beamed.

Selecia didn't speak. Didn't move. Just stared at the unlocked cuff as if it might snap closed again at any moment. After he left, we sat in silence.

Then she whispered, "I don't feel free."

"You're not," I whispered back softly. "Not yet. Chains or not, this is still a cage."

She looked at her ankle, rubbing the red mark the

shackle had left behind. "I thought I'd feel different."

I did too. But I'd learned this much by now: Freedom isn't a gesture. It's an exit. I moved over to sit beside her, voice low. "Let him think we're grateful. Let him think we are adjusting. It's still a step in the right direction."

She raised an eyebrow. "You really think we can convince him."

"I do," I said. "I think eventually he will let his guard down and we can leave." We watched the door together for a long time, neither of us saying a word. Because for the first time, we were both unchained. And for the first time in a very long time, escape felt like it was possible.

CHAPTER 26: BATHWATER AND BLOOD

He let me use the upstairs bathroom. Supervised, of course. Blake stood just outside the door, the knob removed, listening. The water was lukewarm. The soap smelled like lavender, something he thought I'd like. I scrubbed hard, too hard, until my skin turned red and raw, like I could wash away my time in the basement. Like I could wash away the time between now and my first night here.

I stared at the reflection in the spotted mirror. Gaunt cheeks. Hollow eyes. Pale lips. And under it, something more complex. Stronger. Not Isadora Amber Rose, the daughter of surgeons. Not Isadora, the waitress. A girl who learned to survive beneath concrete and chains.

When I came out, a towel wrapped tight around me, he smiled like I'd handed him a ring.

"You look radiant," he whispered. I smiled back. Then I bit the inside of my cheek until it bled.

CHAPTER 27:
THE DRAWER

He left me alone in the kitchen one afternoon. Five minutes. That's all I needed. I scanned the drawers: knives, tools, a corkscrew. I slipped the small knife into my waistband beneath my sweater. Later, while lying in bed, my face toward the edge, I slipped my hand under the mattress and slowly hid the knife, more than aware of the camera blinking in the corner. I wasn't sure if it could see us with the lights off, but I wasn't taking any chances.

Selecia's eyes widened when I told her what I had done. "We're going to kill him?" she questioned.

"No," I said. "Not yet."

"Then why—"

"In case we run out of time."

CHAPTER 28:
THE FEVER

Selecia got sick. Her skin burned with fever. Her small body trembled on the mattress. She coughed so hard she choked.

"Blake," I said, panicked." She needs help." He frowned, watching from the stairs.

"She'll recover. Kids are resilient," he spat.

"She's twelve," I snapped. "You kidnapped her! You want your family to die?!" My anger clouded my vision. My hands shook with the force of my rage. I couldn't control myself. I wouldn't watch Selecia die. Something dark flickered in his eyes.

"Fine," he muttered. "I'll bring something." I could tell by his eyes that I would regret my outburst later, but if Selecia was okay, it didn't matter. He came back later after what felt like forever with a bottle of antibiotics with his name on them and a damp towel. He said she was probably getting pneumonia, and they would help.

I sat by Selecia's side all night, spooning water between her lips, wiping sweat from her forehead.

"I don't want to die here," she whispered once.

"You won't," I promised. "Not if I have to burn this place down myself."

Selecia's fever had finally broken. I wasn't sure how long

she had been sick, but if I had to guess, I would say at least a week. I was just so relieved that she was okay.

My relief was short-lived. I had been right that Blake was still angry. He didn't like how I had spoken to him, and he wasn't about to let it go. He had waited until Selecia was better and acted normally until then. Then, suddenly, he was beside me, asking me to come upstairs. He seemed calm, but I knew something was simmering beneath the exterior. I sat up and moved to follow him. I should've resisted. Should've screamed. But I didn't. I knew better.

Upstairs behind the locked door, he didn't speak for a long time. Just stared at me. Circling like I was something I had to fix.

"You humiliated me," he said finally. "In front of her."

"I told the truth. I couldn't just watch her die. She's family." His hand flew so fast I didn't see it coming. He backhanded me, sharp across my mouth. I staggered, blood blooming against my lip.

"You don't get to accuse me. You don't get to poison her mind against me." I didn't answer. I couldn't. The metallic taste filled my mouth, but I forced myself not to cry. That's what he wanted. He wanted to see me crumble.

"You're supposed to be the heart of this family," he growled. "But maybe I made another mistake. Maybe I chose wrong." He didn't hit me again. But he didn't need to. His words shook me to the core. His words scared me more than his actions. Because what would he do if he decided I was the wrong choice for his family? He would kill me.

CHAPTER 29:
BLAKE'S RULES

Blakes POV

They don't see it. The way Isadora looks at me now, it's real. She used to flinch, now she doesn't. She listens. She smiles.

She's softening. She is beginning to understand. She is embracing her part in this family. I'm doing it right this time.

Not like with Paige. Not like the ones before. I was too impatient with them. I wasn't picky enough. I was too desperate.

But Isadora's different. And Selecia... she was never part of the plan, but she's made things better. Less lonely. She completed us.

A daughter. A real family. I walk down the stairs and catch them huddling together, whispering. Again. Always whispering. I smile anyway. Because soon, they won't whisper anymore. Soon, they'll thank me.

CHAPTER 30: A GAME OF TRUST

I started playing a game with Blake. I'd ask him questions, little ones. "What's your favorite color?" "Did you always want to be a husband?" "What would our wedding look like?"

I feigned interest in every word and smiled where I should. I learned every detail of his life. I asked what he did for work before us. He said he had been a contractor. I asked him what his dream vacation was. I asked him everything I could. Hoping that it will make him trust me more and more.

His eyes lit up like I had handed him a key to heaven. It wasn't hard to listen. Just painful. Sometimes he'd brush my hand. Other times, he'd kiss the top of my head. Every time I smiled, I wanted to cry.

He gave me more freedom. More time upstairs. And I used it. I studied the locks. The patterns. Where he put his keys. The direction his truck was always parked. Freedom was an illusion—but information? That was real.

CHAPTER 31: LATE-NIGHT VISIT.

He came into the basement at night. Late. Quiet. I pretended to sleep, curled next to Selecia. He walked to the side of the mattress and knelt. I felt his fingers touch my hair.

"You're mine," he whispered. "You just don't know it yet." Then he left. I didn't breathe again until I heard the door click shut.

Selecia shifted beside me. "You awake?" "Yes."

"I hate him."

"So do I." She was silent.

"Are we going to make it?"

I didn't answer. Because I didn't know

CHAPTER 32: THE PAPERCLIP

I found a paperclip in the drawer with the junk tools. It looked like nothing. But it was everything. I bent it carefully. Hid it in my bra. Selecia didn't ask what it was for. She just nodded.

We no longer say the word "escape." It was too dangerous. Too sacred. But the look in her eyes said it all. Soon.

CHAPTER 33:
THE STORM

Rain poured one night, loud and violent. The power flickered. Blake came down carrying a flashlight. "Don't worry," he said, calm as always. "We're safe here." "Why don't you ever leave?" I asked suddenly.

He looked surprised. "Everything I need is here."

"What about work? Groceries?"

"I plan ahead."

"And if you get caught?"

His smile didn't reach his eyes. "I won't."

Selecia stared at him. "People don't notice."

"No," he said, crouching beside her. "No one's looking. I made sure."

He looked at me. "We're all we need. I can provide for you." For now, I let him believe that.

CHAPTER 34: THE CRACK

Later that night, when the power finally failed, the basement went completely dark. No camera. No light. No Blake. Just the sound of wind and our shallow breathing.

In the silence, I whispered, "We're going to do it."

Selecia's hand found mine. "How?"

"I don't know yet. But soon. I can feel it." She squeezed tighter. The darkness wasn't comfortable. But it was honest. And I'd learned something Blake never understood: Truth lives in the shadows. And we were ready to rise from them.

CHAPTER 35: CONTROL

It wasn't the chain that held me anymore. It was the balance. The delicate, terrifying balance between making Blake trust me just enough and not letting myself forget who he really was.

That night, he brought down dinner like always, but he lingered longer. Watched me eat. Watched me breathe.

"You seem calmer lately," he said, setting the tray aside and sitting on the edge of the mattress.

I forced a soft smile. "I'm getting used to things."

"That makes me happy," he said, reaching out to brush my hair from my face. I didn't flinch. He took it as a sign. He stayed, talking about pointless things—movies, music, and some childhood memory about a dog. I listened. I nodded at the correct times. I even laughed once.

All while memorizing the way his eyes shifted when he got too close. He wanted me to be soft. So, I became soft. He wanted a wife. So, I played along. Not because I believed it. Not because I cared. Because power isn't always physical, sometimes, it's in the knowing.

And I knew I'd get my chance. Not today. But soon. I'll walk upstairs someday. And when I do, I won't be coming back down.

CHAPTER 36:
JOURNAL ENTRY

Blakes POV

Isadora smiled at me tonight. Not a forced smile. A real one. Her eyes didn't look like they were searching for a way out. They looked... warm.

She's softening. It's happening. I knew she'd come around. Love just takes time. And now that Selecia's here, it feels like a family. Like I imagined.

Sometimes I sit at the top of the stairs and listen. The way Isadora talks to her—so gentle, so protective. She's going to be a great mother. I can see it in her. She needs a child. Not just to take care of—but to heal her. We all need healing.

Selecia is still... resistant. Stubborn. But she'll adjust. She just doesn't see the big picture yet. She doesn't understand how good this can be. I don't want to punish them. I hate when I have to raise my voice, or skip a meal, or lock them in for longer. But I won't let chaos creep in. Rules matter. Structure saves lives.

And love? Love is worth waiting for. I'm getting through to her. She let me touch her hair tonight: next time, maybe her lips. We're almost there.

CHAPTER 37:
HER SHADOW

Selecia was asleep, her small frame curled tightly on the mattress across from mine, one hand still clutching the edge of the blanket. Even in sleep, she looked alert, like her body had forgotten how to rest fully.

I watched her for a long time. She is barely a teenager. I had promised to celebrate her birthday, but I wasn't even sure what month it was. It could have been a couple of months since she got here, or it could have been a year.

She should've been worried about spelling tests and school dances, not counting the footfalls on the stairs to predict our captor's mood. She hadn't said much all day. Not after Blake had come down and praised me for being "so cooperative" and offered me a book as a reward. She didn't say it out loud, but I saw it in her eyes: she thought I was giving in.

I wasn't. But she was too young to understand the layers it took to survive a man like Blake. I waited until the lights were off upstairs and the silence settled like dust. Then I whispered, "Selecia?"

Her eyes opened. "I'm not asleep."

"Thought so."

She didn't sit up. "You smiled at him today."

"I know."

She turned her face away from me. "You're starting to like him."

"No." I sat up slowly. "I'm starting to learn how to stay alive."

She rolled over. "It's hard to tell the difference." I didn't respond. Because sometimes, she was right. Sometimes the line between manipulation and surrender blurred between pretending and losing a part of yourself. I hated that she could see it happening.

But I hated it more that I understood why she looked at me with that mixture of resentment and fear because I had once looked at myself the same way.

CHAPTER 38: SHELTER

I heard him yelling upstairs before the door even opened. Selecia was frozen on her mattress, her hands trembling, eyes wide and locked on the stairs. I got up quickly and moved between her and the door, standing even though my legs didn't want to.

The lock clicked. Then creaked. He came down heavy-footed, muttering to himself, jaw tight, fists clenched. Something had happened—something outside this basement that he couldn't control.

And when Blake couldn't control something, he came down here to find something he could.

"Get up," he snapped, pointing at Selecia. She flinched. Didn't move. I stepped forward before he could repeat it.

"She's sick," I lied. "She barely touched her food. Been throwing up all night."

His eyes darted between us. "Really."

"Yeah." I didn't blink. "I was going to tell you. She needs rest."

His lip curled slightly. "You think I can't tell when you're lying?" I said nothing. But I didn't back down.

After a long pause, he scoffed and dropped a water bottle onto the table. "Fine. But if I find out you're covering for her, there will be consequences." He turned and stormed back up the stairs, slamming the door so hard it shook dust from the rafters.

I waited until the silence returned before turning to her. Selecia's lower lip was trembling.

"You didn't have to—"

"Yes," I said, kneeling. "I did." She launched into my arms, wrapping her arms around my neck like she was five years old instead of twelve. Her breath hitched against my shoulder. It was a stark reminder that this was a child. A terrified child who was only here because of me. It was my responsibility to protect her.

"I'm sorry," she whispered. "I should've said something. I just froze."

"I know," I said, stroking her hair. "You don't have to explain." We sat like that for a long time. And for the first time since she arrived, she fell asleep without fear written on her face. And I stayed awake, guarding her. Because she was my reason now, and I would burn this place to the ground before I let him break her too.

CHAPTER 39:
THE TRADE

The next morning, he brought down breakfast and stood in the doorway longer than usual, watching us with a distant kind of calculation. Selecia stayed tucked behind me. She hadn't spoken a word since last night.

Blake placed the tray on the floor. Oatmeal. Apples. Two protein bars. Then he straightened. "You've been... cooperative, Isadora," I said, nothing. "I'm considering giving you the privilege of a shower today," he continued, his voice smooth like it was some divine offering. "But it comes with a condition."

I didn't like the way his eyes flicked to Selecia.

"No," I said instantly.

"You don't even know what I was going to say."

"I don't need to. If it involves her, the answer's no."

His jaw flexed. "You're not in a position to be making demands."

"And you're not in a position to use a child as leverage."

A long silence stretched between us. Then Blake crouched, leveling his eyes with mine.

"She's not a bargaining chip," he said coolly. "She's part of this family. But families contribute. They follow rules. They don't get to sit out forever."

I met his eyes in defiance. "She's a child. If you want something, you deal with me."

He stood again and turned toward the stairs. "Think about it. I'll be back in an hour. And if you want that shower, maybe consider what you're willing to give." Selecia looked up at me as the door slammed.

Her voice was small. "I can do something, if I have to."

I shook my head firmly. "No."

"But you haven't showered in forever. You—"

"I'm fine." I pulled her close, hand protectively around her shoulders. "He doesn't get to take more from you so that I can feel clean for five minutes. I'll survive." She stared at me for a long time, like she didn't understand how anyone could give something like that up for her. But I meant it.

Every time he tried to use her against me, I'd make sure he lost. He didn't realize it yet, but I'd die before I let him touch her.

CHAPTER 40:
NOT ALONE

Selecia's POV

Before I came here, I used to hate silence. Now it's the only time I feel safe. When Blake is quiet, when the stairs don't creak, when the light upstairs stays still—that's when I can pretend I'm just hiding. That this is some game of survival, I'm good at. That there's an end coming.

I used to count the days by scratch marks in my mind. However, the numbers slipped away after a while, falling like pages ripped from a calendar. Now I just count breaths. Hers and mine. Isadora. She's the only good thing here. Maybe the only good thing I've had in a long time.

Back in Phoenix—before all of this—I was the quiet girl. I ran track. I liked rules because they kept people predictable. But then he came. Blake. With that fake smile and sad eyes. Said he was a family friend picking me up from school. Said Mom forgot to call. I didn't believe him. But I got in the car.

I don't know why; maybe it was because I was tired. Maybe because part of me wanted to see if I mattered enough for someone to come looking. No one did. But Isadora was here. And she stayed.

She keeps shielding me and telling lies on my behalf. She gave up food once, so that I wouldn't lose mine. She brushes my hair with her fingers sometimes, like a big sister would. I haven't told her, but I pretend she is. I like how it feels when she calls me "kiddo," even though I try to act older than I am.

Today, when Blake brought down the oatmeal and said nothing, I watched Isadora freeze until he left. Then she laughed as if it were nothing. But I saw her shoulders shake. I lay next to her that night, and I didn't say anything. I just reached for her hand in the dark. And she held it. Not for me. For us. Because we were still here, and that had to count for something.

CHAPTER 41: THE HAIRBRUSH

I didn't cry anymore. It wasn't that I didn't want to, I just couldn't. The tears had dried up sometime after the seventh time he had locked me in here without food. After about a month of isolation. After I realized no one was coming to save me. After I watched Selecia stare at the wall, stomach growling loudly, pretending she wasn't hungry.

She never asked why I gave her my share. She just looked at me with those wide eyes like she couldn't understand why anyone would bother. Why would anyone give up something so crucial for her, just to protect her? But I did. Because I remembered what it felt like to be alone in this place.

He brought down a hairbrush today. Just dropped it on the bed without a word, like it was nothing. A cheap plastic thing with bent bristles and a cracked handle. But to us, it might as well have been gold.

On shower days, we'd sit in silence trying to comb through weeks of knots, filth, and dried sweat with our fingers. We'd wince, flinch, and nearly cry from the pain of pulling through the matted clumps. We wasted precious water on other days trying to detangle the strands. Our scalps would be sore for days. All we wanted was to feel somewhat normal. Even if we never did. We tried to keep our hair braided most days to minimize the damage. It didn't always help.

Selecia picked up the brush like it might disappear. She didn't say anything, just held it close, blinking too fast like she was trying not to cry. I sat beside her, legs crossed, pretending not to notice the way her body leaned slightly into mine. We didn't talk much anymore; we didn't need to. Our bond had become its own language. A glance, a sigh, a shared silence could communicate so much now.

"You ever think about the sky?" she asked softly, fingers running over the cracked handle as if it were fragile.

"All the time."

"I miss it."

"Me too."

She paused. "You think we'll see it again?"

I didn't answer right away. I just wrapped an arm around her and pulled her close. "We will," I whispered into her hair. "I promise." She didn't reply, but she didn't let go either. And in that moment, in a basement meant to break us, we held on like the stars above us still remembered our names.

CHAPTER 42: MEASURED OBEDIENCE

Blake hadn't yelled in weeks. But he didn't need to. His silence was sharper than any blade. Ever since the night I screamed about Charlotte—when he came dangerously close to losing control—he had changed, not softened. Not really. Just… adjusted. Smoothed out the violence and replaced it with something quieter. Slimier. Measured.

He still wanted me. Not just as a possession. As a wife. That word made my skin crawl. He came down the stairs like always, smiling like he was returning home from work, not descending into the basement where he kept two girls captive. "Good morning, darling," he said to me, ignoring Selecia entirely. "Did you miss me?"

I didn't answer. He didn't expect me to. My silence was part of the game now.

He knelt beside me and tucked a strand of hair behind my ear. "You're prettier when you don't cry." I flinched without meaning to. He noticed.

"I brought something," he added cheerfully. "Breakfast. For Selecia only." My heart twisted, but I didn't react. I couldn't afford to.

Selecia blinked at him. "Why just me?"

Blake gave her a sugary smile. "Because your sister's been distant lately. Wives don't get to sulk when their husbands are trying." I clenched my jaw.

Selecia glanced at me, unsure. "She's not—"

"Shh," I cut her off gently. I knew better than to let her finish that sentence.

When he left, Selecia pushed half her toast onto my tray. "You're not his wife," she said fiercely. "You're not."

"I know," I said softly. But the knot in my stomach didn't go away. That night, Blake returned with a cheap nightgown. Pale pink. Faded lace.

"I saw this and thought of you," he said, laying it on the mattress like it was silk. "Try it on tomorrow, alright? I want to start having dinner together. Upstairs. Like a real couple." I didn't move. My throat went dry.

He stepped closer and cupped my cheek, thumb brushing just under my eye. "I need to know you still love me, Isadora. Even after everything."

"I never said I did," I whispered. I knew I shouldn't defy him, but my stomach revolted at the idea of telling him I loved him. I knew he would punish me for this. I prayed he would leave Selecia out of it.

He smiled. "Not with words." Then he left. And I sat perfectly still, heart hammering like a drumbeat of dread.

CHAPTER 43: SILENCE BETWEEN US

We hadn't spoken in two days. Not since he took away the bucket and made us sit in our own filth. Selecia clung to my side like a shadow, silent, shivering, scared. I tried not to cry in front of her anymore. She needed me to be steady. If I broke, she'd fall apart too.

Blake hadn't touched me in a while—not like before. No cuts. No burns. No metal bed. But that didn't make it better. It made it worse.

The silence was punishment now. The way he'd watch me without saying a word. The way he took food away from us, just to "remind me who was in charge." The way he'd slam the tray on the floor so hard the water spilled out, and then smile like it was my fault.

He was more dangerous now than ever—calm, calculating, waiting. I still remember the night he almost killed me. It was after I'd snapped. He told me Charlotte would forget me. That even if I got out, she'd be older, different, and I'd mean nothing to her.

I lost it. I screamed. I tried to throw the bowl at him. I yelled that he'd never understand what it meant to love someone who really mattered. That he was alone because he deserved to be.

And then the straps came out. The chair. The blade. The familiar smell of alcohol wipes and rust. He carved slowly this time, deliberately. And he didn't speak until it was over. The cut wasn't deep. But it was long. My arm throbbed for hours.

He left me there, strapped to the bed, bleeding. The cut on my arm was the worst one, but he had sliced small slits all down my back, arms, and stomach. I couldn't remember everything he had done to me in that room, but I remembered afterwards. How badly it hurt every time I moved. How raw my throat was from screaming. How he smiled at my pain.

When I came to, he was pacing. He looked at me like I was some glass doll with a crack down the middle. Like he hadn't done it himself. His hands trembled as he cleaned the wound. He whispered, "You scared me," like I was the one who had gone too far.

Since then, he hadn't touched me in anger. But his control? It never left. Now, he punished us with silence, with isolation, with watching me starve while Selecia cried in my lap and begged him to stop. And the worst part? He'd say it was because he loved us.

CHAPTER 44:
THE THREAT

He came downstairs humming. Not his usual, cheerful, and obnoxious humming, this time it was eerie and tuneless. I stiffened where I sat on the mattress, and I saw Selecia do the same from across the room. She had the sketchbook open but wasn't drawing. Just holding the pencil like it might become a weapon if she needed it.

Blake walked in with something behind his back. I didn't ask. I didn't breathe.

"I brought you something," he said. His voice was warm. Too warm. It made my skin crawl. He stepped toward me and revealed a small black velvet box. The kind that usually holds engagement rings. My stomach flipped.

"This," he said with a grin, "was in your room. I remembered how much you used to wear it." I didn't want to open it. But I had to. Because not opening it would be worse. My fingers shook as I lifted the lid.

Inside, there was a silver locket. My mother's. Oval-shaped, engraved with faint vines, tarnished at the edges. I hadn't seen it in years. I remembered how it used to lie warm against my chest, how I used to hold it between my fingers when I was nervous. Inside was a photo of my mom on one side and Charlotte on the other. My baby sister was only five years old the last time I saw her. Probably seven now. My vision blurred instantly.

"I thought you might want a piece of home," Blake said. Home. He'd gone there. He'd gone to my house. To my room. He'd been near Charlotte. I couldn't breathe. My chest rose and fell in uneven gasps, and I tried to turn away, but the locket was already in my hands.

"She still sleeps with a stuffed bunny," he added casually. "At least, she did when I looked through the window." That broke something.

"You—" My voice cracked. "You went near her?"

He tilted his head. "Of course. She looked peaceful. You should be proud. She's doing just fine." I curled in on myself, clutching the locket like I could crush it. I wanted to scream, to throw it, to claw at his face until it bled.

But I didn't move because Selecia was watching, and because if I broke now, he'd win. I glanced at her, expecting confusion, but what I saw was horror. Her eyes were wide, her lips parted. "He went into your home?" she whispered, voice small and shaking. I nodded, still trembling.

She shook her head, like she couldn't believe it. "He was near your family..." There was pain in her voice—real pain. Because Selecia didn't have a family of her own, but that didn't mean she didn't understand what it meant to have someone worth protecting.

"I always wanted a sister," she said softly. "But not like this. Not at the cost of someone else's." I could see the disgust on her face—not just for Blake, but for the violation of something sacred. Even with all she'd endured, she understood what it meant to belong to someone and how cruel it was for Blake to poison even that.

But I didn't just see a gift. I saw what it really was. A threat. He'd been inside my world. He knew where Charlotte slept, what she clung to at night, what gave her comfort. He wasn't just trying to win me over—he was showing me what he could take away.

Blake smiled, satisfied. "I thought you'd like it." Then he left, just like that. The door shut behind him with a soft thud, but the silence that followed felt loud. I didn't look at Selecia. I just held the locket to my chest and cried without sound.

Because he'd touched my memories, he'd walked into my past and turned it into something ugly. And worse, he knew exactly what he was doing.

CHAPTER 45:
FRACTURES

I didn't sleep that night. Selecia did, eventually—curled up under the fleece blanket, her knees to her chest, one arm across her eyes like she was blocking out the world. But I sat against the wall, the locket still clutched in my hand, fingers numb from holding it too tightly.

Blake had been inside my room. He had seen Charlotte. Maybe not up close—but enough. Enough to tell me what color her pajamas were, what she still cuddled at night. Enough to plant fear like a seed and walk away smiling.

I stared at the blinking light on the camera, feeling like it was blinking straight into me. Was he watching now? Was he replaying my reaction? He didn't need to hurt me anymore. He just needed to remind me that he could.

When morning came, the basement was quiet. The kind of quiet that's heavy—thick with things unsaid. Selecia stirred but didn't say anything right away. When she finally did speak, her voice was hoarse.

"Do you think he'd actually hurt her?" I didn't answer. Because I didn't want to lie. And I didn't want to tell her the truth. Instead, I stood and crossed to the corner where we kept the small pile of supplies he'd let us have, mostly scraps. I reached for the radio and turned it on low, pretending I wanted to listen to music.

But what I really wanted was distraction. I needed to

think. To plan. To survive. Because now I knew—Blake was raising the stakes. He was escalating. And I had to move faster.

Selecia came and sat beside me without asking. Her arm brushed mine. "He's getting worse," she whispered.

"I know."

"We have to get out."

I turned to her. "We will."

"But how?"

I looked down at the locket, still in my palm. The face of my mother stared back at me, frozen in time. Charlotte beside her, beaming with her crooked baby teeth. I closed it gently. Set it in my pocket.

"He made a mistake," I said.

Selecia frowned. "What?"

"He showed me the one thing I can't let him take." I met her eyes, steady this time.

"And that means I'll do whatever it takes to end this." She didn't speak. But she didn't look away either. Because she understood now, this wasn't just about survival. It was war.

CHAPTER 46:
THE SWITCH

I smiled when he came down. It wasn't real, of course —not the kind that reached my eyes—but it was the kind he wanted. Soft. Warm. Grateful.

"Good morning," I said lightly, smoothing the corner of the blanket with practiced calm. Blake looked momentarily stunned. Then pleased.

"Morning, sweetheart," he said, setting a tray on the table. Pancakes. Fruit. A single rose in a chipped mug. "I thought we could eat together today."

"I'd love that. I missed you." His eyes lit up. Like a child handed a gold star. I waited until he sat, then joined him, legs tucked beneath me, hands folded neatly. I tilted my head slightly—enough to mimic affection without looking rehearsed.

He poured juice into plastic cups. "I've been thinking," he said, not meeting my gaze. "Maybe it's time we change things up. Let you come upstairs once in a while. Sleep somewhere more comfortable." My heart clenched. Not from hope—from fear. Because I knew what that offer meant.

But I didn't flinch. "I'd like that," I said, keeping my voice even. "I miss being close to you."

He blinked, startled. "You do?"

"Of course." I picked up a slice of banana and bit into it,

forcing a smile. "You've taken care of me. Of us."

I glanced at Selecia. She sat silently on the mattress, still waking up, rubbing sleep from her eyes. She didn't speak. She didn't need to. One look told me she knew I was putting on a show.

Blake followed my gaze. "She's been quiet lately."

"She's still adjusting," I said gently. "It's hard to feel safe when the world outside is so cruel. But she trusts me. And I trust you. "The words felt like ash in my mouth. But they worked.

Blake leaned back, pleased. "You've changed."

"I've realized what matters." I met his eyes. "I've been angry for so long. I think I forgot what it feels like to... belong."

He reached out and brushed a strand of hair behind my ear. "You do belong. Here. With me." I nodded.

"Maybe," he said, glancing at Selecia again, "we'll move you two to the guest room. So, you'll be closer to me." The implication stung—but I smiled.

"If that's what you want."

He beamed. "Dinner tonight. Something special. I bought you a red dress."

"You are so sweet."

He stood and walked to the door, glancing back once. "I knew you'd come around." The lock clicked shut behind him. I stayed still for a moment. Let the silence settle. Let Selecia process what she'd just witnessed.

Then I turned. "I meant every word," I whispered. "Not because I believe it, but because he needs to."

Selecia's jaw was tight. "Do you think it's working?"

I nodded. "Yes. And when he trusts me enough, I'll end

this."

CHAPTER 47: THE PERFORMANCE

It started with a knock. Not loud. Not urgent. Just a soft, polite knock at the top of the stairs, we lived in a house with rules and doors and respect. Like this wasn't a basement he'd kept us locked in for nearly two years.

Selecia looked at me, eyebrows raised. I stood, brushing off invisible dust from my skirt. "Get ready," I whispered. "Remember what we talked about." She nodded once, tight, sharp. She understood now. This wasn't just surviving anymore. It was a strategy.

Blake came down holding a tray, a smile already fixed on his face. "There's my sunshine girls," he said. "Dinner time."

I returned the smile, warm but modest. "Hi, Blake," I said, sweetening my tone just enough. "We were just talking about you."

His eyes lit up. "All good things, I hope."

"Of course," I said, stepping forward to help. "Let me take that." He let me grab the tray, and for a second, I saw the flicker in his eyes. He liked it. The obedience. The ease. I set the tray down on the foldable table and laid out the food—macaroni, toast, and apple slices.

"Is this for all of us?" Selecia asked gently, stepping beside me.

Blake looked surprised but not upset. "Of course.

Families eat together."

She smiled. Not too much. Just enough. "That's nice." I almost flinched. She was good. Natural. Her voice had lost its edge, its resistance. She didn't look afraid—she looked like a girl humoring a tired parent, like this was all... normal.

We all sat. A loving family sitting down for breakfast. Progress. "Today went really well," I said brightly, twirling a piece of toast between my fingers. "We cleaned and organized. I even taught Selecia a card game."

"She's a quick learner," Blake said, smiling at her.

"Thank you," she replied softly. "It helps... having people who care." The way she said it almost fooled me.

Blake looked between us, glowing. "This—this is what I've always wanted. A real family. Not forced. Chosen."

I reached across the table and touched his hand. "You made this possible." He practically melted. Over the next few minutes, we ate together as if we were in some suburban kitchen, instead of a concrete prison. Selecia played her part well, laughing at a joke, thanking him when he passed the juice, and asking questions about the upstairs, as if she were curious, not desperate.

When the plates were scraped clean, Blake leaned back in his chair and said, "You two make me proud. Really." We both smiled.

"You've earned something special," he added. "I've been working on the guest room upstairs. Lavender walls, white trim. I was thinking you could move up soon."

I didn't let my smile fade. "That sounds amazing."

He turned to Selecia. "And you'll stay with her. Sisters should stay close."

Her eyes lit up just the right amount. "I've never had a

sister before," she said quietly.

Blake's hand pressed over his heart. "Now you do."

When he stood, he kissed the top of my head. Then, to my surprise, he turned to Selecia and did the same. Her jaw tightened for just a second, but she didn't flinch. She leaned into it. When the door clicked shut behind him, silence settled.

Selecia leaned forward. "That was disgusting."

"But effective," I whispered.

She nodded. "If I play the daughter, and you play the wife..."

"We get out."

"Do you think he suspects anything?" she asked.

"No," I said. "Not yet. But we have to stay sharp. Every move counts."

She exhaled shakily. "I'm with you. For real." I reached across the table and squeezed her hand.

"We're not victims anymore," I said. "We're actresses. And the curtain just went up."

CHAPTER 48: CRACKS IN THE SCRIPT

The next morning, Blake brought down board games. He balanced the stack like a proud dad on Christmas morning, beaming as he lowered them to the floor: Monopoly, Clue, and a battered copy of Uno. He knelt like we were kids at a sleepover, not prisoners in a bunker.

"Thought we could all do something fun," he said, clapping his hands together. "Family game day."

Selecia's smile was nearly perfect. "That sounds great."

I nodded, mirroring her. "It's been a while since we did something together."

Blake's eyes softened. "You girls... you're finally starting to see it." We played for hours. Selecia played along with wide eyes and sweet laughter, giving up fake groans when she landed on Blake's property. She let him win a few rounds, but then beat him with a dramatic giggle that made my skin crawl —but it worked. He laughed. He let her win.

I sat next to him on the floor, close enough for him to brush against my arm and feel me not recoil. This was the performance. And it was working.

After the third game, Blake stood to stretch. "I'll go make lunch. Sandwiches and apples?"

"Perfect," I said.

He started up the stairs, then paused. "You two are

becoming something really special. I knew it was in you." He left without waiting for a reply. As soon as the door clicked shut, Selecia dropped her smile like a coat.

"Is it bad that I feel proud of that?" she whispered.

"No," I said. "You should."

"I think he believes us."

"I know he does."

She leaned back, breath shaking. "It's just... creepy. How easy it's getting."

"I know."

"But if this gets us out—"

"We keep going." A pause.

"Do you think he's ever really loved anyone?" she asked suddenly.

I shook my head. "I think he confuses love with possession."

Her brow furrowed. "He said his mom used to lock him in the closet."

I blinked. "When did he say that?"

"A few nights ago. When he brought me tea. Said it was to 'make up' for the chains."

My throat tightened. "He's grooming you."

Selecia's face hardened. "He's trying. But I'm not stupid. I know what this is. I know what he is."

"You're smart," I said. "But don't let your guard down."

"I won't." We sat in silence for a moment, listening to the faint clatter from upstairs.

Then Selecia whispered, "Sometimes I feel like we're

winning. And that scares me."

I nodded slowly. "Because it means we're getting closer."

"Closer to what?" I looked up at the blinking red light in the corner—the camera.

"Closer to being free." She didn't smile. But she reached for my hand and squeezed it hard. The show would go on. But now, cracks were forming in Blake's script—cracks we planned to split wide open.

CHAPTER 49:
THE SMILE AND
THE SILENCE

Blake didn't say a word when he brought dinner down. No strange commentary. No pet names. Just silence. He set the tray down carefully on the table—two grilled cheese sandwiches, a handful of chips, and a glass of juice—and stood there for a moment, watching.

I kept my smile light. Gentle. I'd mastered it now—the perfect blend of affection and submission. Not too eager. Not too cold. A performance tailored to keep him predictable.

"Thank you," I said softly, folding my hands in my lap.

He gave a slight nod. "You're welcome." Selecia sat across the room, cross-legged with a coloring book open. She didn't glance up until he turned to leave. When he reached the stairs, she stood and walked over beside me.

"You okay?" she asked.

I nodded. "He's testing the water."

She frowned. "What does that mean?"

"He's waiting for me to slip up. To prove I didn't mean what I said yesterday."

Selecia looked down at the food. "Then we don't slip." I smiled. Not because I felt joy, but because she understood. She sat with me and took half the sandwich. We ate in silence.

That was the new language we'd adopted—quiet cooperation. A shared understanding that every bite, every gesture, every breath was being recorded somewhere in his mind. We had to be perfect for now.

After dinner, I folded the napkins and wiped down the table with the edge of my shirt. Selecia returned to her coloring book, but this time, she filled the page with a picture of a staircase. One that led to an open door. A little figure stood at the top, reaching for the light.

"You really think we'll get out?" she asked after a while, barely above a whisper.

"Yes," I answered, with no hesitation. She didn't ask how I was so sure. She just smiled. We had learned not to count the days anymore. That was a trap. Time made it harder. Instead, we counted wins. A smile that convinced him. A day with no punishments. A meal we didn't have to beg for.

Little victories. They would add up. They had to. When the lights dimmed and the camera blinked red, I whispered, "Sleep close tonight."

Selecia curled beside me under the blanket. "One day," she murmured, "you'll never have to pretend again." I stared at the ceiling. And prayed she was right.

CHAPTER 50: THE GUEST ROOM

The upstairs room wasn't large, but compared to the basement, it felt massive. Blake called it an upgrade. A reward. "Real light. Real furniture. You've earned this," he said as he led us in like we were guests at a hotel and not prisoners in our own lives.

The space held a worn queen-sized bed, a dented dresser, and a mirror so cloudy it barely reflected our faces. The walls were beige, dull, stained in some corners, but still better than concrete. The window was bolted shut and sealed with screws, the glass barely letting in light through the film of grime. Still, it was light.

"We'll keep this door locked at night," Blake said, pointing to the heavy-duty bolt installed outside. "Just a precaution. To keep you safe." Right.

He handed me a printed sheet. "Your new routine. Cleaning, laundry, cooking. You'll be making meals together from now on. Breakfast must be on the table by eight. Dinner prepared by six. I expect it on the table when I walk in."

I scanned the list. Chores. Meal prep. Sweep the floors. Scrub the bathroom. Wash dishes. His "traditional" family structure was starting to unfold like a script. Selecia stood beside me, reading over my shoulder. She didn't ask questions. She just nodded.

"We'll get it done," I said quietly.

Blake smiled like we'd just agreed to host Thanksgiving. "That's my girl. Both of you." He looked between us, as if he really believed this was something sacred. And then he left, the lock on the outside of the door clicking into place like a final punctuation mark.

Selecia flopped onto the edge of the bed and sighed. "He really thinks this is normal."

I sat beside her. "We let him think that."

"We're cooking now," she said, almost laughing. "What's next, Sunday game night?"

I forced a smile. "If it gets us closer to the door... We'll play house."

She met my eyes. "I'm in."

We unpacked the few things Blake had left in the corner —some folded clothes, a bag of off-brand toiletries, and a handful of kitchen items for us to start dinner with. Nothing sharp, of course. Nothing useful.

Later, as we stood in the cramped kitchen side by side—peeling potatoes with blunt tools and checking the stove twice for heat—I realized something. This wasn't freedom. But it was new territory. And new ground was harder to control. Which meant Blake had just made his second mistake.

CHAPTER 51: ROLES

The first morning upstairs felt like waking up in a borrowed body. The mattress creaked when I rolled over. I could feel Selecia's elbow brushing mine—she'd curled toward me in her sleep; her face relaxed in a way I hadn't seen since the night she arrived.

I didn't wake her. Instead, I slid out of bed quietly and checked the door. Still bolted. Still locked from the outside. But at exactly 4:30 a.m., the lock turned.

Blake opened the door with a cheery, "Time to get started." He handed me a printed schedule yesterday, but what he hadn't said—what we learned only now—was that we'd be expected to wake up before dawn every day to make breakfast. He also, surprisingly, pointed to the hallway. "There are soap and towels in the bathroom. You'll have time to freshen up before we eat."

It was the first time we'd been allowed real access to hygiene since arriving. My skin itched at the idea of a hot shower, shampoo, even the cheap toothpaste on the counter. The water was actually a pleasant temperature. He didn't have much in the way of products, but it was enough.

I stepped out feeling a little more human and found Selecia already brushing her teeth. We moved quickly—carefully—like inmates testing the weight of looser chains.

"I'll start the eggs," I said.

"I'll do the bacon," Selecia offered. No argument. No need for one. We worked like shadows—choreographed and soundless. I scrambled the eggs while she set the table. Toast browned in the old toaster he'd left us. The smell was familiar. So was the weight in my chest. Because this wasn't just breakfast, it was theater.

When the front door opened again around six, we were already seated. Blake stepped inside like a proud husband returning home. He sniffed the air and smiled.

"Something smells good."

"It's ready," I said with a softness that wasn't quite mine. He sat. Selecia poured the juice. We all ate together. And for the first time, Blake didn't talk much. He just watched. Us. The food. The table. The way I passed him the butter without flinching. The way Selecia thanked him for the meal, like a polite daughter should. It was working.

Afterward, he wiped his mouth and stood. "I could get used to this."

"You should," I said gently. "We're just getting started." He laughed and ruffled Selecia's hair on his way out. Once the door clicked shut behind him, she looked at me.

"He bought it."

"Good," I said. "Because this is how we win." She didn't smile. But she nodded. And in the silence that followed, I understood something deeper: This wasn't just a new room. It was a stage. And Blake had no idea we were rewriting the script.

CHAPTER 52:
INVENTORY

After breakfast, we cleaned like our lives depended on it—because they did. The schedule Blake printed was taped to the inside of the bedroom door. The tasks were typed in bullet points, color-coded, and labeled like some twisted home economics syllabus:

Kitchen: Wash, dry, and put away the dishes. Sweep and mop the hardwood floors.

Living Room: Dust the furniture. Fluff the pillows—no shoes on the carpet.

Bathroom: Scrub the sink. Disinfect the toilet. Fold the kitchen towels neatly and place them in the drawer.

Bedroom: Make all the beds. Organize the dressers. Keep the floor clear.

It was laughably domestic. But we didn't laugh. Not even a little. We cleaned in silence, save for the occasional instruction between us. We didn't rush. We didn't dawdle. We followed every task exactly as listed—like good little daughters. By noon, the house gleamed. And we'd memorized every corner of it.

Selecia wiped down the counter a third time while I stood in the hallway outside the bathroom, slowly taking mental notes. The walls were cheap drywall. The screws on the window frames were tight, but not impossible to remove. The lock on the bathroom door didn't work, but the hinges were rusted. It wasn't much. But it was something.

"Two vents in the hallway," I whispered when Blake went upstairs for a shower. "One in the kitchen ceiling, one under the bedroom window."

"I already checked the one under the sink. It's small, but metal. Could be unscrewed." We weren't just cleaning. We were mapping. Plotting. By the time we sat down for lunch—two peanut butter sandwiches and a bruised apple each—we had more than a routine. We had a blueprint.

Later, Blake came home with a grocery bag and tossed it onto the counter. "You're in charge of meal planning now," he said. "Make it last the week."

"Of course," I replied, taking inventory with practiced ease. Bread. Rice. Canned vegetables. A bag of frozen chicken. A box of pancake mix.

Selecia helped me sort everything, her face unreadable. But when we were alone again, she whispered, "Do you think he's testing us?"

"Yes."

"You think he'll let his guard down?"

"He already has."

That night, after we cooked a bland dinner of rice and peas with pan-fried chicken, Blake let us sit on the couch while he flipped through the TV channels. He didn't touch me. Didn't bark orders. He just smiled at the image we created. Two girls. One couch. A silent dinner. His perfect little fantasy. And we gave it to him, down to the last obedient nod.

But inside, I was watching the lock on the front door, counting the screws, and measuring the silence, because the script was now ours. And we were learning how to write the ending.

CHAPTER 53: DRESS REHEARSAL

The red dress hung in the hallway like it was waiting for applause. Blake had left it on a plastic hanger, hooked on the bathroom doorknob, just before he went to work. No note. No explanation. Just the crimson fabric and a silent expectation. Selecia saw it first.

"Is that for you?" she asked, her voice quiet, wary.

"It's not for fun," I said. "It's a test."

She nodded, and neither of us touched it for hours. We scrubbed the kitchen. We mopped the floors. We boiled pasta for dinner. And all the while, the dress waited—like a spotlight that hadn't yet turned on.

By four, I'd showered and blow-dried my hair, just enough to look polished. Blake liked effort. Not too much, but not too little. I applied the light makeup he'd left in the bathroom drawer last week. Foundation. Mascara. Lip gloss in a shade called "Petal."

Selecia sat on the bed as I got ready, her hands clasped between her knees.

"He'll want you to smile," she said softly.

"I know."

"You're really good at it now."

I paused at the mirror. "So are you."

She gave a tight smile. "He called me his 'little girl' again this morning."

I turned toward her. "How did it make you feel?"

"Like throwing up."

I walked over and knelt in front of her. "I know it's hard. But every time you say what he wants to hear... every time you play your part..."

"I'm giving you more time," she finished for me.

"Yes." We stayed like that—just looking at each other—until the front door creaked open. He was home. I stepped into the hallway, dress swaying around my knees, and met him at the bottom of the stairs with a practiced smile. He froze.

"You look beautiful," he said.

"Thank you." I tilted my head. "I wanted tonight to be special."

His entire body relaxed. "It already is." Dinner was quiet. Too quiet. Selecia played her part perfectly, passing napkins, thanking him for the meal, even laughing once at a dry comment about the pasta being overcooked. He watched her, pleased. But his attention always came back to me. After dinner, he turned on the radio and offered me his hand.

"Dance with me."

I hesitated, just long enough to be coy. "Okay." He spun me once, then pulled me in too close. I didn't flinch. Didn't blink. I lay my head against his shoulder and let him believe the lie.

"You feel different," he murmured.

"Maybe I've stopped fighting what was meant to be." He hummed, pleased, his chin resting lightly atop my head. Across the room, I saw Selecia watching. She didn't look jealous. Or scared. She looked like she understood. And that meant everything. She believed in me. Because tonight wasn't just about dinner. Or a dress. It was a rehearsal for the final act.

CHAPTER 54:
LEVERAGE

The next morning began just as the last one had. 4:30 a.m. The sound of the lock turning. The door creaked open. Blake's voice calling out, too cheerful for the hour.

"Let's get moving, ladies." But this time, he handed me something new, a folded slip of paper.

"Write a grocery list," he said. "You're running low on supplies." Selecia and I exchanged a glance. Blake never lets us make decisions, not like this. He stood there, waiting, so I nodded and took a pen from the counter.

Eggs. Bread. Chicken. Canned vegetables. Apples. Milk. Sazón. Paprika. Italian seasoning.

I added slowly and carefully, as if each item might get us in trouble if it felt too bold. I left off anything that felt like a luxury. No chocolate. No spices. No razors. When I handed it back, he barely looked at it. Just folded it again and slid it into his back pocket.

"Good. This is what a real household looks like," he said. "Responsibility. Routine." Selecia stood near the sink, quiet but alert. I saw the way her hand gripped the edge of the counter.

Once he was gone, she turned to me. "He's getting comfortable."

I nodded. "And that's the most dangerous thing he can do."

We spent the morning scrubbing the kitchen and vacuuming the small living room. We worked in silence, our rhythm almost instinctual now. No wasted movement. No raised voices. Every action is calculated.

After lunch, I found a blank notepad tucked in a drawer near the stove. I didn't say anything—just slipped it under the mattress in the guest room. That night, after Blake locked us in, I used it to start recording things. What time did he leave? What time did he return? What doors he opened. What keys did he carry?

Selecia watched me write and didn't ask questions. She just sat beside me and drew little floor plans from memory—labeling where the doors were, where the squeaky floorboards creaked, where the power box might be. He came home a little later than usual that evening. His mood was off. Not angry, just unsettled.

"You didn't dust the hallway," he said suddenly, glancing up at the ceiling.

"I'm so sorry. You are so right. I completely forgot, and I'll make sure I get it first thing tomorrow," I replied, tone calm and pleasant. His jaw tightened for a moment. Then relaxed.

"See that you do." We ate together. He sat at the head of the table like a king at a feast. Selecia passed him the juice with a quiet "Thank you." He smiled at her, approving.

"This is what I imagined," he said aloud, more to himself than to us. "A family that works. That respect each other. Where everyone has their place."

I looked at him, soft-eyed. "I'm grateful for mine."

He stared at me for a long moment. Then nodded once. After he left and the locks clicked shut behind him, I turned to Selecia.

"We're getting closer."

She reached for the notepad. "Then we keep planning." And so, we did. Because his rules were starting to change, and that meant we were finally learning how to bend them.

CHAPTER 55: THE MASK HOLDS

By the third morning, our routine upstairs was flawless. Wake up at 4:30, shower quickly, brush our teeth, tie our hair back, and button our shirts to the top; we had to be modest. Cook breakfast as if it were a privilege, smile, be pleasant, be grateful. Blake walked in that morning humming. Not eerie like before—pleased. Settled. Like the house was finally becoming what he'd imagined.

"Smells good," he said, glancing between us as he set his keys down on the counter. I passed him a plate without waiting to be asked—scrambled eggs, toast, and a slice of orange. Selecia handed him a folded napkin as if we were hosting brunch.

He grinned. "My girls." We sat and ate together. And when he talked about chores, we nodded. When he mentioned wanting to repaint the living room, I offered a suggestion— soft blue, something warm. He smiled wider. Afterward, he asked if I wanted to pick out the dinner recipe. That was new.

"Yes," I said quickly, careful not to sound too eager. "I think we could make chicken and rice. Maybe with beans if we have them?"

He seemed impressed, like I'd passed some unspoken test. "You've come a long way, Isadora."

"I just needed time to understand what this is," I said softly, lowering my gaze like I was embarrassed by how long it had taken.

His fingers grazed my jaw as he stood. "You'll see. This life will make sense one day."

The moment he left, Selecia let out a quiet breath. "He's buying it."

I nodded. "We don't break character. Not once."

We cleaned for hours. The smell of disinfectant soaked into our palms. Blake had left a short list: mop the floors, clean the bathroom, wipe the windows. He didn't say it outright, but we both knew—he wanted to walk into a perfect house and believe it was because we loved him. Not because we were surviving him.

That evening, after setting the table with care, we ate together again. Selecia passed him the salt before he even had a chance to ask. I laughed at one of his stories. Laughed. I hated the sound of it. But he believed it.

"You're really starting to belong here," he said, cutting into his food. "I knew you'd come around."

"I just needed the right place," I said. "And the right person." He touched my wrist lightly, possessively, like a reward. Selecia didn't flinch. She kept her eyes on her plate, like a well-trained daughter.

Later, as we washed dishes in silence, I whispered, "You okay?"

She nodded. "You?"

"No. But I'm getting better at pretending."

We dried the last cup and turned off the kitchen light. Upstairs, the bolt clicked shut behind us like a final cue at the end of a stage play. We climbed into bed without speaking, both of us exhausted from the show.

And as I stared at the ceiling, I realized something

terrifying: We weren't faking the routine anymore. We were living it. And that's how I knew—we were close. Because Blake no longer saw actresses. He saw his wife and he saw his daughter. He saw a home that he built, but what he didn't know was that homes can be broken.

CHAPTER 56: RED DRESS, RED RULES

The box sat on the bed when we returned from scrubbing the living room floors. A red dress, neatly folded inside, with the tag still attached. The fabric shimmered faintly in the light, soft to the touch—too expensive for Blake's usual taste. He hadn't picked it randomly. This was deliberate.

"Dinner," I told Selecia. "Just me and him."

She nodded once, jaw tight. "Want me to stay close after?"

"I'll be fine," I said. "This is just another step."

"You sure you can do it?"

I didn't answer. I just picked up the dress and went into the bathroom to change. It fit too well. Snug at the waist, soft over my skin, and cut too low in the front. I stared at my reflection in the foggy mirror. I looked like someone else. Someone he wanted.

When I came out, Selecia didn't say a word. She looked at me for a long time, then gently squeezed my hand before stepping out into the hallway. Blake knocked once before opening the door. His eyes widened with pleasure when he saw me.

"You look beautiful," he said, voice low.

"Thank you." I smiled softly, the way I'd practiced.

He led me downstairs, guiding me by the elbow like a

date on prom night. The table was already set. Pasta. Garlic bread. Two glasses of wine. And a candle flickering between us.

"I thought you deserved something special," he said. "You've been so good lately."

I sat with care, crossing my ankles beneath the chair. "It means a lot to be trusted."

Blake poured the wine, watching me as I picked up my fork. "You've changed, you know. Your heart. Your attitude."

"I just realized what mattered," I said evenly. "And what didn't."

He smiled, pleased. "This feels right. Like what we were always supposed to be."

I took a sip of the wine and forced a blush. "I want you to be proud."

"I am." His voice dipped lower. "You're everything I hoped for."

We ate in silence after that, his eyes lingering on me with each bite. I chewed carefully, slowly, never letting my mask slip. When we finished, he walked me back upstairs. I expected him to let me go. But at the door, he paused. His hand brushed my cheek.

Then he kissed me. Lightly. On the mouth. I didn't move. Didn't flinch. I kissed him back—barely. Just enough.

He pulled away, smiling. "Goodnight, sweetheart." Then the door clicked shut behind me.

I barely made it to the trashcan. I dropped to my knees and threw up onto the floor, trembling as my stomach emptied itself. Selecia rushed over, dropping to her knees beside me with a towel. "Don't talk," she whispered. "Just breathe." I wiped my mouth with the towel, eyes stinging.

She crouched close. "He thinks you're perfect. That

means it's working." I nodded, still shaking. We climbed into bed wordlessly. The red dress stayed crumpled on the floor beside the puke, like a costume shed after the final act. And in the dark, I held on to the only truth that still mattered: This isn't love. It's war. And I'm going to win.

CHAPTER 57: PRACTICE MAKES PERFECT

Breakfast came earlier than usual. Blake knocked once and opened the door himself, grinning like he belonged there. "Rise and shine, ladies," he said. "Hope you're hungry." He didn't need to add that we'd better be.

I slid out of bed carefully, brushing sleep from my eyes. Selecia yawned beside me, but neither of us complained. Complaining didn't exist anymore—not out loud. We followed the routine. Shower. Dress. Downstairs. The kitchen was still dim with early morning light, and the air smelled faintly of soap from last night's dishes. Selecia started the toast. I handled the eggs and sausage.

Blake arrived at six sharp, as always. But something was different. He stood at the doorway longer this time, watching me. Not us—me. His eyes followed the movement of my hands, the way I set the plates, the way I wiped my palms on my shirt. I could feel him dissecting every gesture and reading into it.

I smiled like it didn't bother me. When we sat down, he didn't touch his food right away. He reached for my hand instead. I froze for half a second—just enough for it to feel real—but then let him take it. His thumb brushed across my knuckles slowly. Reverently.

"You've been so good," he said. "I knew it was in you."

I smiled again. "Thank you."

He leaned forward slightly. "You don't have to act anymore, you know. I can tell you're starting to feel it." I didn't respond. Just looked down shyly and tucked a strand of hair behind my ear.

After breakfast, Selecia stood to take the plates, but Blake waved her off. "Go rest. I need to speak with Isadora." She hesitated, but I gave her a subtle nod. She disappeared to the bedroom without a word. The silence stretched.

Then Blake stepped closer. "You meant it, didn't you?" he asked, voice low. I hesitated—not because I didn't know how to answer, but because I had to time it perfectly.

"I meant... I want peace," I said carefully. "And I want this to work."

He moved even closer, standing just in front of me now. His hand came up and brushed my hair behind my ear again. His touch lingered. Then, without asking, he leaned in and pressed a kiss to my lips. Gentle. Possessive. My body stiffened, just for a second—but I kissed him back. Just enough. Just long enough. When he pulled away, his expression was soft. Satisfied.

"I knew you'd come around."

I looked down. "I'm trying."

He stepped back, straightened his shirt, and smiled. "You're doing better than try."

When he left, I stood frozen for a moment, the echo of his kiss burning on my lips like shame. I didn't cry. Didn't scream. I just swallowed hard and walked to the sink to start cleaning the dishes. Selecia reappeared at the top of the stairs. Her eyes locked with mine.

"He kissed you, didn't he?" she asked quietly.

I nodded once. "Yes."

She stepped forward, slowly. "Are you okay?" I didn't know how to answer that.

But I said what she needed to hear. "I'm in control." And for now... I was.

CHAPTER 58:
THE RING

It happened right after dinner. Blake had been quieter than usual during the meal, watching me with an intensity that made my skin itch. Every smile I gave him, every gentle "thank you," seemed to be feeding something deeper inside him. Something dangerous.

Selecia cleared the dishes while I wiped the table, both of us in sync, moving like we were born to this routine. Blake leaned against the doorway with his arms crossed, eyes fixed on me.

"I have something for you," he said suddenly.

My hand paused mid-wipe. "Oh?" He stepped forward and reached into his pocket. I didn't breathe. When he opened his palm, my stomach dropped. A ring. Silver. Too big. Too shiny. Probably fake. But it was shaped like a promise. My face didn't change. Not even a flinch.

Blake smiled, like this was a fairytale. "I've been holding onto this for a while. I wanted to wait until the moment felt right."

I swallowed. "It's beautiful." He stepped closer. Took my hand. My pulse hammered, but I didn't pull away.

"I think we're ready now," he said, sliding the ring onto my finger like we were standing under altar lights and not a flickering kitchen bulb. "You've proven yourself to me."

I forced a breath, eyes wide like wonder. "I'm... honored." He brushed his lips against mine. Not hard. Not hungry. Just soft. Reverent. I let him. Selecia, from the corner, turned away instinctively—but she didn't speak.

Blake lingered, his thumb brushing my hand where the ring now sat. "This is a new chapter," he said quietly. "No more doubts. No more fear."

I nodded. "No more fear."

He kissed my forehead like a blessing and stepped back. "I'll be upstairs. Don't stay up too late." When the door shut behind him, I stared at the ring. Cheap metal. Too tight. Heavy with meaning.

Selecia sat beside me silently. After a moment, she whispered, "Are you okay?" I didn't answer. Because I wasn't, but this was what it would take. And I would wear his ring like armor—until it was time to take it off for good.

CHAPTER 59: THE LAST TIME I FOUGHT

The kitchen smelled like garlic and onions. My hands moved automatically—chopping, stirring, plating. Selecia hummed faintly beside me as she measured rice into a pot. The clock above the sink ticked too loudly, as if reminding us how many minutes we had left to make everything perfect. Blake would be home soon.

"You okay?" Selecia asked softly.

I nodded, but my stomach twisted. The scent of sautéed onions always made me think of home, and home made me think of before. And before I reminded me of the last time I tried to escape. Not this careful, deliberate game I was playing now. But raw, desperate rebellion.

It had been early on, months before Blake brought Selecia. I had waited until he left to grab supplies. A butter knife, a few batteries, and a screwdriver I'd hidden beneath the mattress. I worked quickly, my hands shaking, as I unscrewed the back panel of the basement vent. I thought maybe I could crawl out. Or at least jam something in the lock. I didn't make it far.

He came back early. I remembered the sound of his boots hitting the top stair. I remembered running to cover the vent, to hide the tools, to lie. It didn't matter. He knew. That was the first time he didn't yell. He smiled. That smile haunted me more than the beating that followed. More than the hours I spent curled up on the concrete floor, ribs bruised, lip split.

More than the cold.

Because the cold was constant, he turned the temperature down for two days, until my fingers were too stiff to move. No blankets. No water. For four days, he didn't bring food. The lights stayed off, but the radio stayed on—blaring static, metal, country, static again. Twenty-four hours a day. I couldn't sleep. Couldn't think. Couldn't scream. No one would hear it over the music anyway.

I started to hallucinate. I thought I saw my mother sitting in the corner, Charlotte's voice humming lullabies above the noise. I cried until my throat bled, and even then, nothing. When he finally opened the door, I couldn't stand.

He knelt beside me and brushed the hair from my face like I was something delicate. "I forgive you," he whispered. And that was the worst part. Back in the present, I stirred the beans too slowly and burned the bottom layer. The sharp scent of scorched food snapped me out of it.

"Hey," Selecia said, nudging me gently. "You good?" I looked at her. At her wide, careful eyes. At the red ribbon she wore in her hair now because Blake said it made her look "sweet." She'd adjusted, just like I had. But not because we were weak. Because we'd seen what happened when we weren't.

"We're good," I said, and took the pot off the heat. We set the table in silence—forks on the left. Napkins folded. Juice poured. When the front door opened and Blake stepped in with a grin, I met him with one of my own. Not because I wanted to. Because I remembered the dark, and I'd never go back, and Selecia would never experience it.

CHAPTER 60: MOVIE NIGHT

It started at breakfast. Blake set the plate in front of me with his usual, too-cheerful energy—eggs, toast, and a single orange slice like it was some gift. Then, as if he were announcing a weekend getaway, he said, "I think we deserve some alone time. Just the two of us. It's been too long since we had a proper date night, don't you think?"

He said it like we were married. Like this—this prison, this performance—was a relationship.

I kept my voice sweet. "That sounds nice." Selecia stiffened beside me. I didn't look at her. I couldn't.

"After dinner," Blake continued, "we'll watch something together. I picked a movie I think you'll love. Romantic. Light. It'll be good for us." He leaned in and brushed my cheek with his lips. "You'll wear that little red dress I got you. You looked beautiful in it last time."

I swallowed hard and nodded. "Of course." He beamed.

And that night, after we finished cooking and cleaning together, he walked Selecia to the guest room and handed her a small plate with crackers and juice. "You get some rest now. It's a special time for me and your mom." She flinched slightly at the word, but said nothing. When he locked the door behind her, I was already trembling inside because I knew what was coming.

The living room was dimly lit, a blanket draped over

the couch like he was preparing for some twisted sleepover. A candle flickered on the coffee table. The scent was faintly sweet—probably something generic like "vanilla breeze"—but it made my stomach turn.

"Come on," he said, patting the cushion beside him. "Let me spoil you." I sat. Not because I wanted to. But saying no wasn't an option. Not anymore. Not when we were so close. He pressed play. A formulaic romantic comedy started up on the screen, but I barely heard the lines. I was too busy tracking every inch between us. Every movement he made. Every moment, his fingers brushed too close to mine.

He put his arm around me. "I missed this," he whispered, his voice low. "Us. Just being close." I nodded faintly. He leaned in and kissed me lightly at first. I kissed him back. Not because I wanted to. Because I had to, but it didn't stop there.

His hand moved from my waist to my thigh. His lips pressed harder. Hungrier. His delusion deepened with every breath. And I let it happen because I was afraid. Not just of what he might do if I resisted, but of what he might do if he knew I was pretending.

The line between safety and violence with Blake was so thin it was invisible. And being alone with him meant no witnesses. No Selecia. No delay. Just me and his fantasies. He took me to his bedroom.

He didn't yell. He didn't threaten. He didn't have to. He just closed the door and said, "I want to be close to my wife tonight." And then he did what he wanted. I stayed silent because screaming wouldn't help. Because fighting would only make it worse. When it was over, he left me there. Alone. Like I was something spent. Like he'd scratched an itch and moved on.

I made it to the bathroom and turned on the shower. I stood under the spray until my skin turned red. Until the heat stripped away the chill. But it didn't clean anything. It didn't touch the filth he left behind. I pressed both palms to the wall and shook. Not because I was cold, but because I couldn't scream. Because the scream was trapped somewhere between my lungs and my teeth, and I couldn't let it out.

Because if I broke, I might never be able to piece myself back together.

When I returned to the guest room, my hair still damp, Blake unlocked the door without a word. I climbed into bed beside Selecia.

She turned to me, blinking. "Hey. Are you okay?"

I smiled. Too quickly. Too bright. "Yeah. I'm good. It was the same as always. We watched a romantic comedy."

She relaxed a little, nodding. "That's good." I turned off the lamp. She nestled under the blanket and drifted to sleep. And I lay beside her, eyes open, staring at the dark ceiling. Because I had lied, and she believed me. And that was the point.

If she knew what really happened, it would break her. And if she broke, we wouldn't survive this place. So, I lied to protect her. But every lie I told made me feel further away from the person I used to be. Every kiss. Every forced smile. Every "thank you" to the man who took everything from me. They were all a step deeper into a version of myself I didn't recognize.

And the worst part? It was working.

CHAPTER 61: THE PIECES WE PICK UP

I woke before the lock clicked. My body ached in places I didn't want to name. The sheets felt heavier than usual, though I knew they hadn't changed. Nothing had changed—except me. Except what had been taken again. I rolled onto my side slowly, careful not to disturb Selecia.

She was still asleep. Curled up tightly, her face tucked into the pillow like it could protect her from dreams. I watched her for a moment, trying to memorize the soft rhythm of her breathing. It reminded me of normalcy. Of quiet mornings. Of before. But the image shattered the second the bolt on the door slid open.

"Rise and shine," Blake called. His voice was too chipper, like he didn't remember what he'd done. Or worse—like he did, and it had only made him happier.

I forced myself up. "We're coming," I said gently, brushing my fingers across Selecia's shoulder. She stirred and stretched, yawning—no tension in her face. No fear. Because she believed what I told her last night—that everything was fine. That we watched a stupid movie, and he didn't touch me. That it was just another day. And that lie was the only gift I had left to give her.

We took quick turns in the bathroom—washing, dressing, and trying to look presentable. I dabbed concealer under my eyes with trembling fingers. Not because Blake cared how I looked, but because I couldn't let Selecia see the bruising sorrow in my face. The kitchen felt colder than usual. Or maybe I just did.

We cooked in silence—scrambled eggs, toast, and the last few strips of bacon. Selecia hummed softly as she poured juice into glasses. It made me want to cry.

He came in with his usual swagger. "Smells amazing," he said, kissing the top of my head like I belonged to him. My stomach turned.

"Good morning," I replied, and it wasn't my voice. It was hers—the one I'd crafted for him. Sweet. Obedient. Trusting.

He turned to Selecia. "You helping your mom again today?"

She nodded with a quiet, "Yes, sir."

He beamed, as if we were a happy little sitcom family. "That's what I like to hear."

We sat and ate like everything was normal. My hands shook slightly when I reached for the butter. Selecia noticed. "You okay?" she mouthed across the table. I smiled. Nodded. She didn't push. After breakfast, Blake stood and stretched. "I have errands today. You girls be good."

"Of course," I said.

When the door slammed and the lock clicked shut, I finally exhaled. Selecia began clearing dishes, but her eyes never left me.

"Are you sure you're okay?" she asked softly.

"I'm just tired," I said. "Too many thoughts. I'm ready to stop playing this game."

She handed me a plate to dry. "You're doing really well. With him. I don't think he suspects a thing." That should've been reassuring. But it wasn't. Because it meant I was doing it right, even if I was smiling while dying inside.

"Thanks," I said.

We worked in silence again, and I realized: we were building a pattern. A rhythm. Not of survival—of preparation. Each day, we made him believe. Each chore completed, each lie told, was a brick in the escape plan we couldn't speak aloud. But something inside me whispered: How many more bricks will I have to lay before I lose myself completely?

CHAPTER 62: THE CRACK IN THE FRAME

Breakfast looked almost normal. Almost. The table was set neatly, plates already waiting—pancakes, eggs, and a tiny bowl of syrup. Selecia and I moved like we'd done this all our lives. Blake watched us from his seat, smiling like a proud husband and father. I sat across from him, folding my hands lightly. My smile was soft. Practiced. Intentional.

"Blake?" I asked gently, waiting until his eyes met mine.

"Yes, sweetheart?"

"I was wondering..." I paused, reaching for the fork. "If you might leave the bedroom door unlocked at night. Just that one. Not the outside locks, obviously."

His brow furrowed. "Why?"

I glanced down at my plate. "Sometimes I wake up and need water. Or the bathroom. I don't want to knock and wake you. And I've been having nightmares again, and getting up to walk around for a minute helps." He didn't respond at first. Just watched me, measuring something behind his eyes.

I added, "It's just the one door. We wouldn't leave the room or anything. I just... I'd sleep easier knowing I had a little more room to breathe." Beside me, Selecia didn't flinch or interrupt. She just took a slow bite of toast like she was completely unaffected. She was playing her role perfectly.

Blake leaned back in his chair. "You've been doing so

well," he said slowly. "Both of you."

I nodded. "We just want to keep doing well."

He tilted his head, thinking. Then smiled. "Alright. We'll try it. But you don't try anything. If I find out, you did…"

"I won't," I said quickly. "You have my word."

He stood and kissed my forehead. "I trust you." But that trust came with weight. It wasn't a gift—it was another test. Another invisible line we couldn't cross.

That night, he walked us upstairs like always. Brushed a hand across my back as we entered the room. "Sleep well, baby." Then, for the first time, he closed the door without the click of a lock.

Selecia waited until his footsteps disappeared down the hallway. Then she whispered, "Why'd you ask that?"

"Because I needed to know if he'd say yes," I replied.

She frowned. "You're testing him."

I nodded. "And every time he says yes, we get one step closer." I lay awake long after she fell asleep, staring at the door. It was just a piece of wood. But tonight, it wasn't a barrier. It was an open question. And questions had answers.

CHAPTER 63:
SEA OF RED

I felt it before I saw it. A dull cramp low in my abdomen. Not sharp, not alarming. Just enough to make me pause as I folded laundry on the edge of the bed. I didn't say anything at first. I kept moving, sorting through Blake's shirts and our hand-me-down clothes like nothing had changed. Like something wasn't unraveling inside me.

Then I felt the warmth—that sudden, unmistakable shift. I set the shirt down and padded to the bathroom. Not in a rush. Not panicking. Because some part of me already knew. My body knew before my mind could form the thought, before the fear had a name.

When I pulled down my pants, the blood was there. A lot of it. It hadn't soaked through yet, not enough to reach the bed. And thank God for that—Selecia was still in the room. Still humming quietly to herself as she cleaned the little desk space Blake had given us to "journal." She hadn't seen. She wouldn't.

I sat on the toilet and just stared at it. I hadn't even known I was pregnant. I hadn't missed a period because my cycles had been irregular for so long. The stress. The malnutrition. The trauma. All of it had thrown my body into chaos, and I'd stopped trying to keep track. But something had started. Something had been growing inside me, and now... it was gone.

I leaned forward and pressed my elbows to my knees, burying my face in my hands. No sound came out. No sobs. Just my breath—tight and shallow.

I don't know how long I sat there, but the cramps got worse. I kept checking. More blood. More pain. Eventually, I cleaned myself up, flushed everything, and wrapped a rag around my underwear like some makeshift pad. I rinsed my hands, dried them on my shirt, and looked at my reflection in the mirror.

I looked the same. But I wasn't. I stepped out of the bathroom quietly. Selecia didn't look up. She was sketching something, maybe a dog, perhaps a tree. I couldn't tell. My vision felt blurry. Not from tears. Just… disconnected. Like I wasn't quite inside my body anymore.

"You okay?" she asked after a few minutes, not looking up.

I nodded too quickly. "Just tired." She accepted it. She always did because we were always tired, all the time.

That night, I didn't eat dinner. I pushed the food around on the plate until Blake stopped watching, and then I dumped the rest in the trash under the sink. Selecia asked if my stomach was hurting, and I said it must've been something I ate. She didn't press. But Blake noticed.

"You've been quiet today," he said as he locked up for the night. "Everything alright?"

I forced a smile. "Just sleepy."

He nodded and kissed the top of my head like I was some housewife in a 1950s sitcom. "Well, you get some rest. We've got a full day tomorrow." When he left, I climbed into bed beside Selecia and lay there in the dark, eyes wide open. I didn't know what I was supposed to feel.

Relief? Gratitude? Sadness? I didn't even know how far along I was. A few weeks? A month? It couldn't have been much more than that. But it had been real. A possibility. A heartbeat that almost existed. And now it was gone.

And I didn't know whether to mourn it or be thankful. I stared at the ceiling, counting the small cracks in the paint as if they might spell something out. My body still ached, but it was the ache of emptiness now of something lost without a name.

A part of me was glad. Because how could I carry a child in this place? How could I give birth to something beautiful in a world built on violence and fear? It would've been Blake's. A constant reminder. A living, breathing extension of everything I hated. But still... it had been mine too. Mine. And now it wasn't.

That's what kept circling in my mind, over and over, like a cruel whisper. It's gone. You didn't even get to decide. I felt numb the next morning. I went through the motions, cooking, cleaning, smiling when he smiled. Saying "thank you" when he complimented the eggs. Nodding when he told me I was glowing. Glowing.

I wanted to throw the pan at his face. But I didn't. I kept my hands steady, my voice even, because none of this could slip. That day, I barely spoke to Selecia. Not because I didn't want to—but because I was afraid of what might come out. Because if I started talking about what I felt, I didn't know if I could stop.

I sat in the shower that night long after the water had gone cold, arms wrapped around my knees, chin pressed to my chest. And for the first time since the blood started, I cried. Not loud. Not violently. Just quiet, steady tears that felt like they were being pulled from the center of my ribs.

I didn't want this child, not like this. But I'd lost it. And that still meant something. It meant something because my body had been building a future without asking me. And now that future was gone, and the world hadn't even noticed. That night, when Blake kissed my cheek goodnight, I didn't even flinch. I just nodded and said, "Sleep well."

And when I curled into bed beside Selecia, she whispered, "You're shivering."

"I'm fine," I said. "Just a little cold." She reached over and tucked the blanket tighter around me. I closed my eyes and pretended to sleep. But I didn't. Not for hours. I just kept thinking...

If something inside me can die without warning—without even being named—what else will I lose before we make it out?

CHAPTER 64: HOLLOW DAYS

The days after the miscarriage blurred. They weren't even days, really—just pale periods smudged together by repetition. Wake up. Cook. Clean. Smile. Sleep. Repeat.

I moved like a shadow of myself, careful not to let anything slip. Not the fatigue. Not the cramps that still lingered. Not the ache deep in my chest every time Blake called me beautiful. I didn't flinch when he touched me. Didn't freeze when he brushed his lips against my temple. That was the performance now: not reacting. But something in me had shifted. Something essential had gone silent.

On the third morning, I stood at the stove flipping pancakes and caught my reflection in the small, grease-smudged window above the sink. My hair was tied back. My eyes were blank. I looked older—like the girl I used to be had left, and someone else had stepped into her place. A version of me that had learned how to keep breathing without actually living.

"You okay?" Selecia asked from the table, her voice low.

I nodded. "Just tired." It was my new script. The safe one. The one that didn't invite questions. Selecia didn't push. She just watched me with a softness that made it harder to breathe. I wanted to tell her. I wanted to say I'd lost something. That something had died inside me, and I didn't know how to grieve it without unraveling completely. But if I said it out loud, she would cry. She would ask questions I didn't have answers to. And worse—she might stop believing we were strong enough to get out.

So, I kept it buried like everything else. Blake came into the kitchen humming that afternoon. Some upbeat melody that didn't match the staleness of the air. He clapped his hands once and said, "Tonight, I'm thinking spaghetti. Something warm. Comfort food." Comfort.

I smiled. "We'll make it special."

He winked. "That's my girl."

The spaghetti boiled, and the sauce simmered. The kitchen smelled like a memory, like a house I hadn't seen in four years, like a mother who used to hum while she stirred noodles in a pot. I blinked hard and stirred faster. I wouldn't let that feeling in. Not now. Not here. When dinner was done, Blake pulled out a deck of cards and said, "Let's have a little fun tonight. A family game night. Like old times."

There were no old times. But I nodded. Selecia sat beside me on the couch, silent but cooperative. We played Go Fish and Crazy Eights like we were two kids and a father enjoying an evening in. Every time Blake laughed, I forced one of my own. Every time he reached over and touched my arm, I held still and smiled.

Inside, I felt like I was watching someone else wear my skin. By the time the game ended, Blake looked genuinely happy. He rubbed his eyes and yawned. "I'll let you girls turn in early tonight. You've been doing great. I'm proud of you." He didn't kiss me goodnight. Just ruffled my hair and walked off humming the same cheerful tune.

When we were alone in the room, I changed into my nightclothes and sat on the edge of the bed. My hands wouldn't stop shaking. I pressed them flat against my thighs, willing them still.

"You sure you're okay?" Selecia asked again, this time in a softer tone.

I nodded. "It's just been a long week."

"Nightmares?" she guessed. "You're not sleeping much."

I looked at her. The way her hair curled slightly at the ends, the way her cheeks had filled out with the extra meals. She was stronger now. More alert. But she was still a kid. Still hoping. Still fragile.

"Something like that," I said. "They'll pass." She lay down and turned away from me. I slid under the blanket beside her and stared at the ceiling. Sleep didn't come.

Instead, memories did. Flashes of that moment in the bathroom. The blood. The disbelief. The way the silence felt heavier than any scream. I hadn't cried since that night in the shower. And even then, I'd cried without sound. As if making noise might give it too much power. Might make it real.

But it was real. It was a loss. And I hadn't let myself feel it.

I turned onto my side, facing the wall. My hand slid over my lower abdomen, pressing gently against the spot that had once held possibility. And for the first time since it happened, I whispered to the darkness, "I'm sorry."

Sorry for not knowing. For not wanting. For not protecting something that had already started forming inside me. I didn't say it out loud again. Just once. A quiet confession to the part of myself that still believed in mourning. The next few days, I went numb again, not on purpose. It just happened. Selecia noticed.

She started doing more around the house—taking over the dishes, folding the laundry, even when it wasn't her turn. I saw her watching me, her eyes searching for something she didn't know how to name. She didn't say anything. But she was there. She stayed close.

Blake didn't notice. He was too busy reveling in our "progress." He talked more now. About adding curtains to the kitchen. About putting a radio in the bedroom so we can fall asleep to it. About trying for a baby. The words dropped like acid in my chest.

"We're doing so well," he said one night, his hand on my lower back. "I think it might be time. Time to grow our family." I froze. I didn't breathe.

"You're already a wonderful mother," he added, nodding toward Selecia. "It would be perfect."

"Maybe," I said, my voice tight. "But maybe we should enjoy this stage a little longer first."

He smiled. "You're right. I always rush things. We'll wait. For now." For now. I nodded. But inside, I was screaming. That night, I couldn't sleep again. I sat at the desk and stared at the journal Blake insisted we keep. "Write your dreams," he said once. "They're important." I didn't write dreams.

I wrote a list. Things I Had Lost:

My freedom.

My body.

My name (he only calls me "darling" now). Unless he was angry.

My voice.

The baby I didn't know I had.

The right to mourn.

The list grew. And then I tore the page out and burned it over the stove when no one was looking. Because if Blake ever read it, we'd lose everything. Still, the act of writing it felt like something. A rebellion. A crack in the mask.

149

The next morning, I woke up before the alarm and stood at the window, staring out into the backyard. The trees were still bare, their branches like arms stretching toward a sky that never seemed to brighten. Winter was coming. So was something else.

I didn't know what yet. But I could feel it like pressure building under the surface of things. Like the part of me that had died in that bathroom wasn't entirely gone—it had just changed. Hardened. And maybe, just maybe, that hardness would help keep us alive long enough to get out.

CHAPTER 65: BLINDING

The front door opened without warning. Blake didn't speak—just motioned for us to follow with a quick flick of his wrist. I exchanged a glance with Selecia, her eyes wide and wary. He hadn't mentioned errands. No promises. No threats. Just, "Come on."

We hesitated. Neither of us moved right away. Then I took a step forward. Barefoot. We didn't have shoes anymore —we hadn't needed them. We hadn't been beyond the front porch since we were brought here. Not since the basement. Not since captivity became our normal.

The threshold felt like a barrier between two worlds. As soon as we stepped outside, the sunlight struck me like a blade. Sharp. Blinding. My eyes burned and watered instantly, squinting against a brightness I'd almost forgotten existed. The sky was too open. The air is too cold. Everything felt like too much.

I raised my hand to shield my face, blinking rapidly. My skin flinched at the chill of the porch beneath my bare feet. The boards were rough, splintering. It felt wrong. Foreign. Three and a half years indoors will do that to you.

Selecia gripped my arm lightly. Her breathing had quickened. She didn't say anything; she didn't have to. Her silence told me everything. She felt it too. The smallness of the world we'd lived in until this moment. The sudden vastness of the one we'd forgotten.

Blake stood on the gravel driveway with his keys in one hand and a paper bag in the other. "Come help," he called, like we did this every week.

There were no neighbors in sight—just dense woods hugging the edge of the house. A cracked road wound off into silence. No cars passing. No voices. No escape. We stepped off the porch, gravel biting into the soles of our feet. We didn't complain. Didn't wince out loud. Pain was familiar. Blisters were nothing.

We carried bags of food, including canned soup, cereal, and powdered milk. Nonperishables. The kind you buy when you're preparing to stay locked away for months. Inside, the air felt thick again. Safer, maybe, but not comforting.

As we passed through the hallway, something caught my eye. A calendar. One of those oversized ones with inspirational quotes and big boxes for each day. It was flipped to August. The quote at the top said, "The best view comes after the hardest climb." I stared at it, numb.

August. But not just August. August 2024. Almost four years. Four years since the crash. Four years since he dragged me into his world and locked the door behind us. We'd passed unmarked birthdays. Missed holidays. Lost track of entire seasons. All that time, gone. Like the world kept spinning and forgot to take us with it.

I didn't mention the calendar. Not to Selecia. Not to Blake. I just memorized the way the numbers looked. I let the silence hang in the air as I helped unpack and put things away. That night, I moved like a ghost. I chopped vegetables and stirred the soup. Set the table. Ate silently. When Blake smiled and called me "his sunshine," I didn't flinch. But I didn't smile back, either.

"You okay?" Selecia whispered once we were alone in our room.

"Yeah," I said, too quickly. "Just tired." I lay beside her, staring at the ceiling. My thoughts felt like wet cement—heavy and hardening. I had seen the sun today. Really saw it for the first time in a long time. And it hurt.

It reminded me of everything we'd lost. Everything we might never get back. It reminded me that even if we got out… we wouldn't be the same. I wasn't the same. Hope felt brittle. Like something that might snap if I held it too tightly. I'd been faking normal for so long, I didn't know what real even looked like anymore.

And the worst part? Blake hadn't forgotten to lock the door that morning. He'd done it on purpose. To make us believe this was a gift. A privilege. Kindness. But it wasn't. It was a leash. And we were still tied to the post.

CHAPTER 66: UNRAVELING

We heard him before we saw him. The front door slammed—hard enough to rattle the cheap dishes in the cabinets—and the sound of Blake's boots against the laminate floor echoed like thunder. Selecia and I froze. She dropped the dish towel she was folding, and I slowly turned off the burner, sliding the pan of eggs to the back of the stove.

He hadn't slammed a door like that in months. When he rounded the corner into the kitchen, I could tell something was wrong. His eyes were wild. His shirt was half untucked, and there was a scratch running down the side of his neck— fresh, angry, like he'd been in a fight. His breathing was too fast. Erratic.

"Everything okay?" I asked, keeping my voice soft. He didn't answer right away. He just stared at me. Then at Selecia. Then back at me.

"Don't talk to me like I'm a guest in my own home," he snapped. "Dinner isn't even on the table yet."

I blinked. "It's breakfast." Blake didn't respond. He pushed past me, grabbed a cup, and poured himself a glass of orange juice with shaking hands. His knuckles were white. Selecia stood frozen near the fridge. She didn't even breathe until he turned and walked back toward the hallway, muttering something about people taking him for granted.

When the door to his room shut, Selecia whispered,

"What was that?"

"I don't know," I said, moving toward her and handing her the towel she'd dropped. "But we need to be careful." She nodded and got back to drying dishes, her hands trembling slightly. By midday, Blake hadn't come out again. We finished our chores in silence and made a simple lunch—canned beans, rice, and a few old vegetables that were starting to go soft. The storm in him had gone quiet, but we knew better than to relax.

That evening, he came out smiling. Calm. Like nothing had happened. He kissed me on the forehead and told me I looked beautiful. The pattern started to shift after that. One day, he was cheerful and generous, bringing home bags of discount groceries, letting us eat together in the living room, even joking about taking us out one day "when things settle down."

Next, he was unpredictable, angry, distant, and silent. He started locking the door from the outside again—not every night, but often enough that I noticed. He forgot to check our journal entries. He forgot meals. Once, he forgot to come home at all. And each time he slipped, my mind worked faster.

What could I hide? Where could I stash extra food? How could we use his unraveling against him? But while my mind raced, my body slowed. Again. The nausea crept in quietly, soft waves that I blamed on nerves. But the second time I gagged while brushing my teeth, I knew. The tenderness in my chest. The way the smell of bacon made my stomach flip. I didn't need a test. I knew.

Pregnant. Again. I didn't tell Selecia. I couldn't. It was too fresh. Too uncertain. I didn't even want to think the word, let alone say it. It felt like a curse, as if I were calling something into being just to watch it vanish.

I started counting the days—secretly, on a page I tore from the back of the journal and tucked into the lining of the dresser. One scratch mark for each day I didn't bleed. One for each day, the ache in my lower back remained steady. I made it to thirteen before it happened.

The second miscarriage was different. It started with pain—sharper, more insistent. I woke up in the middle of the night and couldn't breathe. My hands clutched my abdomen, and I bit my fist to keep from waking Selecia. She shifted beside me, murmured something in her sleep, and rolled the other way.

I slipped out of bed and into the bathroom. I didn't need the light. I knew what I'd find. Blood. Thick, red, and already pooling. I sat on the floor, my back against the tub, and cried. Not quietly this time.

I let the sobs out, choking on the sound of them, pressing my forehead to the cold porcelain and wishing it would all stop. The pain. The fear. The pretending. Everything. I didn't know how long I stayed there, but by the time I stood up again, my legs were numb, and the tears had dried in itchy streaks on my face. There was nothing to bury. Nothing to hold. Just blood. And silence. Selecia noticed the next morning.

"You're pale," she said, watching me stir oatmeal.

"I didn't sleep well."

"You didn't eat yesterday either."

"I wasn't hungry." She didn't press, but I saw it in her eyes. Worry. The kind that comes from knowing someone too well. I smiled, but it didn't reach my eyes. She didn't smile back. Blake didn't notice.

He walked in, kissed my cheek, complimented the food, and asked if I'd changed my shampoo. I said yes. He liked it. I said thank you. The words tasted like ash. That afternoon, he left to "run errands." He didn't say when he'd be back. We waited an hour. Two. Three.

Then I noticed it. The lock on the front door? Not engaged. I stood there, staring at the knob, heart hammering.

"Selecia," I whispered. She came over and followed my gaze.

"Is it...?" I nodded.

"We could go now," she said, voice shaking. "We could just walk out." My hands hovered over the knob. My pulse thundered. And for a moment, I saw it. Freedom. Trees. A road. The outside world. But I pulled back.

"No shoes. No plan. It's broad daylight. He could come back any second."

Her shoulders slumped. "So... we wait."

"We plan," I corrected. "We hide food. We map the area. We wait for night. And then we run." That night, I noticed a small calendar tacked to the wall. It was old. Stained. But the pages were marked. Scribbled. Tracked. And it hit me. We'd been here for nearly four years. Almost four years of waking up to the same walls. The same voice. The same hunger. And I wasn't sure how many more months I could take. But maybe I kept hesitating because I wasn't sure of my role outside of these walls. And I couldn't bear the thought of telling Selecia we could leave and him catching us. He would kill her just to hurt me.

I looked at Selecia—her head resting on the pillow beside mine. Her hair was matted from sweat. Her arms curled around herself. She deserved better. We both did. Later that week, Blake brought home a pair of secondhand shoes.

"Figured you two might need these soon," he said. "The floor's getting cold." Selecia's eyes flicked to mine. He was slipping. Offering tools, he didn't even realize we could use them. And still, the third pregnancy came.

This one, I knew from the start. The heaviness. The way

my body felt like it belonged to someone else again. I didn't keep a calendar this time. I didn't name it. I didn't allow myself to imagine anything at all.

And like the others, it came to an end. Quietly. One night, I woke up soaked in blood, shaking so hard I nearly passed out in the bathroom. I cleaned it up in silence. Tucked away the rag I used. Hid the pain behind my eyes. And in the morning, I made pancakes. Smiled when he said they were "perfect." Nodded when he called me his wife.

Because even if my body was failing, even if pieces of me were being stolen every day, we were still here. Still alive. Still waiting. And one day, he would forget something bigger than a lock or a pair of shoes. One day, he would slip so severely he couldn't recover. And when that day came, we'd be ready.

CHAPTER 67: THE SPLINTER

The coffee pot hissed on the stove as if it were angry. I stared at the rising steam; my hands still wrapped around the chipped mug like it was something sacred. Selecia moved behind me, setting the table, quiet as ever. She didn't ask why I hadn't spoken all morning. She didn't need to.

Something had cracked. Not broken—not yet—but I could feel the fracture deep beneath my ribs. A splitting down the center of who I used to be and whatever this shell was now.

"You want sugar?" she asked gently.

I nodded. Then shook my head. "No. I'm fine."

That was the problem. I said that too often. I'm fine when I wasn't. When I was aching, when I was hollowed out, haunted. I used to be able to lie and feel nothing. Now the lies scraped their way up my throat.

Blake came in late. The lock clicked louder than usual. He looked… disheveled. His hair stuck up in places like he hadn't slept, and the buttons on his shirt were uneven. His eyes darted between us, lingered on the untouched eggs, and the missing smile on my face.

"You girls okay?" he asked, his tone light but edged.

Selecia smiled. "Breakfast is still warm."

He didn't sit right away. Just walked around the table, slow, calculating. Then he grabbed my mug and sniffed it.

"Smells burnt." I didn't say anything. I didn't flinch either. That's what he was waiting for.

"Something feels different," he muttered. "Like... maybe someone's not appreciating everything I do." He dropped the mug on purpose. It hit the floor and cracked straight through. The silence that followed the shattering of the glass was louder than the noise itself.

"I'll clean it up," I said quickly, bending to my knees. The sharp edge of the ceramic sliced the side of my thumb. I didn't even react.

When he left for work, Selecia helped bandage my hand. "He's getting worse," she whispered.

"I know."

"What do we do?" I didn't answer. Because I didn't have an answer yet, but we couldn't wait much longer. That afternoon, I went to put away laundry and found a splintered piece of wood in the closet floorboard. Jagged, almost sharp. I didn't know how long it had been there, but I didn't put it back. I wrapped it in a rag and slid it under the bed. Mini goals. That's how I kept sane. Small wins. A sharp edge hidden. A pattern memorized. A weakness observed.

Later that week, while I was washing dishes, the TV in the living room caught my eye. Blake always left it on, background noise. Usually sports or news. This time it was a missing person special. I don't know what made me walk closer—just instinct. And then I saw it—my face.

The photo was taken in school during my sophomore year. Hair long, makeup light, the smile barely mine. But it was me. And underneath, in bold letters:

STILL MISSING. ANY INFORMATION, PLEASE CALL—

The rest blurred. My knees buckled.

Selecia rushed in behind me. "What—"

I turned the channel fast. "Nothing. Just... just something dumb."

She stared at me, uncertain. "You okay?" That word again. Okay.

"No," I whispered. "But we're not forgotten." I didn't sleep that night. I just stared at the ceiling, counting down the days in my head again. Almost four years. Almost. That calendar in the hallway had confirmed it. And we couldn't afford a fifth.

Blake began to slip and forget small things. Leaving the stove on and losing his keys. He even forgot to relock the cabinet one night after dinner—inside it, we found batteries. We hid them behind the sink panel.

He would sometimes start muttering and pacing the hallway. Accusing me of "thinking about someone else." Said my eyes "looked too distant lately." Said he "could feel me slipping away."

"You're mine," he hissed once when I brought him a drink too slowly. "You think I don't see what you're doing?" But then he softened, kissed my forehead. "Don't worry. We'll be together forever." I smiled when he said it. But I looked at Selecia across the room. And I saw the same panic in her eyes that I felt in my chest. We had to run. Soon. Even if it killed us.

CHAPTER 68:
THE KEYS

Blake set the table with unusual care that night, humming low under his breath like he'd won something. He wasn't angry today. He hadn't slammed a door or accused me of anything. In fact, he'd been eerily calm and composed in a way that made my skin crawl. The kind of calm that always came before something worse.

Selecia and I stood side by side in the kitchen, working in rhythm like we always did—me seasoning the chicken, her arranging plates and silverware. We didn't talk much anymore unless we had to. Not because we didn't want to, but because every word carried risk. One wrong phrase, one misstep, and Blake's mood could crack like thin ice.

He sat down before we did. "Smells good," he said, reaching for the napkin and placing it neatly in his lap like we were at a restaurant. "I'm proud of you girls. You're making this house feel like a home."

I smiled. Tight. Controlled. "Thank you."

Selecia didn't speak. She was getting better at playing the quiet daughter and playing safe. Then it happened. Blake reached across the table to grab the salt and knocked something off the edge of the table. It clattered against the linoleum with a dull metallic thud. My eyes darted down. His keys. My chest clenched. He didn't notice.

"Oops," he muttered, scooping up the salt with one

hand, but not the keys. He set the shaker back in place, took a bite of his food, and never looked down again. The keys stayed there, resting just beside the table leg, nearly out of sight. Selecia's eyes flicked to mine. Fast. Fleeting. I gave the tiniest shake of my head. Not yet. Not while he was still here.

Dinner passed slowly after that. Blake chatted about the news—some politician, a storm coming, maybe snow. He seemed distant. Distracted. Not entirely present.

We cleared the table like always. Washed dishes. Wiped counters. I dried my hands on a towel and turned to find Blake already in the hallway, stretching. "Think I'm gonna head to bed early," he said with a yawn. "Don't stay up too late."

"Of course not," I said. "Goodnight." He didn't come back to lock the bedroom door. Selecia and I sat on opposite ends of the bed for a long time, frozen, listening. Waiting. I counted his footsteps down the hall, the creak of his mattress, and the flick of the lamp turning off. Then… silence. Just the hum of the fridge, the tick of the thermostat, and my own heartbeat slamming against my ribs.

An hour passed. Two. The moonlight filtered through the crack in the curtains, casting faint shadows across the carpet. I stood up slowly, as if even that could wake him. Selecia followed, her bare feet silent on the floor. We stepped into the hallway like ghosts.

I moved first, inching down the hallway toward the kitchen. The keys were still there. Still lying in the same spot where Blake had dropped them hours ago. I reached for them, trembling, and clutched the ring so tightly the metal bit into my palm.

Behind me, Selecia hovered near the wall, her breath coming fast. I turned and nodded once. We crept to the front door. The bolts were loud. Too loud. I turned them one by one, flinching at every click. Every shift in the metal made my stomach knot tighter. My hands were slick with sweat. I kept glancing over my shoulder, expecting to see his silhouette at the end of the hall. But nothing came. No footsteps. No shouting. Just the sound of our freedom, unlocking itself one click at a time.

Finally, the door opened. The cold air hit me like a slap. For a second, I froze. Just stood there in the doorway, staring out at the darkened field beyond the porch, where the woods loomed like silent witnesses. I had dreamed of this so many times. But it never felt real, not like this.

"Go," I whispered. Selecia didn't hesitate. She grabbed my hand, and we ran barefoot across the frozen ground, rocks and thorns slicing our skin. We didn't stop to cry. We didn't stop to scream. We ran like the ground behind us was on fire. I didn't look back. Not even once.

CHAPTER 69: THE FIELD

The ground tore at our feet—sharp twigs, frozen grass, tiny rocks slicing skin that hadn't touched the outside in years. I didn't care. Every stab of pain was proof: we were out. Free. Alive.

We didn't speak. Our breath came in fast gasps, clouding in the frigid air, and the only sound between us was the soft slap of soles against dirt. We ducked under branches, leapt over a broken fence, and pushed forward through the darkness with nothing but moonlight to guide us.

My lungs burned. My legs screamed. But I didn't stop. I don't know how long we ran—time lost meaning out there. Minutes could've been seconds or hours. The only thing that existed was motion—forward, forward, forward—because the second we stopped, we would hear him.

Selecia stumbled once, and I caught her by the arm. She winced, but didn't fall. We didn't dare slow down. Not until we saw it. Headlights. Distant. Small. But real.

"A car," I choked, grabbing her hand tighter. "Come on!" We cut across another patch of field, emerging near the edge of a narrow two-lane road. There it was—a gold sedan rolling slowly down the shoulder, like some kind of miracle. I ran straight for it, waving both arms wildly in the air, heart pounding so loudly I could barely hear myself scream.

"Stop! Please stop!" The car hesitated, then pulled over to

the side of the road. The driver's side door opened. A woman—maybe in her fifties, with short hair and a heavy coat—stepped out cautiously, holding up her phone like a shield.

"Are you girls okay?" she called out. Her voice was wary, but kind.

"Yes," I gasped. "No. Please—we need help. Please." She looked at us—at our bare feet, our ragged clothes, our faces twisted with panic—and something shifted in her expression. She moved forward.

"Oh my God. Okay. Okay, get in the car. I'll call the poli —" Bang. The sound cracked through the night like a whip. The woman's body jerked, once, twice—then crumpled to the ground. Blood sprayed across the side of the car.

"No!" Selecia screamed, lunging forward. But I grabbed her, held her back with everything I had. And then he stepped into the headlights. Blake.

His silhouette was wrong—arms stiff, legs mechanical, like he wasn't even human anymore. Just rage and madness stitched together in the shape of a man. He raised the gun again.

"Run!" I screamed. Selecia didn't. She broke from my grip and ran straight for him.

"Don't touch her!" she yelled. "Don't you touch her!"

"Selecia!" I shrieked. She threw herself at him, hands clawing, teeth bared like some wild thing. Blake grunted, shoved her hard, then— Another shot. She dropped. I couldn't breathe. Couldn't move. The world tilted.

"No..." I whispered.

Blake stepped over her like she was trash on the ground. He looked at me, eyes glazed, mouth twisted in a grin that didn't reach his face.

"You thought you could leave me?" he asked softly. I didn't answer. He pointed the gun at my chest. But he didn't fire. "Get back in the house," he said. I didn't move. He lunged. And then—Blackness.

CHAPTER 70: FALSE DAWN

I shot up with a scream lodged in my throat, choking on air that didn't feel real. Sweat clung to my skin like oil, and my hands trembled violently as I clawed at the blanket. My chest heaved. I looked around—wildly, desperately.

I was in the bedroom. Still here. The same furniture. The same walls. My breath hitched. It had been a dream. Just a dream.

Selecia stirred beside me, half-awake now, frowning as she rubbed her eyes. "What—what happened?" I couldn't speak. My throat burned. My whole body ached with the ghost of motion. Every part of me was still there—in the field, on the road, in front of that woman, covered in blood. I could still feel Selecia's hand slipping out of mine. Still hear the gunshot. I could still see her fall. Tears streaked down my face before I even registered that I was crying.

"Isadora?" she whispered, sitting up fully now, voice soft and uncertain.

" I-I thought you were dead," I managed to choke out, pulling her toward me in a grip that was too tight, too desperate.

She froze in my arms for a second, then slowly hugged me back. "I'm not," she said. "I'm here." But the truth was, in that moment, I wasn't. I was still out there, still on the asphalt. Still screaming and still trying to throw myself over her body.

And when I looked at her now, safe and alive beside me, all I could think was: What if next time, it isn't a dream? What if he really does kill her? What if I really lose her? I couldn't stop shaking.

We sat like that for a long time—me holding her like she was already gone, and her whispering, "I'm here, I'm here," over and over like she was trying to pull me out of the nightmare.

Eventually, she pulled back just far enough to look at me. "What did you see?" I didn't want to tell her. But I did. Every horrible detail. The escape. The road. The car. The woman. The blood. The way she ran at Blake. The way she dropped. How I couldn't stop it. How I didn't even get to scream her name one last time. When I finished, she was pale.

"That's what you're afraid of?" she whispered. "That he'll kill me?" I nodded, jaw clenched.

She swallowed hard, then took my hand. "Then we make sure he doesn't." There was no fear in her voice. Just resolve. I stared at her—this girl who had every reason to break—and I realized something terrifying. She wasn't afraid of dying. She was scared of me dying for her. And I didn't know if I could protect us both anymore. But I had to try.

CHAPTER 71: NO ROOM FOR GHOSTS

The morning after the dream was too quiet. Like the house was holding its breath.

Blake left early, muttering something about errands. His keys jingled loudly in his pocket, like he needed us to hear the reminder—he still held all the power.

I stayed on the bed long after the door shut behind him, arms wrapped around my knees. I hadn't changed out of the oversized T-shirt he liked. Couldn't bring myself to move. My mind kept flashing to the road, the blood, the gun. Selecia's body collapsing like a ragdoll. My hands slipping in the cold as I tried to reach her.

Selecia gave me space. She always did when she knew I was unraveling. But eventually, she sat beside me.

"You know it wasn't real," she said. I nodded. But it didn't matter. The ache didn't know the difference. The grief felt real. The terror still lingered in my muscles, coiled and ready to strike.

"I keep seeing it," I whispered. "You running away. I keep hearing the sound of the shot."

"You don't have to do it alone," she said. I looked at her. Really looked. And for a second, I couldn't believe she was alive, that she was sitting here, whole and warm and breathing beside me. I pulled her into a hug, clinging to her like a lifeline.

She hugged back, fierce and steady. "We're still here," she whispered.

Later, I found myself scrubbing the kitchen sink as if trying to erase something. Selecia sat nearby with one of the old coloring books Blake brought down weeks ago, the tip of her pencil never really touching the page. We were both somewhere else.

The dream had left more than a scar. It had lit a fire. The kind of fear that didn't shrink with time—it multiplied. And it was screaming at me now: You're running out of time.

By the time Blake returned with groceries and a fake smile, I'd buried the panic. He handed me a bag of apples and made some joke about "his girls eating healthy," and I smiled like I wasn't mentally counting down how many nights we might have left.

During dinner, Selecia and I played our roles. I laughed once, because I had to. Blake noticed and looked pleased. But my eyes kept flicking to the window above the sink.

Later, after Blake locked himself in his office, I grabbed Selecia's arm. "We need to check the back window." She nodded immediately. We crept through the hallway, avoiding every known creak in the floor. In the laundry room, I reached for the small window above the shelves. The bolts were still in place —four of them, drilled directly into the frame. But one had rust around the edges, the metal beginning to flake like brittle snow.

"Look," I whispered.

Selecia leaned in, running her thumb along the rust. "If we can loosen this one..."

"We might be able to pull the whole frame apart."

"Not tonight," she said.

"No. But soon." We didn't have tools. Not yet. But we

had time. And desperation. And that was enough. Back in the bedroom, we lay under the covers, our shoulders pressed together, facing the same direction. Not quite touching. Not quite apart.

"I thought I lost you," I said, voice low.

"You didn't," she replied. "You won't." I didn't answer. My brain was already turning, running simulations of bolt patterns and hiding places and how many seconds it might take to undo a screw with a spoon.

Sleep didn't come easily. But when it did, there was no field. No gun. No blood. Just the sound of my own breathing, even and slow. And when I woke up, it was still quiet. Not peaceful. But focused. We weren't ghosts yet.

CHAPTER 72: ANOTHER DAY

The morning began like any other. Blake brewed coffee in his chipped ceramic mug, humming under his breath. I scrambled eggs in a pan slick with oil, the scent clinging to my clothes like smoke. Selecia wiped down the counters in small, anxious circles. The air in the kitchen was thick, buzzing with static. We spoke only in murmurs.

"Pass the salt."

"Watch the pan."

"Grab the bacon."

The routine felt too perfect. Too smooth. Like a dream being reenacted by people pretending to be alive. Blake sipped his coffee and glanced at the paper, something about rising food costs or failing crops. I couldn't focus. My hands were clammy. The eggs stuck too fast to the skillet. That's when Selecia stilled.

I looked up and saw her staring, wide-eyed, blood draining from her face. Her gaze was locked on the table. I followed it, and the breath punched out of me. There they were. The truck keys. Sitting out in the open, next to Blake's mug. Not in his pocket. Not in the drawer. Just... there. As if they belonged to us.

He had left the keys before, but I thought we hadn't had enough time to run. I wouldn't make the same mistake twice. We had to go. We couldn't keep waiting for the perfect opportunity. It was never going to come.

My heart stuttered. Blake didn't seem to notice. He just leaned back in his chair, arms stretching wide. "Gonna run out after breakfast," he said casually. "Need nails for the gutter and maybe a fuse for the garage." He stood, grabbing his coat. "You girls clean up. Be good." He left the keys.

Selecia and I locked eyes. Neither of us moved until the front door clicked shut and his footsteps faded off the porch. Still, we didn't breathe. My ears strained for the sounds of him outside. There was nothing.

Selecia's fingers twitched at her side. Then, quietly, as if reaching through water, she grabbed the keys. We stood frozen for another full minute. I don't know why. Maybe we thought he'd come back. Maybe we thought the universe would revoke the opportunity. But he didn't. And it didn't. So, I said it—soft but certain.

"Now." We didn't have time to think. No time to pack. No bags. No supplies. No plan. We hadn't been preparing to leave today—we'd just been preparing to survive.

I darted toward the bedroom and pulled the old knife from beneath the mattress. It was dull, barely more than a piece of scrap metal, but we'd hidden it weeks ago during one of Blake's starvation spells, just in case. Not for an escape. Just in case he tried to make us animals again.

Now, it would be all we had. I tucked the blade into my hoodie, wrapped it tight against my stomach. Selecia was standing in the hallway like a statue.

I grabbed her hand. "We have to take this chance," I whispered. "We might not get another one. If we wait, if we let fear keep us here... we'll die in this house."

Her lips trembled. "What if he comes back?""Then we'll be gone before he does." We moved quickly. Bare feet padded silently across the cold tile. Every floorboard creaked like a warning shot. We didn't speak. Just breathed and moved.

When we reached the front door, my hands shook. There were four locks: top bolt, middle deadbolt, bottom turn, and a chain. I took a deep breath and started at the top. Click. The sound was deafening.

Selecia flinched behind me. Her fingers dug into the hem of my sleeve. Click. The second lock gave way. Click—one more. Only the chain is left. I slipped it free, slowly. It rattled like bones in a box. Then I turned the knob. And opened the door.

Light. Real, unfiltered daylight. Blinding and warm and terrifying. The porch looked just like I remembered from my dreams. Old boards. Weather-beaten railing. The world beyond was too bright. Too open. It almost didn't feel real. I blinked, stepping outside with Selecia behind me. We were halfway down the steps when she gasped.

"Don't move," I said instantly. She pointed. Across the yard—just beyond the tall grass—Blake was crouched over someone. A woman. Maybe in her thirties. Dirty blonde hair. Bare feet. Wrists bound behind her back. Her cheek was bleeding. Her eyes were vacant. My heart stuttered. Who was she? We didn't have time to help her.

Blake was holding a knife. And for once, he didn't know we were there. I slapped my hand over Selecia's mouth and slowly backed us onto the porch again.

"We go for the truck," I breathed. "Right now. Quiet." We turned. Every step down the stairs felt like a bomb could go off. The gravel bit into our feet as we crossed the yard. The truck sat idle in the drive, dusty and dented, but promising something sacred, escape. I clicked the unlock button.

The lights flashed. Blake looked up. Our eyes met. The blood drained from my face. He stood upright, knife glinting in his hand.

"Go!" I shouted. We threw ourselves into the truck. My hands fumbled with the ignition. The engine groaned once, twice, and caught. Blake was sprinting now. I slammed my foot onto the gas. The tires squealed, throwing up gravel. We tore down the driveway, hit the road, and didn't look back.

Trees blurred past the window, branches lashing like reaching hands. The engine roared beneath us, shaking the truck with every gear shift. My foot stayed heavy on the pedal. Every ounce of my mind, muscle, and breath was focused on staying ahead of whatever was behind us.

Beside me, Selecia sat curled up, knees to her chest, arms wrapped tightly around her legs. Her lips were white. Her eyes didn't blink.

"He was going to kill her," she said finally, her voice barely a whisper. "That woman... he was going to kill her." I nodded. My jaw clenched until it ached.

"We could've stopped him."

"No," I said, eyes fixed on the road. "He would've killed us, too."

"But what if she was still alive?"

"She isn't now." Silence. I hated having to say it. Hated that it was true. The speedometer crept past 65—the road wound in tight turns through dense forest. There were no signs. No lights. Just miles of narrow asphalt and dark trees.

"I'm scared," Selecia said, finally.

"I know."

"Do you think he's behind us?" I didn't answer. I didn't know what to say. Knowing Blake, he was never going to let us leave. He would follow me forever. Could I even go home? Did I even want to if I was leaving one monster only to return to another? I would never let someone victimize me again. I wanted my mom, but I would leave her, too, if I had to see my father as well.

She turned to me, her voice shaking. "Do you?"

"I don't know. I didn't see his other car move. But he's resourceful..." I trailed off. She began to cry. Quiet at first. Just the shaking kind—the kind that builds like pressure in a bottle. Her fingers clenched into fists. Her face pressed against the window like she couldn't look at me, like she was afraid of what I'd say next.

I wanted to comfort her. To say it would be okay. But I couldn't lie. Because the truth was—we didn't know if we were safe yet. We drove for hours. I don't even remember when we passed into a new county or crossed state lines. I just kept moving. My body ached. My eyes burned. But I didn't dare stop.

It wasn't until the sky began to darken, the clouds staining purple and red, that I finally slowed down. The fuel light had come on.

The road carved sharply through the woods, hemmed in by dense underbrush and towering pines. My hands were cramping from how tightly I gripped the wheel, every nerve screaming to stay alert. The fading light turned the pavement into a ribbon of shadows, and I took the next bend too fast. The tires shrieked in protest as they lost traction, skidding across the gravelly edge.

"Isadora!" Selecia screamed, bracing herself against the dashboard. I yanked the wheel hard, barely regaining control, just in time to see a pair of headlights explode around the curve behind us—a silver car.

No. I knew that car. It was Blake. Before I could react, he was on us—his car swerving aggressively, closing the distance with terrifying speed. I saw him through the windshield, just for a second—his face twisted in fury, his arm out the driver's side window as he shouted something I couldn't hear.

"Pull over!" he screamed, his voice cutting through the wind like a blade. "Stop the goddamn truck!" Then he rammed us. The first hit slammed into the rear bumper, jolting us forward. I fought to keep the truck on the road, but he didn't let up—another hit. Metal crunched. The steering wheel buckled in my hands.

"He's trying to kill us!" Selecia cried. I pressed the gas harder, heart racing, but Blake was relentless. His car darted in again, striking our bumper like a battering ram. We were nothing but prey now trapped between the cliffs of the road and the madman behind us. Another hit. Louder. Closer.

The truck fishtailed, wheels screaming across the asphalt. Then... the world turned white. The final impact was bone-shattering. Glass burst around us like shrapnel. The truck spun, my scream lost in the deafening cacophony of metal and motion. We slammed sideways into something solid.

The bridge. Everything jerked to a stop. My hands were welded to the steering wheel, knuckles bone-white, body locked in place. And then I saw it. The front wheels hanging over the edge. Nothing beneath us but open air and a long, black drop into the river below.

The front of the truck crunched against the metal railing of a bridge. We were tilted. I looked out the windshield—and froze. The front wheels were dangling over the edge. There was nothing beneath us but water. The river. Oh God, we might die. I wouldn't accept that we went through all of this just to die on a bridge.

Selecia moaned beside me. "Isadora... what happened..."

"Don't move," I whispered. Scared to move and push us further over the edge. My breaths came in short pants. The metal beneath us creaked. The truck shifted an inch forward.

"Are we going to die?" Selecia yelled.

"No. we are going to be ok. Just breathe. You have to trust me. I will get us out of this. I promise."

"I don't want to die, Isadora. I'm scared."

"We're not dying here," I yelled back, trying to snap her out of her panic. I unbuckled myself carefully, slowly. The click of the belt echoing like a gunshot. There was only one option where Blake didn't get to us, and where we might live. If we were in the truck when it fell, it would kill us.

"We have to jump," I said. "Out the window. Into the water."

Selecia's head shot up. "No. No, I can't."

"It's the only way. The car's going to fall. We can't wait for the fire rescue. Blake will get to us first."

"What if I hit the rocks? What if I drown?"

"You won't."

"I'm scared!"

"So am I!" I said, louder than I meant to. "But we're here. We're this close. We made it this far—we are not dying on this bridge." She began to sob. I reached for her. Held her face in my hands.

"You trust me?" I asked.

"Yes," she breathed.

"Then do exactly as I say." The window was already cracked from the crash. I kicked it once, hard. Glass splintered and scattered into the river below. I climbed onto the door, balancing my weight. I watched as Selecia did the same, climbing slowly to the driver's side. The truck groaned again, and one tire slipped forward, screeching against the rail. The truck jolted with our moving weight but didn't fall.

"We jump together," I said. "Far and fast."

"Okay," she whispered, her hand gripping mine like a lifeline.

"One." She shook her head.

"Two." Her breathing stuttered.

"Three." We jumped. The water hit like concrete. Cold. Hard. Merciless. I sank fast, the weight of my hoodie dragging me under. I kicked upward, flailing until my head broke the surface. Gasping. Screaming Selecia's name. There, ten feet away, her head bobbing, coughing, gasping.

"I'm here!" she choked.

I swam to her, threw one arm around her waist. "Kick. Keep kicking!" The river pulled us fast. I couldn't see where we were going. Just darkness and motion and the terrible roar of the current. Then—rocks. Shoreline. Mud. I dragged us toward it with everything I had. My arms burned. My legs screamed. And then... Land. We collapsed, coughing and heaving on the muddy bank, soaked and shaking.

Selecia curled into me like a child, sobbing. "We're alive." I nodded, unable to speak. Overhead, the truck groaned one last time. And fell. With a crash so loud, it shook the bridge above, it exploded into the river. Water surged. Glass and metal rained around us. We crawled farther up the bank, sobbing. The truck was gone. Our captor, we hoped, thought we were too.

CHAPTER 73: THE LONG WALK

I don't remember crawling out of the river. Just the cold. The absolute, bone-deep cold that clawed at every inch of my skin as I dragged myself onto the muddy shore, coughing and gasping, my limbs numb and useless. Behind me, Selecia emerged next, her soaked hair clinging to her cheeks, eyes wide with disbelief. We had survived.

The car and Blakes truck were gone, swallowed by the black water beneath the bridge. There had been no explosion, no fire—just the deep, echoing splash and the silence that followed. No more tires. No engine. No screams. Just quiet.

For a long time, we didn't move. I sat in the mud with my knees to my chest, arms wrapped tight around my shivering body. Beside me, Selecia shook violently, her face pale, her breaths short. Every few seconds, she looked at me like she needed confirmation that we were still real. Still alive. And I didn't blame her. Because I didn't believe it either. We had done it. We had really done it.

"We're alive," I whispered. The words didn't even sound like mine. "We're alive."

Selecia nodded slowly, her eyes filling with tears that mixed with the river water still clinging to her lashes. "We made it," she whispered back. "We made it out." But we weren't safe yet. Not really.

It was still early morning—maybe 9 a.m.—but the sun

barely filtered through the gray clouds above. We were in the middle of nowhere, miles from anything. And barefoot. Soaking wet. Cold. We had no food. No money. No idea where we even were. But we had each other. And that had to be enough. We had to move.

At first, the terrain was all riverbank and jagged rock. Then came tall grass, thick with brambles and vines that caught on our clothes and scratched at our legs. The cold air bit at our skin as the wind picked up, whistling through the trees. Our soaked clothes clung to us like a second skin, and the mud squelched beneath every step. The rocks tore into our bare feet. It was miserable, but we didn't stop.

Every noise made us jump. A bird. A squirrel. A snapping branch. At one point, a deer bolted across our path, and Selecia let out a scream, collapsing to her knees. I had to pull her up, remind her over and over, "It's not him. He's not here. He's not here."

We hiked for hours. The sun crept higher, but its warmth barely touched us. Our wet clothes eventually dried, but stiffly, leaving us itchy and uncomfortable. Selecia's teeth chattered, and my fingers turned red and cracked. I didn't know how far we'd walked—maybe ten miles? Maybe more. But I could feel the burn in my calves, the aching in my hips, the profound exhaustion clawing up my spine. I could feel my feet bleeding, cuts and scrapes littered our arms from the branches that slapped us as we walked.

We didn't talk much. Every so often, I'd squeeze her hand or whisper, "Almost there," even though I had no idea if that was true. And then—around midnight, maybe later—we saw it—a gas station.

It stood alone on a corner where two roads met, its flickering yellow lights casting eerie shadows on the pavement. There were two old pumps, a single red pickup parked out front, and the buzzing neon OPEN sign in the window. We stood across the street, staring.

"It's real," Selecia whispered. Her voice cracked. "It's not a dream?"

"No," I said. "It's not." Though I wasn't sure I fully believed that. We crossed the road slowly, blinking against the artificial light. I reached for the door handle—and paused.

We must've looked insane. Our hair matted and tangled, our clothes stiff and stained with river mud, our bare feet raw and bruised. My hoodie was torn at the sleeve. Selecia's face was streaked with dried tears and grime. We didn't even look like people anymore—just two ghosts who had clawed their way out of hell. Still, I opened the door.

A small bell chimed above us as we stepped inside. The gas station attendant—a young guy, probably in his twenties, with shaggy brown hair and earbuds in—looked up from behind the counter. He blinked. Once. Twice. Then pulled out one of his earbuds, his mouth slowly falling open.

"Holy shit," he muttered. "Are you guys okay?"

"We need help," I said, my voice cracking. "Please." He stared at us for a few more seconds, like trying to figure out if we were real. Then, all at once, he jumped into action.

"Okay. Okay. Come in. Sit down." He scrambled around the counter and pointed to a bench near the coffee machine. "You're freezing. Let me grab something." We collapsed onto the bench, and he returned a moment later with two scratchy gas station-branded hoodies from the clearance rack. "They're huge, but you're soaked," he said, pressing them into our hands.

"Can we use your phone?" I asked, my voice shaking. "I need to call my mom. I don't know if she still has the same number, but—"

"Yeah, of course. Here." He handed me his cell. "Do you

want water? Food? There's a microwave in the back—I can heat something up." I shook my head, holding the phone as if it might disappear. My fingers trembled as I dialed. I hadn't dialed her number in years, but it came back to me like muscle memory, etched into the deepest part of my brain.

It had been four years. What if she changed her number? What if she blocked every unknown call out of grief? What if I lost her forever? Please... please still have the same number...

The dial tone rang once. Then twice. Three times. My chest felt like it might split open. I held my breath as I listened to the dial tone.

"Hello?" It was her voice. Older. Fragile. But unmistakably her.

I collapsed against the counter, gripping the phone so tightly it might shatter. Tears spilled down my face so fast I couldn't even breathe. "Mama?" My voice cracked. "It's me. It's Isadora. I'm alive." Silence.

"...Who is this?"

"It's me. It's Isadora. I- I need help. Please don't hang up. I'm at a gas station. I don't know where we are. I stole his truck, and it crashed, and—Mama, we made it. I made it. I'm alive." More silence. Then a sob. Raw and real.

The gas station clerk was watching with wide eyes now. His earlier nervousness had shifted to full-blown disbelief. Selecia stood frozen, clutching onto me.

"This isn't funny," my mother said. "Who the hell is this? What kind of sick joke is this?"

"Mama, please!" I sobbed. "Please, I'm at a gas station. I don't know where. But I'm out. It's me. I swear it's me. Please believe me. I'm alive. I made it out. We made it out."

"Oh my God. Oh my God. Isadora? Who's we?" She gasped, a sharp, strangled sound. I could hear the disbelief in her voice.

"It's me," I said again, wiping my face. "I'm with another girl. Selecia. She's fourteen. We escaped together. We need help. Please."

"I—I thought this was a prank," she whispered. "I thought—I thought you were dead."

"We almost were."

She cried harder. "Where are you?"

I turned to the clerk. "What's the name of this place?"

He blinked, "Cherry Hill. Off Route 19. Just past Maple Creek," he said quickly.

"Cherry Hill," I repeated. "Don't tell the news. Just call the police. Only Dad and the cops. No one else. He still thinks we're dead. It's our only chance to stay safe."

She was still crying, but I could hear her moving, grabbing something, maybe a pen. "I'm coming. I'm sending help. Isadora, sweetheart, I thought you were dead. I thought I lost you forever."

"I love you," I whispered. "I'll see you soon." I hung up and stared at the receiver for a second, like it was a mirage. The room felt too small now. I could feel the clerk watching us. For the first time in four years, I let myself fall apart. Beside me, Selecia rested her head on my shoulder. She didn't ask to make a call. She didn't ask for anything.

Selecia stepped closer. "She believed you?"

"She's sending someone. Don't you want to talk to someone?" I asked softly. She let out a tiny breath, half sob, half laugh, and wrapped her arms around me. I held her tightly, felt her damp clothes clinging to mine, our bones aching with exhaustion. We were a mess; muddy, scraped, damp, broken, but we were alive.

She shook her head. "There's no one to call," she whispered. "I just want to stay with you."

The clerk finally found his voice. "Holy shit," he breathed. "You're those girls... from the news. You're the ones who went missing."

"Please," I said, shaking. "No cameras. No phone calls. Not yet. Just let the police come."

He raised both hands. "Yeah. Yeah, of course. I just — Jesus Christ. I thought you were about to pass out. Do you want water? Food? Blankets? You're safe now." He walked around the counter and grabbed water bottles from the fridge. Selecia's hands shook as she opened one.

We sat on the floor, hunched between a rack of motor oil and a mini fridge of soda, sipping warm water and waiting for help. My body was wrecked. My head pounded. But for the first time in almost four years, I had hope. I wrapped my arm around Selecia. We weren't safe yet. But we were out. And for the first time, we had a future ahead of us.

CHAPTER 74: AFTERSHOCK

The gas station had fallen silent again, except for the low hum of a cooler and the occasional flicker from the buzzing neon sign in the window. The clerk—Ryan, we'd learned—sat on a milk crate across from us, his eyes darting between the door and us, like he was trying to convince himself we wouldn't vanish. "I locked the front just in case," he said, voice quiet. "Didn't want anyone wandering in before help got here."

I nodded numbly. My legs were cramping, but I didn't want to move. If I stood up, it might feel too real. Too vulnerable. As long as we stayed behind the counter, we could pretend no one could see us, and that we were still hidden. That we were safe.

Selecia sat pressed against my side, knees drawn up to her chest. Her hands trembled faintly in her lap, the hoodie sleeves too long for her small frame. She hadn't spoken since my phone call. Her eyes remained locked on the floor.

"Do you want another water?" Ryan asked. His voice cracked, like he wasn't used to talking this much. "Or, um, I think I have protein bars in the back. Or—whatever you want, really." I opened my mouth to answer, but the sound of sirens pierced the quiet—three distinct bursts—low, fast, coming from a distance. We froze. Even Ryan jumped.

"Is that—?" he started, but I was already moving, peeking cautiously over the counter. Through the expansive windows, I could see it: red and blue lights dancing in the foggy darkness, growing brighter with each passing second, their beams illuminating the tires on gravel. Doors opening. A voice on a megaphone.

"Hello? This is the Police Department. We received a call from this location—" My legs gave out again. Not from fear—this time, from relief.

"They're here," I whispered. "They actually came."

Ryan moved quickly, pushing open the locked door and waving frantically. "They're in here! They're inside!"

The door opened fully, and suddenly the small gas station filled with people—officers, EMTs, and a woman in a gray blazer with a notepad. One of the officers crouched down in front of us immediately, his face a mix of shock and gentleness.

"My name's Officer Delaney," he said. "You're safe now. We've got you." But I couldn't answer. My mouth was dry, and my body felt too heavy. Selecia clung to my arm, her eyes wide with panic.

"No one's going to take you," I said quickly, shielding her instinctively. "We're not letting go of each other."

The officer nodded. "That's okay. You can stay together. We want to get you warm and check you for injuries, alright?" I didn't realize I was crying until I tasted salt on my lips.

They wrapped us in thick silver thermal blankets and helped us out of the store. The cool night air hit me like a wave again, but this time it didn't scare me. It smelled like asphalt and pine and gasoline—everyday things. Alive things.

A female EMT leaned toward us gently. "Do you remember your names?"

"I'm Isadora Amber Rose," I said. "She's Selecia. She's fourteen. We were taken by a man named Blake."

"Okay, Isadora. Thank you. You're doing great." She helped guide us toward an ambulance, her hands warm and steady on my back.

"We're going to take you to a hospital nearby," she said. "Just a check-up. To make sure everything's okay. We've already contacted your mom; she's on her way. Should be here in a few hours."

"She's coming?" My voice broke.

"She is," the EMT confirmed with a soft smile. "She's been on the phone with our dispatcher. She hasn't stopped crying." Selecia's grip tightened on my arm.

"I don't want to leave her," she whispered. "Please. Please don't separate us."

"You won't be separated," the EMT promised. "We'll make sure of it." They lifted us carefully into the back of the ambulance. The lights were bright—too bright—and for a moment I couldn't breathe. My eyes squeezed shut, and I waited for the pain, the punishment, the voice yelling for obedience. But none came—just the gentle rustle of blankets.

Just the hum of the engine starting. Just safety. The ambulance bumped gently along the dark backroads, and I sat hunched beside Selecia on the cot, wrapped in a warm blanket that still couldn't quiet the trembling in my bones. The EMT —Kara—sat across from us, scribbling notes on a clipboard, occasionally glancing up to make sure we were still breathing.

"How are you feeling, sweetheart?" she asked softly. I didn't have the words. My throat felt rubbed raw from the river water and screaming. From crying. From surviving.

"I'm okay," I whispered, but it didn't sound convincing, not even to me. Selecia didn't answer at all. She had curled into herself beside me, her head against my shoulder, her eyes vacant.

"She hasn't said much," I told Kara. "She's overwhelmed."

Kara nodded. "That's normal. You both are in shock. Your bodies are coming down from survival mode. You've done something almost no one ever gets to do. You got out." I looked down at my scraped hands, still red from gripping the steering wheel and the rocks on the riverbank.

Got out. Not rescued and not saved. We had done it ourselves. We had taken the risk. And now... now we were here. It felt like my soul was limping behind my body, struggling to catch up.

The hospital lights were jarring after the still darkness of the night. Everything inside smelled like antiseptic and stale air, but even that felt clean. Safe. The kind of sterile that came with locked doors, security cameras, and nurses who didn't raise their voices.

They kept us together—thank God. Kara had whispered something to the nurses about trauma bonding and not separating us under any circumstances. I didn't know what I would've done if they'd taken Selecia from me, even for a moment.

They gave us a private exam room—sterile, windowless, and pale blue—and gently peeled the wet clothes from our bodies. Everything we'd worn was sealed into evidence bags and whisked away. I didn't ask where. I didn't want to look at those clothes ever again.

Someone brought us warm gowns. Thick socks. Hot tea in little foam cups. I wrapped my hands around mine to feel the heat. They took blood samples. Swabbed cuts. Checked for bruises and fractures. Took pictures of injuries. I flinched at every flash. The nurse who examined me didn't ask unnecessary questions. She just moved slowly, kindly, like she knew exactly what she was looking for—and precisely what not to say.

"You're safe now," she murmured, over and over like a mantra. "You're safe now." When she stepped out, Selecia finally turned to me.

"Are they going to arrest us?" she asked, her voice barely audible.

My heart cracked. "No. No, baby. We didn't do anything wrong."

"But we took his truck. And the knife…"

"You defended yourself," I said firmly. "We escaped. That's not a crime." She nodded, but I could see the war behind her eyes. All the rules Blake had drilled into us—about obedience, about silence, about loyalty—were still tangled in her brain. They were still tangled in mine—a soft knock. The door creaked open.

"Isadora?" a voice said. And then I saw her. Mom. Her hair was shorter than I remembered, streaked with gray at the temples. Her face was thinner. Her eyes were bloodshot and wide with disbelief. She looked like she hadn't slept in years. For a second, I didn't move. I couldn't. Then she crossed the room in two strides and wrapped me in her arms.

I broke. Every wall I'd built, every shred of strength I'd faked—it all collapsed. I sobbed into her shoulder, clinging to her like I was five years old again. She rocked me gently, stroking my hair, whispering my name through her own tears.

"My baby," she kept saying. "My sweet baby girl. I thought—I thought I'd lost you forever."

"I missed you," I choked out. "Every day. I didn't think I'd see you again." We stayed like that for a long time, until my body stopped shaking. Until I could breathe again without sobbing. Then Mom looked up and noticed Selecia.

"And this is…?"

"This is Selecia," I said. "She saved me as much as I saved

her."

Mom stood and knelt in front of Selecia. "Can I hug you?" Selecia hesitated, then nodded once. The moment Mom wrapped her arms around her, Selecia burst into tears.

"You're safe now," Mom whispered. "You're safe. I promise."

I woke up to the beeping of machines. My body felt like it had been filled with sand—heavy, aching, slow. A fluorescent light buzzed overhead, soft but sharp enough to make me squint. The room smelled like antiseptic and cotton. Somewhere nearby, a heart monitor beeped in time with my pulse, too steady to match how chaotic I felt inside.

My throat burned. My ribs ached. My legs felt like they were carved from lead. But I was alive. And I was warm. Clean. Covered in a blanket that didn't smell like mildew or blood. Dressed in a hospital gown that didn't cling like a second skin.

I turned my head slowly. Selecia sat in the bed beside mine. Her knees were pulled up to her chest, her eyes half-shut. Someone had given her clean clothes—sweatpants and a hoodie two sizes too big—but her hair was still a tangled mess. She looked like a child, barely clinging to sleep.

"Selecia," I croaked.

She stirred instantly, jerking upright with a gasp. Her eyes met mine, wide and terrified. "You're awake." I tried to nod, but it hurt. Everything hurt.

She reached for the call button beside the bed. "I'll get the nurse—wait—should I?" Before I could answer, the door opened. A nurse entered with a clipboard and a gentle smile.

"Welcome back, Isadora," she said kindly. "You're in Cherry Hill Medical. You've been unconscious for almost a full day."

I blinked. "Is she okay?" I gestured weakly to Selecia.

"She's fine. Dehydrated, bruised, exhausted. But she's tough." Selecia smirked faintly, but her eyes stayed locked on me.

"I'll let the doctor know you're awake," the nurse continued. "He'll want to go over some things with you." Minutes passed—maybe more. I drifted in and out. Then a knock came, and a tall man in a white coat entered, his face somber.

"Isadora?" he asked gently. I nodded.

"I'm Dr. Patel. You've been through a tremendous amount, so we're going to take everything slowly. But I do need to review a few things from your bloodwork." He flipped through a chart, then paused. "Would you like your... friend to leave the room?"

"No," I said quickly. My voice was firmer this time. "She stays."

Dr. Patel nodded. "All right." He looked at me closely, like he didn't want to say the words. Then:

"You're pregnant." Time didn't stop. But my breath did. Pregnant. Again. The word echoed like a scream in a cavern, bouncing off the walls of my skull. I shook my head slowly, like that would undo it. Like I hadn't heard him right.

"No," I whispered.

"It's early," he added gently. "Just a few weeks, based on HCG levels. But yes, it's confirmed."

I felt like I was falling through the bed. The air thinned. My chest tightened. I was barely out. Barely safe. And now this?

Selecia's hand reached for mine. "Isadora..." And that's when it hit me—she was hearing this too and learning everything I'd never said. Everything I'd tried to protect her from. Her eyes welled up, but she didn't cry. Just squeezed my hand tighter.

"I didn't know," I whispered to her. "I didn't want you to know. Not like this."

"I figured," she said quietly. "I'm not stupid. I just... I hoped I was wrong."

Dr. Patel cleared his throat softly. "You don't have to make any decisions right away. We'll have a counselor speak with you, and—"

"I don't want to talk about it," I snapped. My voice cracked again, but the edge was there. "Not now."

He nodded. "Understood. I'll give you space." He left. The silence felt suffocating.

"I'm so sorry," Selecia whispered. I pulled her onto the bed beside me and held her close.

"We got out," I said softly. "But we're still bleeding." She didn't answer. She just held me tighter. I didn't know what the future held. But for the first time, I wasn't facing it alone. And even with the weight of that word—pregnant—pressing down on my chest, I knew one thing: We survived. Now, we had to figure out how to live.

CHAPTER 75:
THE WEIGHT OF
MY SECRETS

The fluorescent lights overhead buzz faintly, too sterile, too sharp. I lay curled on the hospital bed, blanket pulled tight up to my chin, trying to stay grounded. My fingers twitch against the scratchy edge of the sheet, finding no comfort in the fabric. The IV in my arm itches beneath the tape. I can still feel the river water on my skin, the mud between my toes—even though I know it's long gone.

Across the room, Selecia is in her bed. The nurses insisted we both rest, but I couldn't sleep, and I don't think she has either. Her eyes stay half-lidded, her body still. But I see the way her fingers twitch. The way she peeks at me when she thinks I'm not looking. The door opens gently—a woman steps in—soft cardigan, clipboard, visitor's badge.

"Isadora? I'm Jennifer. I'm a trauma counselor here at Cherry Hill Medical." I nod slowly. I don't sit up. I don't think I could if I tried.

She glances toward Selecia. "Would you like some privacy?"

"No," I say, voice low but firm. "She stays."

Jennifer gives a gentle nod and sits in the chair beside my bed, close but not too close. She knows how to navigate a room like this. That should make me feel safer, but it doesn't.

Nothing really does yet.

"The doctors asked me to check in with you after the results of your bloodwork. I know you've been told. I want to talk through it, at your pace."

Pregnant. The word echoes again in my head, like it's carved into the air above me. I nod. "I know. They told me."

"How are you feeling about it?"

I stare down at my hands. They're red, cracked, trembling. "I don't know. I'm angry. I'm sick about it. It's his. That makes me feel like there's poison inside me."

Jennifer nods, calm, nonjudgmental. "That makes sense. That feeling is valid." I hesitate. My eyes flick toward Selecia.

"I've been pregnant before. Three times."

Silence. Selecia slowly sits up. Her eyes widen. "What?"

I don't look at her. I can't. I keep my eyes on the blanket. "Three miscarriages. I didn't tell you because I didn't want you to carry that. I didn't want you to know how bad it was. I didn't want you to see what he did to me."

She moves, her bare feet touching the floor, then the soft shuffle of her steps. I feel the mattress shift as she crawls into bed beside me. Her arms wrap around me, and for a second, I can't breathe.

"You didn't have to protect me from that," she whispers. "You were hurting too."

Jennifer speaks gently again. "Isadora, you have every right to feel conflicted. To be scared. This isn't a decision you have to make today. You can take time. You have options, and you're not alone."

I close my eyes. I want to scream, but it catches in my throat. "I want the baby. I do. That's the worst part. I'm not sure if I can be a good mom. I don't even know if my body will let me." Jennifer doesn't rush to respond. She lets the weight settle.

"Wanting the baby doesn't make what happened okay," she says. "It means you're choosing something different. It means you're reaching for something that's yours. That can still be yours." I cry. Not loudly. Just steady tears that slide down my cheeks and into my hair. Selecia holds me tighter.

"I'm here," she whispers. "I'm not going anywhere."

Jennifer stands quietly. "I'll give you both some space. When you're ready, we'll talk again." She leaves, and the room grows still again. My mother isn't here yet. I'm glad. I don't want to answer more questions. I want to feel what I feel without being told how I should feel.

"You'd be a good mom," Selecia says after a long time.

I turned my head toward her. "How do you know?"

She shrugs, her chin trembling. "Because you already are. You've been taking care of me the whole time, even when you were hurting. Even when you were scared. You still tried to protect me. That's what moms do." I pull her close. The weight of survival doesn't lift. But it shifts. And now I'm carrying it with someone beside me. And maybe, just maybe, that's how healing begins.

CHAPTER 76: CONTROL

The room is too quiet now. Selecia's breath is slow and steady against my shoulder; her head nestled into the crook of my neck as we lie curled together in the narrow hospital bed. The blankets don't feel as cold with her weight beside me; her hand is still looped loosely in mine. But sleep doesn't come. Not really. Every time I close my eyes, I see his face. Hear his voice. Feel the nausea twist in my gut—not just from the pregnancy, but from the memory of who put it there.

I stare at the ceiling and count the dots in the tiles. One, two, three, four... anything to keep my mind from spiraling. I try to pretend we're somewhere else. Somewhere safe. But even the humming machines and the sterile scent of antiseptic can't erase four years of conditioning. Every time the door handle rattles, I flinch. Every footstep outside sounds too heavy, too close. My body still expects pain, even here.

A soft knock breaks the stillness. Not loud. Just a gentle tap, like someone's trying not to wake a child. Selecia stirs but doesn't sit up. My mother peeks inside, her eyes swollen from crying.

"Still awake?" she whispers. I nod.

She steps in, holding a paper cup of decaf tea and a small container of crackers. "Didn't think you'd be ready to eat, but I figured maybe something plain."

I take it with a faint smile. "Thanks." She moves slowly,

like she's afraid to disturb the fragile peace in the room. I don't blame her. I feel like glass myself. One wrong move and I'll shatter.

Selecia opens her eyes sleepily. "Hi," she murmurs.

"Hi, sweetheart," Mom says. "Want anything?" Selecia just shakes her head and burrows back into my side.

"I talked to the nurses," Mom says, settling into the chair beside the bed. "They said there's a social worker on staff who handles... special cases. They'd like to set up a time for her to visit. To check in."

"Like the counselor?" I ask, my voice hoarse.

"She works more with the legal side of things. Detectives, court, advocates for survivors." The word survivor hangs in the air. It feels heavy. Too big for me. I don't feel like one. I feel like a ghost—half here, half somewhere, still stuck in that basement. I glance down at Selecia. Her arms are wrapped tight around her stomach, like she's trying to hold herself together.

"Not yet," I say. "I don't want to talk about him yet."

"I told them that might be the case," Mom says gently. "They won't rush you. You call the shots." You call the shots. God, when was the last time I felt like that was even possible? I press my hand to my abdomen, barely able to feel anything through the hospital gown. Still so early. Still unreal. But it's there. Something alive inside me. And the thought alone sends a wave of nausea and guilt and longing rolling through me.

"I asked the nurse earlier if I could have an ultrasound," I blurt out.

Mom blinks. "You did?"

I nod. "I don't know if I'm ready. But... I need to see. I need to know it's real. That I'm not just... broken." There's silence for a beat too long. Then Mom stands and gently places her hand on my head.

"You're not broken, Izzy. You never were." My throat tightens. I want to believe her. I really do. But how can something that came from so much pain ever be anything but tainted?

Selecia shifts beside me. "If you want me to stay in the room... I will. For the ultrasound."

I nod slowly. "I do. I want you there." The nurse comes in a little later and wheels in a portable ultrasound machine. She's soft-spoken, gentle. She asks if I'm okay with her touching me. She explains every movement before she makes it. She even warms the gel between her hands, so it won't sting when it hits my skin. The screen lights up in front of me, grainy and gray. My heart races.

"Let's take a look," she says. I hold my breath. For a moment, I see nothing. Just static. Then a flicker. A tiny pulsing blur.

"There," she whispers. "That's the heartbeat." Selecia squeezes my hand. I can't speak. I don't know what to say. A single tear slides down my cheek.

The nurse prints the image and places it in my hand before cleaning the gel from my stomach. "Whenever you need to talk," she says softly, "we're here." She leaves us alone. I stare at the photo. It's small. Incomplete. But it's real. That flutter of life—however fragile—is real.

"I don't know if I can do this," I whisper. "What if I'm not a good mom?"

"You will be," Selecia says firmly. "You already are. You took care of me when no one else did."

"But I'm so angry," I admit. "I hate what he did to me. And I'm scared. Scared of losing it again. Scared of failing. Scared of it being him. Of looking into a face and seeing his eyes."

"I'll be here," she says. "No matter what. You won't do it alone." And for the first time, I let myself believe that maybe—just maybe—he didn't get to take everything from me.

CHAPTER 77:
MY STORY

We've been at the safe house for nearly four months. It's strange how time can pass and still feel stuck. The days are quiet, but not peaceful. The news cycles fade. The phone doesn't ring as often. Therapists rotate in and out. But every creak of the floorboards or shadow on the window still sends my heart racing. And the nausea hasn't stopped—not entirely.

I'm four months pregnant now. There's a slight curve to my belly that wasn't there before. It catches the fabric of my shirts. It's real in a way it wasn't in the hospital. I feel it when I wake up too fast or when I bend too low. I haven't felt any movement yet, but my doctor says I will soon. Selecia keeps saying it's a good sign that the baby's still here. Still growing. Still mine.

I want to believe her. Mom's still here, too. She takes calls in the other room, pacing softly. She does laundry like it's therapy. Sometimes she brings me hot tea and sits beside me without saying a word. We've been waiting—for what, I don't know. Maybe for Blake to be found. Maybe for the fear to fade.

Then the letter came. It was delivered by hand. Detective Ramirez stood on the porch, face tight and pale, holding a sealed manila envelope like it was a bomb.

"Where did that come from?" my mom asked immediately.

"A precinct officer named Sarah Adams," Ramirez said.

"Her daughter was taken two nights ago. Fourteen. Blonde. Blue eyes. We believe it's Blake." The world shifted under me. I took the letter with trembling hands.

Inside was a neatly folded page. No smudges. No fingerprints. Just Blake's handwriting—smooth, familiar, sickening.

My girls,

I know you're scared. I know you're confused. But I forgive you.

I understand why you ran. I know the fear that made you leave. But families fall apart sometimes. That doesn't mean we don't fix them.

Isadora, you're carrying a piece of me. A piece of us. That means something. And Selecia, I know you're scared too. You're still my daughter, no matter what they've told you. We can start over. We can be better. I forgive everything.

Come to the place where we first became a family. You know where. I'll be waiting. Bring her. I miss you both.

Tell the police if you want. It won't change anything. You belong with me. You always have.

Blake

I didn't realize I was shaking until the page dropped from my hands.

"He's taunting us," Mom whispered.

"No," I said. "He believes it. Every word."

Ramirez gathered the letter, already calling it in. Sarah Adams' daughter—Emily—was missing for less than forty-eight hours. No ransom. No note. Just gone. Taken from her home while her mother was on night duty. Another girl with blonde hair. Blue eyes. Petite frame. She looked like me.

"He's escalating," Ramirez said. "We're mobilizing every available team. If he reached out to you, he's planning something. He wants to be seen." I looked at Selecia, who hadn't spoken since I read the letter. Her face was pale, her hands clenched in her lap.

"He wrote to you too," I said softly. "He still thinks you're his daughter."

"I know," she whispered. "I read it." We sat on the couch, the weight of his words pressing into the room like fog. He hadn't let go. Not of me. Not of Selecia. Not of the fantasy. And now, someone else was paying the price. Emily Adams was out there somewhere. And Blake was waiting. For us

CHAPTER 78:
THE PLAN

We started planning an hour after we received his letter. The envelope he had given us was plain, but the moment Sarah Adams walked into the safe house and handed it over, something inside me twisted. There was no return address. Just our names scrawled in sharp, obsessive ink across the front. Inside was the message. Blake's message. Delusional. Dangerous. But unmistakably his.

He still believed we were his. Still thought this was a misunderstanding, a betrayal he could fix if only we came to our senses. Emily Adams had been missing for two days. We were past the forty-eight-hour mark. The detectives didn't say it outright, but we all knew the truth—every second we delayed, the odds of finding her alive dropped.

"He's unstable," Ramirez said, her voice low and even. "But if he's still reaching out, he's trying to reconnect. That might be the only leverage we have left." So they suggested it.

A letter. One that would play into his fantasy. One that would lure him out. Not because we believe in him. Not because we forgive him. But because we need him to think that we do. Selecia and I sit cross-legged on the floor of the safe house living room, surrounded by rejected drafts and scattered pen caps. Her knees are bouncing. I keep chewing on the inside of my cheek until I taste blood. Every word we write has to feel like the truth. Like his truth.

And that's what makes it so hard. I stare down at the

blank sheet of paper and take a trembling breath.

"We have to sound like we want to go back," I whisper.

Selecia swallows hard. "I can't pretend I miss him."

"You don't have to. We just need to say what he needs to hear." We write.

Dear Blake,

We miss you. We didn't think we would, but we do. Every day has been harder without you than the one before. It's like the world outside doesn't understand us, what we had. What we were. A family. Your family.

We should never have run. We see that now. Everything you said... You were right. The world is cruel and fake and full of liars. But you were honest. You gave us something real. You gave us each other.

They're not letting us leave. They keep watching us and following us. Like we're prisoners. But we've never stopped thinking about you. Wishing we could go back. Wishing we could fix it. We made a mistake. We believed the lies they told us. That you were the enemy. But you're the only one who ever loved us.

Please forgive us. Please come. Meet us. We want to be a family again. We want things back the way they were. We need you.

You were always right. We'll be at the old Crescent Ridge Grocery parking lot, near the trailhead. There's a bench by the side entrance. You remember. We'll be there on Wednesday at 11:00 A.M. Just the two of us. Please come.

Love always, Isadora & Selecia

I reread it three times before I set the pen down. My hand is cramping, my heart pounding. It's a knife disguised as a hug. And it must be convincing. I glance at Selecia. She's pale. Her lips are tight. She nods without speaking.

"It's perfect," I say, though it makes me sick to admit it.

Sarah Adams is waiting outside the door. Her hands shake when she takes the letter. She will drop it off at a gas station where Blake first approached her.

I touch her arm. "Please be careful."

She nods. "We're running out of time." Back inside, the house feels too quiet, like the walls are listening.

"He's going to come," I say. Selecia climbs onto the couch beside me. Her hand finds mine.

"You think so?"

"I know so." Because this is what he's wanted all along. To be wanted. To be right. Now we have to make him believe it. Long enough to save a life. Long enough to help Emily. We had to do this because no one had been able to help us.

The hours pass in thick silence, broken only by the occasional creak of the house settling or the soft murmur of a police radio outside. The letter is gone. Sarah delivered it exactly as planned. Now all we can do is wait.

Detective Ramirez returns mid-afternoon with a whiteboard and a plastic folder filled with aerial photos. "We'll stage units here, here, and here," she says, pointing to the grocery parking lot. "There's an abandoned maintenance shed near the tree line. That'll be SWAT's base. We'll keep comms open. You'll be wearing hidden microphones. We'll have eyes on everything."

I nod slowly. It all feels mechanical. Technical. Like we're planning a movie scene. But this isn't fiction. This is our lives. And we only get one shot.

"Will he bring her?" Selecia asks quietly, still sitting on the couch beside me.

Ramirez doesn't answer right away. "He might. If he believes you... If he thinks it's safe."

Selecia's throat bobs. "What if he kills her before he even gets there?"

"He won't," I say before Ramirez can speak. "He needs her. That's his leverage."

Ramirez glances at me, something unreadable in her eyes. "We'll be ready either way."

Later, we rehearse. Not what to say, but how to move. What to wear. The sound equipment is small—tiny mics clipped under our collars; transmitters tucked into our waistbands. The tech team runs checks. The SWAT commander briefs us three times on the danger. And every time, the air in the room thickens.

At dinner, I can barely eat. My stomach feels like it's folding in on itself. The nausea is constant now, pregnancy and fear fighting for control of my body. I stare at my plate until the food goes cold. Selecia eventually takes it from me and sets it in the sink.

"You're not going to be alone," she says. "Not tomorrow. Not ever again." I want to believe her. But I can still feel his shadow pressing in around me.

The house is quieter than usual tonight. Even the floorboards seem to hold their breath. Outside the living room window, the police cars have dimmed their lights. A single beam glows faintly from the porch, but everything else is cloaked in shadow. Time crawls. I sit on the bed with a brush in my lap and a section of Selecia's hair looped between my fingers. She's sitting cross-legged in front of me, her shoulders stiff.

"Tell me if I pull too hard," I murmur.

She shrugs. "You're fine."

I start braiding slowly, my fingers moving through the strands with the ease of muscle memory. She used to braid mine when we were bored, twisting and retwisting until the silence was bearable. I try to do the same now, not just braid but build something between us that fear hasn't ruined.

"I keep thinking," she says after a while, "what if we see him tomorrow, and I can't... move. What if I freeze?"

"You won't," I say. "But even if you do, I'll be there."

She nods, but I feel her body tense again. Her voice is small. "I still see his face when I close my eyes." I pause, hands halfway through the braid.

"I do too," I admit.

My stomach turns—not just from the pregnancy, but from the memory trying to claw its way back in. I close my eyes. The scent of mildew and bleach. The slap of his footsteps on the basement stairs. That time, he brought down a tray and left it on the floor, smiling like it was a gift. We'd gone four days without food. Four days. My vision had blurred. My body shook just trying to sit up.

He set the tray down and said, "Tell me you're grateful, and you can have it."

I couldn't speak. My tongue felt like sandpaper. My lips cracked. Selecia whispered it first. "Thank you." Her voice was barely audible. He made me say it, too. I said it. Just to get her food. Just so she wouldn't pass out again. And then he made me sit and watch while he fed her the first bite. I shake my head to force the memory away.

"I remember when he took the lightbulb," I whisper. "That week, he said we didn't deserve to see."

Selecia nods. "That was the week I started naming the cracks in the wall. To remember something." Silence stretches. I finish the braid and secure it with a small hair tie. She turns to face me. Her eyes are glassy.

"Do you think we'll be safe after tomorrow?" she asks. I don't answer right away. I look down at my belly, curved now beneath my sweatshirt, unfamiliar and quietly alive.

"I don't know what safe even means anymore," I say. "But I think... maybe we'll be free." Selecia inches closer and lies down beside me on the bed, curling up so her head rests near my stomach. She presses a hand against it gently.

"You're not alone," she whispers. "Neither of you." I place my hand over hers.

"I talk to them sometimes," I admit, cheeks warming. "When I think no one's listening."

"I know," she says softly. "I hear you."

My chest tightens. I swallow the lump rising in my throat. "Sometimes I don't know if I deserve to keep them," I say. "It's Blake's. And I'm scared every second that something will go wrong. That I'll wake up bleeding again." I pause. My voice cracks.

"But I want this baby. I want them to live. I want to be someone who can protect them. Who can give them something better." I close my eyes and rest my hands over my stomach. My voice is a whisper, just for the two of us. "I'm doing this for you, little one. So, you'll never know what it's like to live in fear. So, you'll be born into something better than what I had. So, you and Selecia will be safe." Selecia stays quiet beside me. Her hand is still against my stomach, steady and warm.

Outside, the wind picks up, brushing against the windows like fingertips. The house creaks. Somewhere down the hall, a floorboard shifts under someone's weight, probably one of the officers pacing near the front door. Inside, we don't move. Eventually, our breaths begin to sync. In. Out. In. Out.

I feel the baby flutter—so faint I think I imagined it. But I didn't.

Selecia lets out a quiet gasp. "Was that...?"

I nod, eyes wide with shock. "I think so." She smiles. A real one. The first in weeks. We drift into silence again. For the first time in a long time, I feel the slightest flicker of hope. Tomorrow, we will face him. But tonight, we hold each other through the dark.

CHAPTER 79: HOPE

Blake's POV

The gas station off I-17 smells like diesel, burnt coffee, and desperation. I wait in the truck with the engine running. The afternoon sun cuts through the windshield, baking my arms, but I don't shut it off. I want to stay ready. I need to be prepared.

A woman walks in. Brown hair in a bun. Gray hoodie. Her movements are quick but not panicked. She doesn't look at anyone. She heads straight to the counter, speaks briefly with the clerk, then leaves an envelope on the display stand next to the gum. Casual. Innocent.

I don't move until she's gone. Then I go inside. I keep my head down. Sunglasses on. No one pays attention—just another customer looking for a snack or smokes. I stroll up to the display and pick up the envelope like it's nothing. My name's not on it, but I know it's for me. I can feel it in my bones. It's thin. Light. My pulse hammers in my ears.

Back in the truck, I rip it open with shaking fingers. Two pages. Handwritten. Their handwriting. Isadora. Selecia. I freeze. They wrote to me. They remembered. I reread it once. Then twice. My hands tremble.

They miss me. They understand now. They see what I've known all along—this world, this broken place, doesn't deserve them. But I did. I protected them. I gave them a purpose. Love. Structure. And yes, sometimes love hurts. But only because I cared so much. Too much.

They're trying to come home. I let out a shaky breath, running my fingers over their names. Isadora. My beautiful girl. My salvation. Selecia. Still mine. Still, my daughter.

They're reaching out. Not because anyone forced them —no, no one could fake this kind of devotion. I know Isadora's heart. I see the way her voice shakes when she tells the truth. I recall how Selecia used to draw pictures of the three of us at the table. We were a family.

I press the pages to my chest and close my eyes. They'll be waiting at the grocery store. I don't remember it, but that doesn't matter. They chose it. They'll be there.

I look over at the passenger seat. Emily is still unconscious, head lolled against the window, duct tape over her wrists, bruises just beginning to bloom along her arms. She looks like Isadora used to. Same fragile frame. Same pale hair. Not quite the same. Not the same heart. But she'll serve her purpose.

They'll see. They'll see I'm still capable of love. That I never stopped. That I forgave them. And when we're together again—when they see how much I've done to bring us back to what we were—everything will fall into place. Families heal. And this one's almost whole again.

CHAPTER 80:
THE STING

I can't stop staring at the clock. Each second seems louder than the last, like the ticking is vibrating through the floorboards and straight into my chest. It's nearly 5:00 p.m. now. One hour before we leave. One hour before everything either ends... or begins again.

The house is quiet, too quiet. The kind of quiet that suffocates instead of soothes. My mother was pacing outside on the porch again, whispering into her phone. I think she's praying or maybe talking to my grandmother—someone who might understand the way grief turns into fear and wraps around your throat. I can't hear the words, just the way her voice trembles.

Inside, Selecia is curled on the couch, hugging a throw pillow to her chest. Her knees are tucked up beneath her, and her eyes keep flicking toward the window, toward the road, toward the direction where Blake might already be waiting. Her face is pale but determined, and she hasn't spoken since lunch. I know what she's thinking, though, because I'm thinking it too.

What if he doesn't believe us? What if he sees through the letter? What if he brings a gun? What if we're not enough to save Emily?

The front door opens with a low creak, and Detective Ramirez enters, followed by two techs in navy jackets carrying cases of equipment. They move with careful precision, like every step matters. No one smiles—no one jokes. There's no space for anything light today.

Ramirez kneels in front of us. Her voice is soft but steady. "We're going to wire you up now just like we practiced. Tiny mics under the collar, transmitters in your waistband. We'll be less than a block away the entire time. Eyes on you. Guns ready. You're not alone."

I nod and feel the way my neck tightens when she opens the case and lifts the microphone. The tech beside her hands me a small white cloth and asks me to lift my shirt just slightly, fingers shaking as he adjusts the clip. It's cold against my skin, clinical, not intimate, but it still makes me flinch.

"Try speaking," Ramirez says.

I swallow and clear my throat. "Testing?"

Her voice crackles softly through a handheld receiver, and she gives me a thumbs-up. Selecia's next. She flinches a little too when the mic is secured, her lips pressed into a tight line. When they're done, the techs double-check everything, then pack up the cases.

"You'll drive your mom's car," Ramirez says. "Unmarked police vehicles will follow at a distance. We'll be monitoring your movements, your voices, and Blake's approach. The moment he exits the vehicle, SWAT will move. He won't get close." I want to believe that. I need to accept it. But my fingers won't stop curling into fists in my lap, nails biting into my palms.

We gather the last of our things—IDs, our phones, a bottle of water—and step into the hallway. My mom meets us there. Her eyes are wet but proud, and she wraps her arms around both of us at once.

"You don't have to do this," she whispers. "You can back out. We'll find another way." But I shake my head.

"This is the way."

We're doing this for Emily. For every girl like us who never got to come home.

The ride to the store is nearly silent, the car humming beneath us like it's holding its breath too. I keep both hands on the wheel, my knuckles pale from the pressure. My mother's car smells like lavender air freshener and something faintly metallic, like old coins or dried blood. I don't know which memory is mine and which is my body reacting to the weight of what's coming. The microphone itches against my collarbone, a constant reminder that this isn't just a ride. This is a setup. A trap. A risk.

The unmarked SUV behind us stays close enough to feel protective, but far enough not to draw attention. I catch a glimpse of it in the rearview mirror, its headlights steady, a symbol of the silent net we've cast around ourselves.

Selecia sits beside me, her posture stiff, her hands resting in her lap like she's afraid to move. She keeps glancing down at her microphone, checking and rechecking the wire at her hip. She hasn't said a word since we left the safe house.

"You okay?" I ask, my voice barely above a whisper.

She swallows hard, then nods. "Just don't want to screw anything up."

"You won't," I tell her. "You couldn't. You've already survived the worst."

The parking lot comes into view as we crest the final hill. It's mostly empty, save for a few scattered cars and the rusted remnants of a shopping cart corral on the far side. The grocery store itself is old, faded, and its sign is missing half the letters. It looks abandoned, forgotten. Which makes it the perfect place for this—an end to something we never asked to begin.

I pull into the spot near the bench. The one mentioned

in our letter. The bench doesn't look like much—chipped paint, bolts rusted at the edges—but as we sit down on its slats, I feel every eye on us. The police. The SWAT team hidden behind the maintenance shed. Ramirez in her car, fingers on her radio. We're not alone. But we have to look like we are.

"Okay girls," Ramirez's voice crackles softly in our ears through the earpieces. "Stay relaxed. Keep your eyes open. We'll handle it." I glance at Selecia again. Her shoulders are drawn tight. She's hugging herself, trying to keep still, but her leg keeps bouncing, betraying the fear she won't say out loud.

"Breathe," I whisper. "Just keep breathing." And we wait. Minutes crawl by, slow and clinging. Each car that passes makes my heart skip a beat. Each breeze that rustles the trees sounds like footsteps. I try not to fidget. Try not to let my gaze drift toward the tree line where the others are waiting. If he sees anything, this is over.

Then we see it. A dark-colored truck pulls into the far side of the lot. It pauses. Lingers. The driver doesn't get out right away. The engine cuts off, and for a moment, everything stands still.

Then the door opens. And he steps out. Even from this distance, I feel my stomach seize. Blake looks the same and completely different. His hair is longer and tangled. His clothes are worn, but still tucked and clean like he's trying to pretend he hasn't been living like a ghost. He moves with purpose. Slowly. Deliberately. Like he's not afraid. Like, he still believes this is real.

My hand finds Selecia's on the bench. She grips it, white-knuckled. He walks toward us. Each step closes the gap, the sound of his boots against the pavement louder than anything else in the world—my pulse thuds in my ears. My chest feels like it's about to collapse. I don't know how long this will last, or if he'll speak to us. Or if we'll have to lie again. But we never get the chance.

"Now," a voice says over the earpiece.

Suddenly, shadows move from behind the shed. Officers pour into view—silent, fast, practiced. Blake doesn't even have time to turn before he's tackled to the pavement. He hits the ground hard, yelling—something about betrayal, something about lies, about love—but it's swallowed by the sound of commands, of metal on metal, of wrists in cuffs.

He's restrained. Shouting. Struggling. But he's caught. He's caught. I don't realize I'm sobbing until Selecia turns toward me, tears already on her cheeks, and throws her arms around me. We cling to each other, breathless, shaking, laughing, and crying all at once.

"He's gone," she whispers against my shoulder. "He's finally gone."

We don't move until a female officer approaches slowly, her voice gentle. "We found her. Emily. She's alive. She's in the trunk, but she's breathing. We've got medics on the way."

My knees buckle. I sit hard on the bench, my whole body shaking from the inside out. Alive. We did it. He's gone. And she's alive. And for the first time in four years, the air doesn't feel like it's trying to strangle me.

CHAPTER 81: HOME AGAIN

It's strange how home can feel both like a memory and a question mark. The sun is bright overhead as we pass the Hadleigh city limits sign. It's worn now, the paint chipped at the edges, but I know it by heart. My stomach flips as the landscape changes from the unfamiliar stretch of highway into something that once felt like the backdrop of my life. I know these streets. I know these trees, the way the desert and pine blur into each other here, how the mountains rest gently in the distance like they're keeping watch.

It's been nearly four years. Four years since I left for a job I thought would lead somewhere. Four years since I last saw the curve of Main Street, the old post office on the corner, the school crosswalk signs. Four years since Blake followed me home from Olive Garden, crashed into my car, and made me disappear. And now we're driving back.

I grip the seatbelt across my chest and glance sideways at Selecia, who's curled up beside me, her legs tucked beneath her. She's watching the window like it's a screen to a life she's never known. Because it is, she's never been here before.

"I used to walk past that church on my way to school," I say softly, pointing to the faded white steeple rising above the trees. "They gave out free hot cocoa on Fridays." Selecia smiles faintly, but her eyes are heavy with something I recognize. Caution. Hope. Grief.

My mom is in the front seat, driving. She hasn't said

much since we passed into town. Her fingers are wrapped tightly around the steering wheel, knuckles white. I know she's trying to be strong—for me, for Selecia, for the baby growing inside me. But I can feel her anxiety in the silence. This town is just as haunted for her.

The house appears suddenly, tucked behind a low brick fence and a weather-worn maple tree. It's smaller than I remember. The shutters are still blue. The driveway cracked in the same spot where I once scraped my knee learning to rollerblade. The porch has been swept recently. It feels surreal.

As soon as we pull up, the front door flies open. Tara. She's barreling down the porch steps, her blonde ponytail swinging wildly behind her, arms already open before the car is even in park.

"Oh my God, Isadora!" she yells, her voice cracking. I barely manage to unbuckle my seatbelt before she's pulling open the door and yanking me out into the driveway, hugging me so tightly I can't breathe.

"You're here. You're here. You're actually here," she sobs, her arms locked around my shoulders.

I freeze for a second, caught off guard by the weight of her embrace, the suddenness of it, the emotion crashing into me like a wave. Then I melt into it. My arms wrap around her. I bury my face in her neck and cry.

"I missed you so much," I whisper, the words raw and barely audible.

"I thought I lost you," she says. "Every day I thought—I didn't know if you were alive." I pull back just enough to look at her. Her eyes are red. Her mascara smudged. But her smile is blinding.

"I'm okay now," I say, though I'm not sure if that's true. But I want it to be. Then Tara's gaze shifts behind me. Selecia stands at the edge of the car, holding her hands in front of her like she's not sure what to do. She looks younger today, smaller. She's never met Tara before and has never been part of my old world.

"This is Selecia," I say. "She's—" I pause, unsure of how to label what she is to me. Sister? Survivor? Best friend? "She's family." Tara's face softens. She steps forward and pulls Selecia into a hug without hesitation.

"Welcome home," she says, her voice warm. Selecia stiffens for a second, then relaxes slowly into the embrace. She doesn't say anything. But I see the way her shoulders drop, the way her fingers unclench. Mom comes around the side of the car and wraps her arm around my waist.

"Let's go inside," she says gently. "Someone is waiting." My heart skips. Charlotte. We walk up the porch steps together, Tara's arm still draped around my shoulder. As soon as the door swings open, I hear a small gasp. Charlotte stands at the top of the stairs.

She's older now. Nine. Taller than I remember. Her hair is longer, pulled back with a sparkly blue headband. She clutches a stuffed animal to her chest like it's a shield.

"Hi," I say, my voice trembling. "Charlie?" She doesn't answer right away. Her eyes are wide. There's something cautious in her expression—like she's seeing a ghost.

I take a step forward. "It's me. It's really me." Her lip wobbles. Then she throws the stuffed animal and slides down the stairs.

"Dora!" she screams, arms outstretched. I catch her just in time. She hits me like a cannonball, and I drop to my knees, holding her so tightly I'm afraid I'll crush her. She smells like shampoo, graham crackers, and childhood. I press my face into her shoulder and cry.

"I missed you," she says, her voice muffled against my hair. "I missed you every day."

"I missed you, too," I whisper. "So, so much."

She pulls back and touches my face. "You look different."

"You do too. You got so big!"

Charlotte glances over my shoulder at Selecia. "Who's that?"

"That's Selecia. She's... someone very special. She helped me. She's kind, brave, and funny. And she's family now, too."

Charlotte hesitates, then gives a slight nod. "Okay."

Selecia smiles shyly. "Hi."

"Do you like Barbies?" Charlotte asks.

Selecia laughs softly. "Not really."

Charlotte shrugs. "That's okay. I have puzzles too."

Later that evening, we are in the kitchen with sunlight spilling over the kitchen tiles in soft golden sheets, warm and inviting, but I can't stop watching the way the shadows stretch. Tara's laugh bounces off the walls as she and Selecia set the table for lunch, voices overlapping, teasing each other gently. Charlotte is in the living room with my mom, giggling at some cartoon she insisted on showing her. Everything feels... right. But I can't shake the restlessness in my chest.

"Isadora!" Tara calls. I glance up from the sink where I've been scrubbing a plate for far too long. "You okay over there? That dish isn't going to dissolve."

I force a smile. "Just zoned out."

Selecia looks over from the counter. There's an old pink plastic bowl in her hands, filled with sliced peaches. "You sure? You haven't said more than three words since breakfast."

"I'm fine." But I'm not.

It starts when Tara walks past me to grab something from the fridge. The scent of her shampoo hits me—lavender and honey—the same kind Blake made me use the first month we were moved upstairs. I flinch. Not outwardly. Not enough for anyone to see. But inside, something cracks open.

The room fades for a second. I'm not in the kitchen anymore. I'm back in that upstairs room. The carpet was beige, stained in one corner from when he spilled coffee and screamed at us for the mess. The lavender scent fills the air again, cloying and sticky. "You smell like spring," he said, right before he shoved me back on the bed we had to share.

My chest tightens. My pulse roars in my ears. I feel his hand pressing my wrist into the mattress—the weight of him crushing the air out of my lungs. The silence afterward was heavier than anything else. I blink hard, and the image vanishes. Tara is still standing by the fridge, oblivious, humming to herself.

My stomach lurches. I mutter an excuse about needing some air and step out onto the back porch. The cold hits me like a shock. My hands grip the wooden railing, knuckles white. I close my eyes and count each breath until my lungs stop shaking. The door creaks open behind me.

"You okay?" Selecia's voice. She doesn't need an answer. She already knows.

I nod. "Just... memories."

She steps closer and leans against the railing with me. "It happens. Even when you think you're okay. It sneaks up like a ghost."

"I smelled his shampoo," I whisper. "The lavender."

Selecia swallows, her eyes going distant. "Yeah... I remember that bottle." We fall quiet. Not heavy, just... together.

From inside, Charlotte calls, "Izzy! Come see what I drew for you!"

I wipe my eyes before turning around. "Be right there, baby."

Selecia smiles a little. "She missed you so much. Kept asking your mom if you were off fighting dragons."

I smile too. "She's the brave one." We go back inside, and Charlotte runs over with a crayon drawing in her hands. It's us—me, Selecia, Tara, Mom, Charlotte, and a baby drawn with sparkles and pink hearts around it.

"That's the baby in your tummy," Charlotte says proudly. My chest aches in the best way.

I drop to my knees and pull her into a hug. "Thank you, Charlie. It's beautiful."

She hugs me tightly. "I'm glad you came home." So am I. That night, when everyone's asleep, I lay in bed with one hand resting on the swell of my belly.

"We made it," I whisper. "We're safe now. And I swear, you'll never know what I knew. You'll never feel that kind of pain."

From the twin bed beside mine, Selecia murmurs, "That baby is going to have the strongest mom in the world." Tears slide silently down my cheeks. Because, for the first time in years, I believe her.

CHAPTER 82: AFTER

It's been two months since Blake's arrest. Two months since the Crescent Ridge Grocery parking lot exploded with sirens and shadows, two months since I saw him thrown to the ground like the monster he is. Two months of trying to believe he's gone and that the worst is over. But it's not over—not really. Because now we have to speak. We have to stand in front of strangers and relive everything out loud.

And nothing about that feels easy. I sit on the edge of the couch, my palms pressed into my knees to keep them from shaking. The living room is packed. Ramirez, two detectives, a woman from the prosecutor's office named Lila Hawthorne, and a man introduced to us as the victim advocate—all of them are here to prepare us for what's coming.

"Jury selection starts next week," Lila says, flipping through a beige folder thick with documents. "Blake's legal team has entered a plea of not guilty by reason of insanity."

Selecia stiffens beside me. "Are they serious?" she asks, her voice tight.

"They're trying to say he didn't know what he was doing," Ramirez explains quietly. "But we've got more than enough to prove he did." Selecia looks away, arms folded across her chest. I reach for her hand, and she lets me take it, though her fingers stay cold.

Lila continues, "You're not obligated to testify, but your stories are powerful. If you do speak, the jury will see who he really is—and what he did." There's a pause. I can feel them waiting for me.

I speak slowly. "I'll testify."

Selecia's head turns toward me sharply, then she looks down at our joined hands. Her grip tightens. "Me too."

The words feel final when we say them, like crossing a line we can't come back from. Lila nods, marking something on her notepad. "We'll prepare you thoroughly. It won't be easy —but we'll be with you every step." Outside, the faint murmur of voices rises. Cameras flash against the curtains.

"They found out," Ramirez mutters, pulling the curtain aside. "The press."

Of course they did. The story was too good to stay quiet forever: two missing girls returned after four years, a serial abductor in custody, a pregnancy, and a confession letter. It's sensational, and they're all camped out on the street for a glimpse of the survivors.

My stomach twists. "Do we have to go out there?"

"No," Ramirez says. "Not unless you want to." She pauses. "But when the trial begins, it won't be optional. The whole world will be watching."

I glance at Selecia, and for a second, we're both silent. Then she says, "Let them watch." We are not what he made us. And we are not ashamed.

That was a few days ago, and the house isn't quiet anymore. It used to feel like a cocoon—like maybe we were tucked away from the rest of the world, invisible behind weathered siding and a chain-locked gate. But that illusion's gone now. Every morning, I hear them.

Reporters. They've been parked outside since the story broke. Cameras are lining the sidewalk. Microphones are shoved in the faces of anyone who dares step too close. My name is on the headlines again. So is Selecia's. They call us survivors. Miracles. They plaster our school photos next to

Blake's mugshot, dissecting what happened as if it were a movie.

But it wasn't a movie. We weren't characters. We were girls. Just girls. And now the world knows. I watch from the living room window, fingers curled around the curtain, breath fogging the glass. My mom is speaking to someone in the driveway. Tara stands behind her, arms crossed, trying to look intimidating even though she's wearing slippers. She hasn't left since the story aired. Neither has Charlotte.

They're worried. I know why. I haven't spoken to a single reporter. Not even the ones "just trying to tell our side." I haven't answered my phone in three days. And I've barely left my room except for therapy and court prep. But I'm not shutting down. Not really. I'm trying to survive.

"I don't know how to be normal here," I whisper. "It feels fake."

Selecia's sitting on the couch behind me, hugging her knees. "I don't think we're supposed to be normal. Not yet."

"Everyone wants us to be. They want a happy ending. They want us to smile at the camera so they can say we're okay now."

"I'm not smiling." I turn toward her. Neither of us is crying, but our silence says enough. The knock on the door makes me jump. It's Detective Ramirez. Again. She comes by most evenings now. Sometimes, to check in. Sometimes, to prepare us. Today, it's both.

She steps inside, clipboard in hand. "The pre-trial date is officially set. Jury selection begins next Tuesday. The judge has ruled it a high-profile case. Testimony will be closed to the public, but the media's already petitioning for transcripts." My stomach flips.

Charlotte peeks around the corner of the kitchen. My

mom gestures for her to stay back. She doesn't argue. For once, everyone knows this conversation is too much for her.

"What happens if we testify?" I ask, my voice low. "What exactly do we say?"

Ramirez hesitates. "You tell the truth. As much of it as you can handle. The DA isn't expecting perfection. Just honesty."

Selecia pulls her sleeve over her hand. "Do we have to sit in the same room as him?"

"Yes," Ramirez says gently. "But you won't be alone. We'll be there. The DA. Victim advocates. A protective order will be in place. He won't be allowed to speak to you directly." I nod slowly, heart pounding.

A thousand images flash behind my eyes. The shackles on his wrists when they dragged him from the car. The girl they pulled from the trunk. The sound of Selecia's sobbing when we realized we were finally free. I remember every second. But remembering isn't the same as repeating it aloud. Later, after Ramirez leaves, Mom comes into my room and sits on the bed beside me. She's holding a folder of legal paperwork, but her voice is soft.

"I don't want you to feel pressured, Izzy. You don't owe this to anyone."

"I know."

"But if you do choose to testify," she says, "do it for you. Not for the headlines. Not for anyone else's idea of justice." I look down at my hands. They're trembling again.

"I want to do it," I whisper. "I need him to hear what he did to me. To us." A pause.

"Then I'll be right there when you do." Outside, the reporters are still waiting. But inside, I feel something shift. Maybe it's strength or perhaps it's fear, and maybe they're the same right now.

CHAPTER 83: THE TESTIMONY

The courtroom is colder than I expected. It smells faintly like lemon cleaner and something older—polish on wood that's been here too long, worn from years of footsteps and judgment and tears. The ceiling is high, the lights bright but somehow sterile, casting a muted glow over the sea of chairs, tables, and the heavy bench where the judge sits like a monument.

I can't stop staring at the jury box. Twelve people. Strangers. Some are older, some younger. Two women make brief eye contact with me before looking away. A man near the end of the row scratches his temple like he's nervous, too. I wonder what they know, what they've heard so far, and if any of them have daughters.

My knees knock together beneath the skirt of my dress. It's the first time I've worn something so formal since... everything. Black, long-sleeved, soft fabric with a slight stretch so it doesn't cling too tightly to the bump that's become impossible to hide. I'm almost seven months pregnant now, and it shows. I wear flats because I can no longer manage high heels. My hair is pulled back in a simple braid, no makeup except a bit of concealer beneath my eyes. It doesn't help much. I still look tired.

Beside me, Selecia fidgets in her seat. She's dressed similarly in professional clothing, except instead of a dress, she's wearing a dark skirt and a soft blouse, her hair curled slightly at the ends, just as she used to do before. She hasn't let go of my hand since we walked in. Her thumb rubs over my knuckles in slow, steady circles, like she's trying to keep me grounded. But I can't stop shaking. Judge Carrington, a stern woman with silver hair pulled into a bun, calls my name.

It takes everything I have not to freeze. My hand slowly releases Selecia's as I move to stand. My feet move on their own, slow and heavy. The microphone stand looks too tall until the bailiff adjusts it, and then it feels too close. I sit, and the cushion sighs beneath me. Everyone is watching. I feel it on my skin, a thousand invisible hands pinning me in place.

The prosecutor, Lila Hawthorne, nods kindly at me. "Isadora, I want to start by thanking you for being here today," she says. "I know this is incredibly difficult." I nod, but my throat is tight. I try to speak. Nothing comes out. I grip the edges of the seat.

"Take your time," she says softly. I swallow. Hard. Try again.

"My name is Isadora Amber Rose," I whisper, and my voice cracks. "I'm twenty-two years old." My hands tremble in my lap. I squeeze them together.

Mrs. Hawthorne waits a beat, then prompts gently, "Can you tell us how you first encountered the defendant?" I nod. The courtroom blurs for a second as tears pool in my eyes, but I force myself to speak.

"I... I was working at Olive Garden. I'd just turned seventeen." My voice wobbles. I clear my throat and try again. "He used to come in a few times a week. At first, I thought he was just an ordinary person. He always asked to sit in my section." My heart pounds as I continue. "He was polite. Too polite. He tipped big. Smiled a lot. I thought maybe he was just lonely."

"And when did things change?" Mrs. Hawthorne asks.

I inhale shakily. "He asked me out one night after I brought him his check. I said no. I didn't know him like that. I said he was too old for me. I told him I wasn't allowed to date customers. He laughed. Said he understood. But he looked angry," There's a pause. My stomach twists. "That night, I was in a car accident. Or... I thought it was. He rammed my car from behind. Before I could move, he was dragging me from my car." The courtroom is silent. Even the air seems to hold its breath.

I blink rapidly, trying to hold myself together. "I woke up in a basement—concrete walls. No windows. A chain on my ankle." My voice breaks. A quiet sob rises from someone behind me, maybe Mom. I don't turn to look.

"Did you know where you were?" Hawthorne asks.

"No," I whisper. "I didn't even know what day it was."

"Can you describe what that first week was like?"

I nod slowly. "At first, he brought me food—crackers, once. A bucket. And then he talked. He said I was special, that I'd been chosen to help him start a family the right way. He told me the rules—how to behave, when to speak, how to be respectful. He said he was helping me, saving me. But I was just... trapped. Alone. Scared. Everything he said made it worse." I pause, and the memory hits like a wave.

"I remember counting the cracks in the ceiling just to have something to do. Something to hold on to. I used to whisper to myself so I wouldn't forget what my voice sounded like." Hawthorne's expression tightens, but she lets me speak.

"He kept me down there for over two years. Sometimes he'd bring things—books, a pillow. One time, a drawing pad. He said he wanted me to be comfortable. That this was my new home." I glance at Blake for the first time. He stares at the table.

No remorse. No regret. Just... blank. I look away.

"And then?" Leone asks gently. I know what he's asking. When did he start hurting you? I can't speak yet. I need to explain what happened before.

"It had been more than two years of no change, when he brought someone else. A girl. Her name was Selecia. She was twelve." My voice wavers, but I keep going.

"She didn't know what was happening. She cried the first night. Screamed the second. He said she was a gift for me. That we were a family now." I feel Selecia's eyes on me. I can't look at her right now or I'll fall apart.

"I tried to protect her. I pretended it was okay. I told her to be quiet, to play along, to act like it wasn't so bad. I taught her how to avoid his anger. What not to say. When to hide." I close my eyes for a second. My hands tighten into fists.

"Eventually, he moved us upstairs. Said we'd earned it. That families shouldn't live in basements." The following words are harder.

"That's when he first assaulted me." I hear gasps. A gavel strikes once; "Order in the court," the judge yells. I keep my eyes forward.

"It happened after dinner. He said he was proud of me. That I was finally becoming the woman he always knew I was." I'm crying now. The words are coming faster, messier.

"I didn't scream. I didn't fight. I just... shut down. I couldn't let Selecia hear. I couldn't let her know. So, I pretended to be okay. I acted like it didn't hurt. Like it didn't matter."

"Did the assaults continue?" Hawthorne asks quietly. I nod, barely.

"I lost three pregnancies. Early ones. Before the second trimester. I never told him. Never told her either. I cleaned my blood myself. Hid the pain. Told her I was sick." The jury is silent. Some of them are crying too.

"And now?" Hawthorne asks in almost a whisper.

"I'm almost seven months pregnant," I say. "And I'm terrified every day." There's more to say, much more. But I need to breathe. I need to hold on.

"I did everything I could to survive. To keep her safe. To trick him into trusting me. I smiled when I wanted to scream. I kissed him when I wanted to kill him. I played along for four years. Four years." I stop. The silence wraps around me like a shroud. This is only the beginning.

I pause, my hands trembling in my lap, fingers knotted so tightly together they've gone white. I can feel the sweat at the back of my neck. The courtroom is silent, heavy with breath that no one dares to release.

The prosecutor gives me a moment, then gently asks, "Can you tell us what changed when he brought someone else into that space with you?" I swallow. My throat feels raw.

"I thought... I thought I was his only target. Perhaps I was the only one suffering because of something I had done, something I had triggered. And then..." My voice shakes. "He came down one day with her. A girl. Twelve years old. She looked terrified." I close my eyes. The image rises instantly, crisp and cruel.

"She was so small. So quiet. And I knew—I knew what was happening. He told me she was a gift. That he was giving me a sister." My voice fractures, and I grip the edge of the witness box as if it can keep me grounded. "He wanted a family. A real one. That's what he said."

The prosecutor's voice stays steady. "What did you feel in that moment?"

"Panic. Guilt. Rage. I wanted to protect her, but I was already so broken by then. I hadn't spoken to anyone in months. I didn't even know how to explain to her what was happening because I didn't understand it myself." I blink hard, trying to keep the tears from blurring everything. "She asked me where we were. And I told her we were in hell."

A few jurors shift in their seats. One of the women wipes at her eye.

"She only cried at first. Later, she just sat there beside me. We took turns with the bucket. Shared food. Slept on opposite ends of the hard mattress on the floor. He said we had to earn his trust. We were silent when he was around, too scared to talk. But when the lights were out… we whispered. Her name was Selecia. And she was just a kid."

"Did Blake treat her differently?"

My breath catches. "Not really. At first, he brought us little things—books, pencils. A radio that only played static. He thought he was giving us normalcy. But it was control. Everything was about control."

"And did you feel a responsibility toward her?"

I nod. "She didn't have anyone else. I knew what I had to do: I had to survive, but I also had to shield her from him. From what I knew, he was capable of. I became her big sister, her protector, her voice when she was too scared to speak."

"And how long were you both kept in that basement?"

"Over two years for me. About a year and a half for her. Then he said we had proven ourselves. He brought us upstairs. He called it a promotion, like we had earned it." My voice falters again. "But that's when things got worse." There's a silence. Even the air feels frozen.

The prosecutor's expression softens just slightly. "Would you be comfortable sharing what happened after he moved you upstairs?"

I nod once, but it takes me several seconds to form the words. "That's when the assaults started. We had more comforts, but I felt so much more broken and afraid upstairs than in that basement." A low gasp travels through the gallery.

"He stopped locking the bedroom door during the day eventually. He gave us chores. Told us to smile more. Told us to call him Dad. But after dinner, he would set up 'dates', time for just me and him." I wipe a tear that escapes down my cheek. "It started slowly. Invasively. Unmistakably. And every time he touched me, I felt like I was disappearing." The judge gently adjusts his glasses. A few members of the jury lean forward, completely still.

"I never told Selecia. I couldn't. I needed her to stay strong. I needed her to think we had a chance at getting out."

"Did the abuse continue?"

"Yes. For the last year we were with him." I'm crying now, but I don't stop. "I pretended to care about him. I smiled when I had to. I thanked him for the food. For clothes. I played the part so he wouldn't hurt her. So, he would trust me just enough that maybe, one day, he would make a mistake and we could run."

The prosecutor hesitates, then asks, "Isadora... you said you had multiple pregnancies?" The air leaves my lungs. I grip the edge of the seat, press my fingers into the wood.

"Yes. Three before this one. All miscarriages. All early. All hidden." My voice is flat now. Detached. "I cleaned up the blood myself. I flushed everything before he could see. Before she could see. I told her I had stomach cramps. I told her I was just sick."

"And now?" I rest a hand on my stomach, which curves gently beneath the dress I'm wearing.

"I'm nearly seven months pregnant." A murmur ripples

through the courtroom. The judge gives a sharp look, and it fades.

"Why testify now?" the prosecutor asks, her tone almost reverent. I lift my chin slowly. My voice steadies.

"Because I'm done hiding. Because I want him to see me —not as a broken thing, not as his possession, but as the girl who got away. The girl who fought. The girl who will never let him take anything again."

CHAPTER 84:
SELECIA'S TURN

Selecia's POV

They call my name, and suddenly the world narrows. The courtroom is too cold. My palms are damp, and I keep wiping them against the sides of my skirt, trying to act normal and trying to breathe. Isadora squeezes my hand once before I rise, and I hold on to that tiny gesture like it's the last solid thing in the world.

I walk toward the stand, each step sounding louder than the last. I know everyone's watching me—the jury, the reporters, the people who came to see a show, and the people who came to see justice. But all I feel is Blake's eyes. Somewhere behind me. Burning. Waiting. Like he always did. I don't look at him.

The bailiff asks me to raise my hand. I do. My voice barely works when I say, "I do." Then I sit down, knees together, hands knotted in my lap like I'm trying to hold my body together. The judge's name is Carrington. Her voice is low but not unkind. Still, it's her eyes that shake me. There's something heavy in them, like she already knows the worst parts of this story. The prosecutor is back on her feet, strolling toward me with a legal pad in hand. Her tone is softer than it was for Isadora. Like, she knows I'm younger. Like she knows, I'm still trying not to disappear into the chair.

"Selecia," she says gently, "can you tell the court how old

you are?"

"Fourteen, almost fifteen," I say it quickly, like I want the words to be over. My voice sounds smaller than I expected.

"And how old were you when you met the defendant, Blake Winters?"

"Twelve." There's a pause. People write things down. I keep my eyes low.

"Can you tell us how you came to be in Mr. Winter's home?"

I swallow hard. I hate this part. "I was walking home from school. I lived in a group home. He drove up in a white truck and said my social worker had sent him to pick me up. He... he knew her name. He knew mine. I didn't know any better." My voice breaks. "I got in."

Ms. Keene nods slowly. "And where did he take you?"

"Somewhere far. A basement. It was dark. I thought he'd drop me off eventually, that this was a mistake, but he locked the door. There were no windows. Just cement walls and one flickering bulb. And her." I glance toward Isadora, who's still seated. Her eyes meet mine, shining.

"She was already there?"

I nod. "Yeah. She looked... broken. But she made space for me. She shared the food. Told me to stay quiet. Helped me when I had nightmares." My voice trembles. "I didn't even know her name at first. Just that she wasn't him."

"Did Blake hurt you in the basement?"

"No. Not physically. But it wasn't safe. It was never safe. We didn't know when he'd show up. He played with our heads. Left us down there for days at a time. One time, he turned off the power completely, and it was freezing. No light. No food. For two whole days. Just to prove we couldn't live without him."

"Did he ever say why he brought you there?"

My stomach twists. "He said he was building a family. That I was gonna be Isadora's sister. Then, later, he said that Isadora was his wife, and I was his daughter. He called us that. Over and over. Made us repeat it back to him."

Ms. Keene pauses. "When did things change?"

"When he moved us upstairs," I whisper. "He said he trusted us now. He said we were ready to be a real family. That's when the punishments started if we didn't say what he wanted or didn't smile enough. That's when I started hearing things from the bedroom." My throat tightens.

"You don't have to say anything you're not ready for, Selecia."

I nod but continue. "I didn't know what he was doing to her at first. Just... that she came back quietly. Distant. She always said it was okay, but it wasn't. Then... one night I heard it." A tear slips down my cheek. "And I didn't know what to do." Silence stretches across the courtroom.

"She kept trying to protect me," I say. "She smiled when he was around. She cooked dinner. She cleaned. She hugged him sometimes. It made me sick, but I knew she was pretending. We both were."

"Did Blake ever hurt you directly?"

I shake my head. "Not like he hurt her. But he scared me every day. And sometimes... he punished her to punish me. One time I said the wrong thing, and he didn't hit me —he locked her in the bathroom for a whole night without anything. Another time, I refused to call him 'Dad, ' and he made her eat on the floor like a dog. Just because he could."

"And how did you survive all that?"

"Her," I say again. "She taught me how. We whispered plans into the night. We counted footsteps and watched when he left his keys out. We pretended to believe him so he wouldn't snap. And eventually... we escaped."

"Do you still have nightmares?" I nod.

"And how are you today?"

"I'm alive." My voice cracks. "We're alive. And that has to be enough for now."

Ms. Keene walks back to her table. "No further questions, Your Honor."

The judge gives me a slight nod. "Thank you, Selecia. You may step down." I don't remember standing up. I don't remember walking back to my seat. But I remember Isadora pulling me into her arms as soon as I sat down, and I cried onto her shoulder like a baby. Only now, no one can lock us away. Not anymore.

CHAPTER 85:
AFTER TRIAL

The walls of my childhood bedroom feel unfamiliar. The posters are gone. The furniture was rearranged. The paint's the same pale blue, but the girl who grew up here doesn't live in this room anymore.

I'm curled up beneath my old comforter, knees pulled high, one hand resting over the swell of my belly. The house is quiet—too quiet. No creak of a monitor. No patrol outside the window. Just the soft hum of the ceiling fan and my shallow breathing. I should feel safe. I should feel free. But all I feel is hollow.

The courtroom images are still fresh, blazing hot in my mind. My voice trembled the entire time. My hands never stopped shaking. And when I finally got down from the stand, I thought it would be over. I thought that would be the worst part. But it wasn't. Selecia's testimony followed mine. She was brave. Steady. But then she said it—something I didn't expect, something I didn't know she knew.

"I didn't know what he was doing to her at first. Just... that she came back quiet. Distant. She always said it was okay, but it wasn't. Then... one night I heard it." And suddenly the world tilted beneath me again.

The door creaks open. I don't have to turn to know it's her. Her footsteps are tentative, careful in that way she always is now, like she's afraid of stepping too loudly in a world that already took too much.

She sits on the edge of the bed, silent for a long time. Then, "Izzy?" I say nothing.

"I didn't want to hurt you," she says finally, her voice barely audible. "Not more than you already were." I shift slightly, still turned away, but not pushing her off.

"I didn't know at first," she says. "You'd come back from being upstairs and you'd act like things were fine, but… You weren't. I saw it in your eyes. You'd smile, but it wasn't real. You'd sit beside me, but it was like you weren't even in the room." Tears gather in my eyes, hot and sharp.

"I kept thinking you were just tired or scared. I told myself that. Over and over. Until one night… I heard it. I heard what he was doing." I close my eyes, but the tears slip through anyway.

"You didn't say anything," I whisper.

"I thought pretending not to know would protect you," she says, her voice shaking now. "I thought maybe if I just let you keep pretending, it would give you some kind of peace. Or control. I didn't want to take that away from you." I turn to face her. Her eyes are red too.

"You never looked at me any different," I say, voice cracking.

"Never," she whispers. "Not once." A sob breaks loose from my throat. I cover my mouth with my hand, but the sound still escapes.

"I kept thinking if you knew… you'd see me the way I saw myself."

"I saw someone surviving," she says. "I saw someone who kept going—for both of us." We're quiet for a beat. The only sound is the ceiling fan and our breathing.

"You kept pretending," she adds. "You cooked. You cleaned. You hugged him. It killed me to watch. But I knew what you were doing. I understood."

"I was just trying to keep us safe," I say.

"I know." She reaches out, and I don't hesitate. Our hands find each other and hold tight.

"I don't want to keep any more secrets," I whisper.

"Me either." We sit like that, forehead to forehead, the past between us but not separating us. And this time, I don't feel so alone.

CHAPTER 86:
THE CROSS

The courtroom is quiet again, but not calm. There's a tension in the air, heavy and expectant, like the seconds before a storm. I can feel Blake's eyes on me. Blake Winters. I won't forget that name. I live with it carved into my body.

Judge Carrington clears her throat. "Ms. Isadora Amber Rose," she says, voice steady and commanding. "Please return to the stand for cross-examination."

I rise slowly, like my bones remember every hour of captivity and need to think twice before moving. The jury is watching. Some with pity. Some with unreadable expressions. Familiar strangers who now know parts of me I never wanted anyone to hear. I take my seat and face the court.

Carter Price stands. The defense attorney. Clean-cut. Polished. A practiced calm in his expression, but his eyes are sharp and cold. I can tell the questions have already been planned; he's not here to find out the truth. He's here to twist it.

"Ms. Rose," he begins, smooth and formal, "thank you for being here again. Yesterday, you shared... harrowing details about your time in Mr. Winters' home." He says it like I wrote a ghost story, not a testimony.

"Let's begin with the setting," he says. "You said you were held for almost four years. That's quite a length of time. Now, you'd agree that if someone were being held against their will, signs would eventually appear? Noise. Disturbances. Maybe attempts to escape?"

My jaw tightens. "If someone could escape."

He nods, pretending to be thoughtful. "And where exactly was Mr. Winters' home located?"

"The outskirts of Cherry Hill, Arizona," I answer. "Woods. Dirt roads. No one around for miles."

"So... remote. Not a suburban neighborhood, not close to town?"

"No," I say. "Completely isolated. No neighbors. Hardly any traffic. Just trees and silence."

He scribbles something on his notepad like it means anything. "So, you're saying no one could've heard you?"

"Not unless they had a helicopter," I snap.

He pauses, clearly not amused. "Did you try to scream?"

"In the beginning?" I lean forward. "I screamed until my throat was raw. I cried. I banged on the walls, the ceiling, and the floor. I begged him to let me go."

"And what happened after you did all that?"

"He beat me," I say, louder now. "He beat me until I couldn't stand. He locked me in the dark for days. He cut me. Starved me. Turned the AC to freezing. Turned the heat to scalding. Left me with nothing but silence and the sound of my breathing." A silence falls over the room. One of the jurors' blinks rapidly, clearly shaken.

Price recovers quickly. "Let's talk about the basement. You say you were chained there for over two years?"

"Yes."

"Every day?"

"I was hardly ever unchained," I reply bitterly. "Only when he wanted to punish me. Or when he needed to move me.

He gave me a plastic tub to wash with. Like an animal."

"What kind of punishments?" he asks, with mock concern.

"He'd hit me. Lock me in a closet. Cut me when I didn't obey. Sometimes he'd just stop bringing food. Or turn off the lights and leave me down there until I couldn't remember if it was day or night."

"But he didn't always hit you?" Price presses.

"Not after a while," I say. "He didn't have to. He controlled everything: food, water, air, warmth. When you know someone owns your survival, they don't need fists anymore. They just need to withhold."

He leans back slightly. "You claim you never had a chance to leave, to cry for help?"

"I had no phone. No door. No keys. No way out."

"Still," he continues, "your testimony also mentioned that your father was abusive. Difficult home life. Isn't it possible, Ms. Rose, that you saw Mr. Winters as... an escape?" I freeze.

"No." I couldn't believe he would even suggest that.

"Are you sure? Teenage girls have been known to run away from abusive homes and seek attention elsewhere. You were seventeen. Maybe Blake Winters offered you what your father didn't." I feel my breath catch.

"I never ran away," I say, voice shaking. "I wanted to, but I didn't. I thought about it a hundred times. But I didn't go with Blake. I told him no. He came to my job. He followed me. Then he crashed into my car. Drugged me. I woke up chained to a pipe."

"Objection!" Lila Hawthorne rises. "Speculation and victim-blaming."

"Sustained," Judge Carrington says coldly. "Mr. Price, move on."

Carter holds up a hand in mock innocence. "Of course, Your Honor."

He turns back to me. "Ms. Rose... are there any physical signs that can support your claims of being abused? Scars, perhaps?" My stomach coils.

"Yes," I whisper.

"Can you show the court?" I pause. My hands tremble in my lap. I glance at the judge. She nods. I rise slowly, then turn my back slightly to the jury. With one hand, I lift the hem of my shirt, revealing the raised, jagged letters carved into my skin.

BLAKE.

Gasps ripple through the courtroom. "He carved his name into my back," I say through clenched teeth. "So, I wouldn't forget who I belonged to." I lower my shirt.

"And now you want to stand here and ask me if I wanted to stay?" I glare at Carter, my voice rising. "I screamed. I fought. I bled. He broke my ribs and left me in a closet without food for three days. He cut me over and over just to see me cry. And when I stopped screaming, when I gave up—that wasn't consent. That was survival."

The courtroom is still buzzing from the scar. Even the jury, now familiar strangers, looks stunned. One of them shifts uncomfortably in his seat, eyes wide and hands clenched in his lap. I try not to look at them. I keep my focus forward.

Carter Price clears his throat and adjusts his tie. He's thrown off, just enough to make his voice falter.

"Ms. Rose... let's shift focus to the other young woman— Selecia." I feel a chill creep down my spine.

"You testified that Mr. Winters brought her into the home roughly two years into your captivity, is that correct?"

"Yes."

"So by then, you'd already been in the basement for over two years?"

"Yes."

"You claim she was also chained in the basement—correct?"

"Yes," I say sharply.

"And you... Never tried to help her escape?"

"I couldn't even help myself."

"But you said you protected her."

"I did what I could," I reply. "I tried to take the punishment for her. I tried to shield her from him. I talked to her when she was scared. I held her when she cried."

He raises an eyebrow. "Punishments? Mr. Winters punished her, too?"

"No," I say, voice steady now. "Not really. He punished me. For both of us." There's silence. My heart is thudding in my ears, but I keep going.

"He had chained her beside me. But if she made a mistake, he'd hurt me instead. He said I was the older one. I should be teaching her how to behave."

"So, you're saying... he used you as an example?"

"He knew that hurting her would only make me harder to control. But hurting me? That made her quiet. That made me compliant."

Carter tilts his head. "So, you're saying she resisted... yet he still managed to control her, just like he did you?"

"Yes."

"Even though she was younger, smaller, and—likely less equipped to handle trauma, she still complied like you?"

"Are you trying to say she should've escaped?" I snap.

"I'm trying to understand why neither of you made any attempt to contact the outside world for years."

"Because we had no world," I say. "No sunlight. No windows. He controlled everything—food, light, sound, time. He made us feel like we didn't exist outside of him." Carter walks a few steps closer to the stand.

"Let's talk about when you moved upstairs," he says. "You claim that after three years in the basement, Mr. Winters moved you into the main floor of the house?"

"Yes."

"And that was also when the assaults began?"

"Yes."

"So, you were no longer chained?"

"No."

"You had a bed and access to a kitchen. You cooked meals. Watched movies."

"Yes."

"And yet... You didn't run?"

"We were still locked inside," I reply. "He bolted the doors from the outside. He held the only key."

"You had more freedom, though. That's what you said. Correct?"

"Yes."

"So why didn't you fight back then?"

I feel heat rising in my face. My hands curl around the edge of the stand.

"Because I knew him by then," I hiss. "I knew what he was capable of. If I fought back, he'd kill me. Or worse, he'd kill her."

Carter narrows his eyes. "So, you're saying you chose to comply?"

"I chose to survive," I say. "That's not the same thing." He started to speak again, but I interrupted him.

"You want to know what complying looked like?" I say. "It looked like letting him hold my hand during dinner, like watching movies, and pretending to laugh so he wouldn't get suspicious. Like wearing clothes he picked out and telling him they were perfect. Like smiling through nausea. Like choking down dinner when my stomach was in knots. Like thanking him for 'no more chains.' Like kissing his cheek when he demanded affection." A pause.

"And all the while," I continue, voice tight, "I was waiting. Counting days. Searching for keys. Watching his every move. Trying to find a way out. For both of us." Carter tries to regain control.

"And you never once attempted to escape during that time? Not even once?"

"We did try. Once," I say. "And it cost us everything. But you don't want to hear that part." He adjusts his cuffs, irritated.

"Let's go back again to the start. You were taken after a shift. Yet you never called out? Never screamed?"

My jaw tightens. "I did scream. I begged. I cried. I fought with everything I had. But he drugged me."

"Then why didn't anyone hear you?"

"I was unconscious and once I woke up in the basement,

he beat me so badly I couldn't scream anymore," I snap. "He left me unconscious. He carved his name into my back like I was a possession. He kept me in the dark for days. No food. No sound. Just silence and pain until I forgot what freedom felt like."

"And you're saying this happened... in a suburban neighborhood? With neighbors nearby?"

I narrow my eyes. "He didn't live in some cheerful cookie-cutter suburb. It was a rural town with a dead-end road, dirt, trees, and fields. No neighbors. No cars passing by. No one to hear us scream. No one ever came." Carter opens his mouth, but I lean forward before he can speak.

"And for the first two years," I say slowly, "I was never unchained. Not even to bathe. He brought down a plastic tub and watched while I used it. The only time he ever unchained me was for punishment—like locking me in the closet or dragging me across the floor by my hair. If I looked at him wrong, he'd slap me. If I spoke out, he'd cut me. If I cried, he'd turn off the lights and leave us for days." Carter is visibly uncomfortable now. But I'm not done.

"You can sit there and ask why I didn't run. Why didn't I scream? Why didn't I fight? But you weren't there. You didn't see what he did. You didn't hear the lock turn, or the silence that followed."

My voice shakes, but I let it. "You didn't have to survive him."

Carter looks at the judge. "No further questions at this time."

Judge Carrington gives me a slight nod. "You may step down, Ms. Rose." I rise. My hands are trembling. My back aches from sitting so straight. But I walk off that stand with my head held high. Because the truth, even when it hurts, it is still mine to carry.

CHAPTER 87: CROSS

Selecia's POV

The courtroom feels more suffocating today. Like the air is thick with something invisible, I tug at the hem of my blazer—navy, itchy—and force myself not to fidget. Isadora sits beside me in the front row, her hand resting gently on my knee for support. We haven't said much this morning and just shared a glance. A silent reminder that we're here together.

The door creaks open, and the jury files in—familiar strangers now, all in the same clothes as yesterday. Same polite blank faces pretending not to have made up their minds already. Judge Carrington sits straighter in her chair as she addresses the room.

"Let's resume with the cross-examination of Selecia." My name. Just my first name. That's all I want to hear. Not my past, not what he tried to turn me into. Mr. Price stands, buttoning his jacket. He's even more smug today, his smile tight and eyes calculating. He saunters toward the stand like he's giving me time to squirm. I won't.

"Good morning, Selecia," he says. "Ready to begin?" I nod once. My voice might crack if I try to speak too soon.

He paces a few steps. "Yesterday, you testified that Blake Winters—Mr. Winters—picked you up after school, correct?"

"Yes," I say.

"And you willingly got into the vehicle with him?"

I hesitate, but then answer clearly. "Yes. Because he said

my foster mom had sent him. That she couldn't make it."

"So... no screaming? No running? No fighting back?"

"Not until later."

"Later?" He raises an eyebrow. "Could you clarify that?"

I grip the edge of the witness stand. "When we got to the house, I was confused. But I didn't really fight until I was already in the basement... and saw Isadora. Chained to a pipe. That's when I realized he'd lied."

He nods slowly, pretending to jot something on his notepad. "So, you're saying that despite being abducted, you didn't resist until hours later?"

"I didn't know I was being abducted," I snap. "He lied to me. I thought my foster mom was picking me up." There's a murmur in the courtroom. Judge Carrington glares until it quiets.

Mr. Price's voice stays smooth. "You described the basement as dark. Unfurnished. A pipe where you were later chained. And you say you remained there for over a year?"

"Yes."

"Yet during that time, according to your earlier testimony, Blake Winters allowed you to speak freely with Isadora. Brought you food. Gave you blankets, books, even crayons."

I nod slowly. "Eventually. Not at first. And none of that made it normal."

"But there were comforts, yes?"

"Things to manipulate us," I say. "To keep us quiet. To make it feel like he cared."

He raises an eyebrow. "Did he ever physically harm you?"

"No." I see him ready to jump on that, so I add, "But that

doesn't mean I wasn't punished."

"Punished how?"

"He'd change the temperature. Make it freezing or boiling. He'd leave us in the dark for days. No showers for weeks. Sometimes he wouldn't feed Isadora, but he'd give me food instead."

Mr. Price leans forward slightly. "So you witnessed Blake neglecting Isadora?"

"Yes."

"Did you intervene?"

"What could I do?" I fire back. "I was chained, too. And she told me not to. She didn't want him to hurt me. I tried to share when I could. We both did."

"Interesting," he says, voice slow, "because you claim to have been so terrified of this man, yet you say he brought you upstairs eventually. Unchained. Gave you responsibilities. Let you clean and cook. So, tell me—why didn't you run then?"

I feel heat rising in my face. "Because by then, we knew what he was capable of. He beat Isadora so badly once that she nearly died. I saw her scars. We knew that playing along was the only way we'd survive."

He steps back and gives the jury a pointed look. "So, the theory is—if I understand it—you both made a calculated choice to appear cooperative in order to survive."

"Yes."

He tilts his head. "And how do we know you weren't... enjoying the attention? The approval?"

I blink at him. "Excuse me?"

"Playing house. Being treated like a daughter. Being praised. Fed. That can be intoxicating to a child from the foster system, can't it?" The air drains from my lungs. I feel something twist in my chest.

"I knew it was fake," I say quietly. "I knew it wasn't real. I had to pretend, but I never believed any of it."

He watches me for a beat, then flips a page in his folder. "You mentioned seeing some of Isadora's punishments. But you didn't see physical abuse."

"No," I say. "Not until after we were moved upstairs. I didn't see it... But I knew."

He squints. "How?"

"She came back different," I whisper. "Worse. She stopped talking. She'd freeze if he touched her shoulder. She started having nightmares."

"And you never asked?"

"I did," I say. "She said she was okay. But she wasn't."

His tone shifts—sharp, skeptical. "You never witnessed anything. So, isn't it possible she made it all up? That this entire narrative is exaggerated for sympathy?"

"Objection!" Lila Hawthorne stands abruptly. "Speculative and inappropriate."

"Isadora is nearly seven months pregnant now. I think her baby is proof enough," I snapped.

"Sustained," Judge Carrington says firmly. "Mr. Price, you will refrain from personal attacks on the witness." He backs off, but not before sending one last look my way—like he's still trying to find a crack in my story. There isn't one.

I grip the stand harder, grounding myself. "He took everything from us. We survived. That's all."

Judge Carrington nods. "You may step down." As I walk

back to the bench beside Isadora, her hand catches mine. We don't speak. But we don't have to.

CHAPTER 88: REVISION OF HISTORY

The courtroom is still, every creak of a chair or shuffle of a shoe swallowed by the pressure in the air. I grip the edge of my seat, my knuckles white, as the bailiff calls, "Mr. Blake Winters to the stand." Every breath in my chest freezes.

He stands slowly, calmly, dressed in a button-up shirt and slacks like he's here for a business meeting, not to face the lives he destroyed. His hair is slicked back, his hands neatly folded as he steps forward. There's a faint smile playing on his lips. The kind that makes my stomach churn. He doesn't look at me. Not directly. But I feel his presence like smoke in my lungs.

Judge Carrington—stern as always with her silver bun and icy eyes—watches him descend onto the witness stand. "You may be seated, Mr. Winters." He nods respectfully and takes his seat, shifting slightly as though he's settling in to tell a bedtime story.

His attorney, Carter Price, stands beside him in his dark suit, flipping through his notes. "Mr. Winters," he begins, his voice calm, composed, "you've heard a lot of claims made about your character over the last several days. I'd like to give you the opportunity to tell your version of events. Let's start with how you first met Ms. Isadora Amber Rose."

Blake clears his throat. "Of course." His voice is soft, measured, and coated in politeness like oil on glass. "I first met Isadora at the restaurant where she worked. I was a regular—loved the food—and she was always my waitress. She stood out to me. Not just because she was beautiful—although she was—but because she was kind. She remembered my order and asked how my day was. There was something warm about her." I can feel the tension rising in my chest, feel Selecia's hand inch toward mine beneath the table.

"I eventually worked up the nerve to ask her out," Blake continues. "She said no, which I respected, of course. I didn't push. But I guess... fate had its plans."

He turns his head slightly toward the jury—those familiar strangers who've sat through every tearful word of our testimonies—and softens his voice. "A few days later, I was driving, and... I made a mistake. I didn't see her car in time, and I clipped it from behind. I was horrified. Genuinely. I went out to check on her, and she was shaken, crying. I offered to take her home, to make sure she was okay."

He pauses, lets that sit in the room. "She said yes." I clench my teeth so hard my jaw aches.

Mr. Price nods encouragingly. "So, you're saying Ms. Rose voluntarily got into your vehicle?"

"Yes, sir," Blake replies smoothly. "I think she just needed someone in that moment. She was scared. I drove carefully; I told her I had some food back at my place and a first aid kit. I asked if she wanted to stop there, just to rest, and she agreed." Lies. All lies. I had a concussion. I was disoriented, barely conscious. He didn't ask me. He drugged me.

"And once she was at your home, what happened?"

Blake leans forward slightly, voice softening. "We talked. I tried to help her feel safe. I told her she could stay a while —only if she wanted. I know that might sound odd to some people, but... I've always believed in helping those who fall through the cracks. She told me about her family, her father, and how she'd been hurt before. I thought... maybe she saw me as someone who wouldn't hurt her." My fingernails dig into my thigh beneath the table. That's not what I said. That's not what happened.

"And did she ever try to leave?" Price asks.

"No," Blake says without hesitation. "Not at first. She stayed. She helped around the house. We watched movies. I know it wasn't traditional, but it felt like we were building something... like a family." I want to scream.

"And what about Selecia?" Mr. Price continues.

Blake nods thoughtfully. "I saw her one afternoon walking home from school. She looked... lost. Tired. Just like Isadora had. I asked her if she needed help, if she wanted something better. She said yes. I told her I'd spoken to her foster mother and that I could take her someplace safe. I believed I could offer that."

"You believe you were doing a good thing?"

Blake's voice grows emotional, almost tearful. "Yes. I know people might not understand, but I never hurt those girls. I gave them everything I had. Food. Shelter. Family. The world abandoned them. I took them in."

Carter Price gives a slight nod, his voice turning more pointed now. "So, the images the prosecution painted—the chains, the punishments, the manipulation—none of that is true?"

Blake looks genuinely wounded. "Chains?" he repeats. "I never wanted to restrain anyone. But Isadora had a history of panic attacks. She harmed herself once. I only wanted to keep her safe." The rage in my chest burns like acid. He's flipping everything upside down.

"What about withholding food, or isolating her?"

"She had mood swings," Blake says, frowning. "There were days she wouldn't come out of the room. I tried to encourage healthy routines. I thought that if I gave her space, she'd come around."

"And the claim that you 'carved' your name into her back?"

Blake sighs. "She asked for it. She asked for a tattoo of my name." Gasps ripple through the gallery—my body trembles.

"Thank you, Mr. Winters. No further questions at this time."

Judge Carrington's gavel knocks once. "We'll resume after a brief recess." I can't breathe. My heart pounds in my ears. His lies drip like poison into the room, and I know the worst is still coming.

The courtroom is quiet again when we reconvene, but it's not the kind of quiet that brings peace. It's the heavy, suffocating kind—where the silence hums like a storm in the walls. I grip the edge of my chair again, every muscle tense, my breath shallow. Blake is already seated, as if he never left the stand. Calm. Centered. Like he's enjoying this. Carter Price stands slowly, adjusting his cufflinks with precision before turning to face the jury.

"We'll continue, Your Honor," he says, and Judge Carrington gives him a curt nod. "Mr. Winters, I'd like to revisit a few details—just for clarity."

"Of course," Blake replies smoothly, folding his hands in his lap.

"Let's go back to the living situation. You stated that Ms. Rose voluntarily remained in your home for some time. Can you elaborate on that period?"

Blake nods. "She stayed with me for several months

before things started to change. At first, she was quiet—unsure —but I gave her space. Eventually, she came out of her shell. She helped with meals. We watched movies. I even brought her art supplies. I encouraged her creativity."

"Would you say you formed a bond?"

"Yes," Blake says firmly. "A deep one. We talked about life. About pain. She told me about her family, her absentee mother, and her abusive father. I became someone she could lean on."

Mr. Price flips to another page in his notes. "And you say she never asked to leave?"

"No," Blake says. "She seemed grateful. I never forced her to stay. She had access to the upstairs. There were no locked doors." Another lie.

"And when you brought Selecia into the home, what was the dynamic like?"

Blake exhales slowly. "It was difficult at first. I could tell she was confused. But I tried to ease her in. I gave her space. I bought her things—books, clothes, even let her pick meals sometimes. Over time, she and Isadora grew close. They looked like sisters. It made me feel proud. Like I had created something good." He makes it sound like a Hallmark movie, like we weren't two prisoners trying to survive in a nightmare.

Mr. Price shifts, adopting a more somber tone. "Let's talk about the accusations of abuse. The prosecution claims you used various tactics—control, starvation, even psychological manipulation. How do you respond to that?"

Blake's eyes lowered slightly, as if disappointed. "It hurts. To hear that. I tried so hard. I did everything for them. I know I may have been strict at times, especially when emotions ran high, but I never intended to hurt anyone. Sometimes, Isadora would lash out. She'd stop eating or say cruel things. I thought space and structure might help. I regret how it came across."

"Did you ever withhold food intentionally?"

Blake shakes his head. "Only if she refused to eat. Or if I thought she was putting herself in danger. I was trying to regulate things. She needed help."

Mr. Price nods slowly. "And the assertion that you withheld heat or used temperature as a punishment?"

"I never thought of it as punishment," Blake says. "Utilities were expensive. I live in a rural area. Sometimes we had to conserve. I always gave them blankets. I made sure they had what they needed." I want to scream.

"And the lock on the basement door?"

"That wasn't to trap them," Blake says, leaning forward slightly, voice low and sympathetic. "It was for their safety. The basement was old. There were exposed wires and sharp corners. I didn't want them wandering down there at night and getting hurt."

"You've said you were trying to build a family. Can you explain what that meant to you?"

Blake softens again. "I lost my own family when I was young. No siblings. No parents after a certain point. I spent most of my life alone. But I always wanted to be a husband, a father. Not in a traditional sense, maybe, but I had love to give. I thought... maybe they were meant for me. That I could give them the life no one else did."

"And when they tried to leave?"

He hesitates. "It broke me," he admits. "After everything... I couldn't understand why. I still don't." Mr. Price steps back for a moment, then paces slowly in front of the jury.

"And the scars?" he asks quietly. "The physical evidence?"

Blake meets his gaze. "I won't deny that there were moments I lost my temper. But I never intended to do lasting harm. I patched every wound. I held Isadora when she cried. I was trying to make it right."

"And the carving?"

Blake pauses. His voice drops an octave. "I wanted her to remember I was there for her. That she wasn't alone anymore, she even asked for it. I think it was a kink for her." A beat of silence passes. No one moves.

Then Blake speaks again, softer still. "They weren't prisoners. They were loved."

Mr. Price closes his folder. "No further questions—for now."

Judge Carrington glances toward the prosecution. "Redirect?" The courtroom holds its breath.

Mr. Price adjusts his cufflink and steps back toward the stand. His voice is calm, coaxing, and calculated.

"Mr. Winters, let's talk about the carving on Isadora's back again. The prosecution described it as branding. A violent, controlling act."

Blake nods slowly, letting out a breath. "It wasn't like that."

"Please explain to the court what it was like."

He shifts in the chair slightly, like he's weighing how much to reveal. "It was consensual." The breath catches in my throat.

Blake continues. "She asked for it. Said she wanted something permanent. It was intimate... symbolic. A way to show she belonged to me. Like a... kink thing. She was submissive, and I didn't force her. It wasn't abuse—it was how she expressed loyalty."

My hands curl into fists in my lap. I feel sick. The bile creeps up my throat as he speaks so casually—so confidently—about something that nearly killed me.

Mr. Price nods thoughtfully, pretending to accept it. "So she requested it?"

"Yes. She even picked the location."

"And at no point did she object?"

"No. She wanted to feel closer to me." I want to scream. To stand up and tear down every word that leaves his mouth. But I don't. I sit in silence, feeling the heat in my face as my stomach twists.

Mr. Price switches gears. "Now, Selecia. You testified earlier that you brought her into your home when she was twelve years old. What made you do that?"

Blake sighs lightly, as if this part actually troubles him. "She looked so sad. Broken, almost. Like no one had ever truly cared for her."

"And you say her foster mother gave you permission?"

"She said she wanted a better life for Selecia, and I promised I'd give her one."

"You do understand how that might look to the outside world?"

"Of course I do," Blake says. "I know how it sounds. But in my heart… I wasn't trying to hurt anyone. I wanted to give her stability. Structure. Love."

"Was she happy there?"

A soft smile creeps across his lips. "She flourished. She laughed more. Drew pictures. Ate well. I homeschooled her —taught her everything from scratch. I'm not saying it was conventional, but I know she felt safe."

"Even in the basement?"

"She was never alone. She had Isadora. They bonded. Became sisters. It wasn't like the prosecution is painting it."

Mr. Price lowers his voice slightly, like he's revealing something sensitive. "If you could go back, would you still bring her home?"

Blake hesitates. "I... probably not. Not because I regret loving her, but because the world isn't ready to understand. I didn't want to hurt her. I just wanted to build something that made sense."

"And this was all out of love?"

"I would've died for them." He says it with such conviction, such distorted passion, that I physically recoil.

Mr. Price turns to the jury. "Ladies and gentlemen, you've heard testimony from two young women—clearly emotional, clearly in pain. But emotions can distort memories. And memory is fragile. What Mr. Winters did was attempt to create a family, albeit an unconventional one. He fed them, clothed them, and educated them. He gave them something no one else had: consistency." I stare at Blake, my skin burning with fury.

"Now," Mr. Price says, his voice louder, "is that so wrong?

CHAPTER 89: CROSS EXAMINATION

The second day of Blake Winters' testimony feels heavier than the first. The courtroom hums with tension as we file in; Selecia sits beside me again, her fingers twined in her lap, eyes on the floor. I can feel the press of the cameras outside even from here. I can feel the weight of the world waiting for this man to fall apart. But he doesn't. Not yet.

Blake sits on the witness stand like it's a throne. Back straight, suit crisp, a calm smile resting just beneath his eyes. He's still lying. And I can feel every word like a blade.

Judge Carrington clears her throat. "Cross-examination will resume. Ms. Hawthorne?" Lila Hawthorne rises with quiet authority. Her heels don't click today. They thunder. She's ready for blood.

"Mr. Winters," she begins, pacing slowly, "Let's revisit your claim that both girls came with you willingly. You testified yesterday that Isadora 'asked' to go home with you. After you crashed into her car."

He nods. "Yes. She was shaken. Vulnerable. She didn't have anyone to call. I offered help."

"You didn't call the police. You didn't exchange insurance information. You drugged her," she states flatly.

Blake's smile tightens. "I didn't drug her. She fainted. Hit her head, I believe. I took her to my home to recover." A low sound escapes me before I can stop it.

Lila's voice hardens. "And Selecia? A twelve-year-old? You told this court she was neglected in foster care, and that you thought she 'deserved better.' Did you inform the authorities? Speak to her case worker? Get legal custody?"

"No," he says. "But she told me she was unhappy. She looked... lost. I knew I could give her stability."

"And you think dragging a child into your home without permission was providing stability?"

"She didn't fight me," he says. "Her foster mother had clearly given up on her. I told her I was there to help. She believed me." I feel Selecia flinch beside me.

"And the chains?" Hawthorne asks. "The shackles we've seen in photographs recovered from your basement. You claimed yesterday that neither girl was ever restrained."

Blake folds his hands together like a teacher. "No. I said that Selecia was not restrained. Isadora... only after she began to exhibit dangerous behaviors. She was unstable. Aggressive. She tried to hurt herself."

"She was reacting to being kidnapped," Hawthorne snaps.

He raises his eyebrows, voice steady. "She had deep psychological trauma long before I met her. Her father was abusive. She told me that herself. I was trying to help." I stare at him, stunned. That's not what I said. I told him that my father was strict, which made me think about running away. Not that I did.

"You've claimed that carving your name into her back was part of a consensual kink." Hawthorne's voice drips venom now. "You claimed withholding food, locking them in darkness, denying showers for weeks, was discipline."

"It was structure," Blake says simply. "They needed routine. It's what helped them feel safe." A photo goes up on the screen. One of the basement. The rusted chain. The bucket. The blankets flattened out in a corner. And in the corner of the frame, the plastic tub he gave us to "bathe."

"If you were helping them," Hawthorne asks, "why does this room resemble a dungeon more than a home?"

He doesn't even flinch. "That room was only temporary —a transition space. Isadora was unstable. The locks were for her safety." I rise to my feet without realizing it.

My voice cuts through the courtroom like broken glass. "You chained me for two years! I wasn't unstable—I was starving! I screamed for weeks! You carved your name into my body because I wouldn't smile for you!"

Judge Carrington slams her gavel once. "Miss Rose, I know this is a lot, but please sit down." Judge Carrington's voice booms across the room, sharp and unflinching. "Miss Rose, I will remind you that this is not your turn to speak."

But I can't sit. Not yet. My legs are trembling, but I stand like I've been braced to the floor. "He's lying," I whisper, then louder, "He's lying about everything."

Lila Hawthorne glances back at me, her expression unreadable, before turning to the judge. "Your Honor, I ask for some leniency. This is not a typical witness—this is a survivor hearing her abuser deny her reality."

Carrington pauses. Her mouth tightens, but after a beat, she gives a slow nod. "Miss Rose, one more outburst and I'll be forced to excuse you for the remainder of the testimony. Please sit down." I do. Slowly. The wood of the bench is suddenly ice-cold beneath me. My chest is heaving and my throat is raw. My fists are clenched so tightly in my lap I can feel the bite of my nails in my skin.

Blake clears his throat on the stand. "I understand she's upset. I do. But trauma affects memory. What she remembers may not be what actually happened."

Lila narrows her eyes. "Let's talk about the specific punishments she described. You said she fabricated the story of being locked in darkness for days

"I said she misunderstood," Blake corrects. "I used temporary sensory restriction to calm her down. It's a therapeutic technique used in some treatment settings. I never harmed her."

"And yet you admitted to carving your name into her back."

He smiles faintly, like this is all beneath him. "She asked for it. It was intimate. Symbolic." I see jurors shift in their seats.

Hawthorne takes a slow step forward. "So to be clear: You're stating—on the record—that your victim consented to being branded?"

"I didn't brand her. It wasn't forced. She wanted a mark. She told me she wanted to belong somewhere. That she was tired of being invisible." I turn away, nausea threatening the edges of my vision.

Lila lifts her chin. "And you stand by your decision to bring Selecia into your home, despite no legal documentation, no familial connection, and no authority to do so?"

"She was lonely. I made her feel safe."

"You made her live underground."

"She had books. Blankets. Coloring pencils. I gave her companionship. Stability."

"And what did you do when she disobeyed you?"

He shifts slightly. "I gave her time to reflect. Sometimes I took privileges away—warmth, music, meals—but only temporarily."

"You left her in the cold."

"I taught her discipline. She thrived."

"She was twelve," Lila hisses.

"And she smiled again," he says calmly. "That's more than her foster family ever did for her." A beat of silence swells so thick I can feel it behind my eyes. Lila nods once and turns to the judge.

"No further questions at this time." But the defense attorney—Carter Price—rises slowly, straightening his jacket like this is the moment he's been waiting for.

"Mr. Winters," he begins, walking toward the stand with exaggerated composure. "Let's clarify a few things. You've been accused of kidnapping, false imprisonment, and repeated physical and sexual assault. Do you deny these accusations?"

"Absolutely," Blake says, calm and clear. "I helped them."

Price nods thoughtfully. "Isn't it true that the media has twisted your story beyond recognition? That you're being painted as a monster, despite your efforts to protect these girls?"

"I am not a monster," Blake says. "Everything I did was out of love."

"And you believe Isadora fabricated these claims—why?"

"She was damaged before she met me. She told me her home life was suffocating. Her father was cruel, her mother absent. She didn't want to go back to that. I gave her peace." He says it like he's proud. Like, he still believes it.

"And Selecia?"

"She didn't even ask to leave, not really. She adapted. We had a routine. We had movie nights and game nights. She laughed."

"And yet they claim they were being tortured."

He shrugs. "You can twist anything to sound like abuse if you want. But we were building a family." The words feel like acid in my ears. But I'm already crying because he's still smiling and still pretending and still lying.

"Do not mistake their composure for consent. Do not mistake their survival for silence. These girls didn't come here today because it's easy. They came because the truth deserves a voice."

She turns back to the jury. "Hold him accountable. Not just for what he did to their bodies, but for what he stole from their lives." The silence that follows is like a held breath. Judge Carrington nods, then turns toward us. "The victims may now read their statements before the jury retires for deliberation."

CHAPTER 90: SPEAKING THE TRUTH

My name echoes from the judge's bench—"Isadora Rose, you may proceed with your statement"—but it hardly feels like my own.

I rise slowly, pressing my palms against the edge of the bench to support myself. The courtroom blurs at the edges— my lower back aches. My belly—rounded and heavy now with the weight of a child I never planned for—presses outward beneath my fitted navy maternity dress. I wore it to look strong. Grown. But I feel like I might collapse.

Each step to the witness box feels longer than the last. My heels scuff against the floor. My hands tremble slightly as I grip the printed statement. My throat is dry. I'm aware of every breath I take. Of every eye on me. Especially his. I force myself to meet Blake Winters' stare.

He's relaxed in his chair, his expression unreadable, almost bored as if this is just another part of the show. I won't give him the satisfaction. I settle into the chair. My knees ache. My pulse pounds so loudly it nearly drowns out the silence in the room. The microphone is too close, so I push it slightly away. I try to take a breath. It doesn't help.

"My name is Isadora Amber Rose," I begin, my voice thin, cracking at the edges. "I'm twenty-one years old." I pause. The silence stretches as I search for my place—on the paper, in the room, in my own body.

"I was kidnapped when I was seventeen. I was supposed to graduate from high school, apply to colleges, move out, and start a life. Instead, I disappeared. I lost everything." I look down at the page, but the words blur.

"There was no ransom. No message. No one saw me taken. I just... vanished." The paper crinkles in my hand as I squeeze it tighter.

"For the first few weeks, I begged him to let me go. I screamed until my voice gave out. I cried until I couldn't anymore. The first time I tried to fight him, he beat me so badly I thought I'd die. He didn't even look angry. Just... calm. Like he was resetting a broken toy." My jaw tenses.

"He carved his name into my back with a box cutter. Not because I did anything wrong. Just to prove he could. So that I would remember who I belonged to." I shift in my seat, the baby pressing against my ribs.

"He chained me to the wall. For days, weeks, months, and then years. I wasn't allowed to speak unless spoken to. I ate when he allowed it. Cold cans of food. Crackers. Spoonfuls of peanut butter if I was 'good.'" My voice drops.

"I used a bucket in the corner for a bathroom. He gave me a plastic bin to bathe in, once every two weeks. Maybe. I lost track of time down there. I started whispering to myself so I wouldn't forget how to talk." I look up briefly, swallowing hard.

"There was no light for days. Then there was too much light. He'd control the temperature. Sometimes it was so cold I couldn't feel my fingers. Sometimes it was so hot I couldn't breathe." My fingers tighten around the paper again.

"I thought I was going insane. I counted the lines in the

concrete. I tapped out songs I remembered to stay grounded. I told myself stories to keep from slipping away." A tear slips down my cheek, but I keep going.

"I had no calendar. No clocks. No human contact except for him. The silence... it was louder than screaming. And then, he brought her." My eyes flick toward Selecia, who's seated beside our advocate.

"She was twelve. She was scared. And I knew right then that if I didn't find a way to survive, she wouldn't either." I turn back to the courtroom, back toward the jury.

"So, I smiled. I played the part. I became what he needed me to be. I cooked. I cleaned. I hugged him when he wanted it. And every time I did, I felt something inside me die." The baby kicks inside me. I press my hand to my stomach instinctively, but keep talking.

"I'm almost seven months pregnant with the child of my abuser. I didn't even know I was pregnant until after we escaped. And now... now I get to carry this child, raise this child, and try to separate her from what he did to me." I look toward the jury now, willing them to really see me.

"I flinch when someone reaches for my arm too quickly. I panic when I'm alone in a room. I can't go to work without wondering who might come in. I walk into a grocery store and my chest tightens, because every aisle feels like a trap." My voice trembles.

"I will never know what it's like to live a normal life again. Every day is survival." I pause there, collecting myself before continuing with the second half of the statement.

I take a breath that shudders on the way out. The silence presses down, heavier than before. My fingers are still wrapped around the page, but I don't look at it anymore. These words live inside me now.

"There are nights I wake up screaming. Drenched in sweat. Heart pounding. I forget where I am—think I'm still there. In the dark. In that basement. With his footsteps coming closer." I shake my head slowly, willing the images away.

"I see shadows and I think it's him. I hear the floor creak, and I brace for pain. I sleep with the lights on, the door open, and a chair against the knob. And I still don't feel safe." More tears fall now, but I don't stop.

"There are people who will tell me I'm strong. That I survived, but that's not what this feels like. It feels like I'm broken in ways no one can see. Like there's a version of me that never came home. And I'm supposed to pretend she never existed." I glance down at my stomach again.

"And now... I'm going to be a mom. I'm supposed to raise a child when most days I don't even feel like I can raise my head. I'm supposed to teach her how to feel safe when I don't know how to anymore." I blink hard, trying to stay grounded and trying not to let the emotion crack my voice too much. But it does. It has to.

"I'm terrified that one day, I'll look at her and see him. That she'll ask me who her father is, and I won't have the strength to answer that I'll never be able to trust another man again. That every time someone touches me, I'll feel his hands." I stop, just for a second, to breathe. It takes everything I have to lift my eyes again.

"I want to be clear: I didn't survive this because I'm strong. I survived this because I had no other choice. Because there was a little girl in that basement with me who looked at me like I could protect her, and I couldn't let her down." I glance at Selecia, who's wiping her cheeks, her eyes locked on mine.

"I survived because I told myself every day that one day, we would be free. That we would get to stand here and say everything he tried to erase." I turn back to the courtroom, to Judge Carrington, to the jury, to every face that needs to hear this.

"So here I am. Broken. But not silent." My voice is growing stronger.

"This man took my voice, my body, my freedom, my dignity, and three unborn children from me. He tried to take everything, but he didn't take the truth. And no matter how many lies he tells, that truth stands here today. I feel my shoulders shake as the final words come.

"My name is Isadora Rose. I was his victim. But not anymore." I fold the statement, my hands trembling now that it's done. I look once more at Blake Winters, who stares back at me like he still expects a reaction. But I don't give him one. I rise slowly, the weight of pregnancy and trauma and grief making every inch of me feel heavy, but I rise. This time, I chose to.

As I return to my seat beside Selecia, she reaches over and grabs my hand. I don't have words for what this feels like. But I know we made it. We're here. We're not his anymore.

CHAPTER 91:
SELECIA'S LETTER

Selecia's POV

They call my name, and my stomach flips like I'm hearing a sentence, not an invitation. I glance at Isadora, who sits beside me with her hands clenched in her lap, her eyes already watery from reading her own statement. She gives me a slight nod, one that says I can do this, even if my hands are shaking and my chest is so tight it feels like I might break in half.

The courtroom tilts a little when I stand. I feel lightheaded from nerves, and my legs—thin and still too weak from everything I've gone through—tremble as I step forward. Every footstep echoes louder than it should. Like the floor is mocking me, reminding me of the basement, of the times I'd tiptoe just to avoid his attention, of how sound always came before pain. Now, all eyes are on me. The jury. The press. The strangers on the benches. And Blake.

I haven't looked at him yet. I don't think I can. When I finally reach the front, the bailiff holds out the folded paper I had handed over earlier. I take it, unfolding it with fingers that refuse to stay still. My palms are already damp. I swallow the lump in my throat and lift my eyes for just a second.

Judge Carrington is watching me patiently, hands folded, face unreadable. Her silver hair is still pulled tightly into that same perfect bun as the other days. She's been fair, I think. Strong. Someone I could trust to keep me safe, even if just from behind a bench. I hold my letter close, like a shield.

"My name is Selecia," I begin, and even I hear the tremble in my voice. "I'm... I'm not here today to present facts. I'm here to tell you how it felt. How it still feels." I pause, blink hard, and force my eyes forward. Blake's there. Just a few feet away. His face unreadable, smug even. Like nothing could touch him, I take a shaky breath.

"I was twelve when he took me. Twelve. I thought I was going to a new home. He told me my foster mom sent him. He smiled. He was calm. I had no reason to think... to think anything was wrong. Not until I saw Isadora chained to the wall." My voice breaks on her name. I take a second to breathe.

"She looked at me like she'd seen a ghost. And I think... I think a part of me became one right then and there. I knew I wasn't going home." I grip the paper harder, but I'm not even reading it anymore. The words are already burned into my mind.

"There was no window. There was no way to know what day it was or what time it was. If the world was still out there." My voice is steadier now, not loud, but no longer trembling.

"I was chained up next to her that first night. We didn't talk much; we just exchanged glances. We were strangers. Trapped. Alone, but not alone. That's a different kind of horror. When you can hear someone else suffering, but you can't help them. And they can't help you." I pause again, licking my dry lips, staring straight ahead.

"He punished us differently," I say. "Sometimes he would withhold food or turn the heat off in the winter. Or the air conditioning in the summer. He'd make us go weeks without showers. He'd give me a full plate and give Isadora nothing. Or he'd feed her while I watched, starving. It was about control. Power. Making us feel helpless." I glance down again.

"I used to pretend it wasn't real. I made up stories in my head about how this was temporary. That someone would find us. That this was just a weird dream, and I'd wake up at school with my friends laughing around me. But months passed. Then a year. Then another. And the longer we were there, the harder it became to remember who I was before." I clench the letter with both hands now, knuckles pale.

"I had a name—a life. I used to like drawing animals. I used to want to be a vet. I don't even know what I want anymore. I don't know how to sleep without checking if the doors are locked. I still flinch when someone raises their voice. I panic when someone touches me from behind. I don't like the dark. I don't like silence. I don't like birthdays anymore either, because I spent two of them pretending they didn't exist." My throat is burning, but I keep going.

"There were good moments. Moments when Isadora made me laugh. When we'd whisper to each other at night and pretend we weren't scared. When she'd tell me stories just to pass the time, she protected me even when she couldn't protect herself. And for that, I'll always love her." I finally look at Blake.

"I'm not your daughter," I whisper. "I never was. And I never will be. You didn't give me a better life. You stole the one I had."

"I don't know if I'll ever feel safe again," I say, and it's not dramatic. It's not exaggeration. It's just the truth. "I look over my shoulder constantly. I lock the bathroom door even when I'm home. I sleep with the light on. I still wake up thinking I hear the basement door creaking open." There's a pressure in my chest I can't swallow back.

"I don't remember what it felt like to be a kid. You took that from me. I don't know how to be normal anymore. I don't know how to go back to school, or laugh at dumb jokes, or trust that when someone is nice to me, they're not just waiting to hurt me. And maybe I never will." I lift the page again with a trembling breath.

"But I'm still here. You didn't break me. Not completely. And that means something. You tried to turn me into your daughter, to rewrite the truth with rules and routines and threats. But I still know who I am, and I'm not who you said I was. I'm not your child. I'm not your possession." I can hear a soft sniffle in the gallery behind me. Probably Isadora. Maybe even Mom. I keep my eyes forward.

"There is no sentence long enough to fix what you did," I say, stronger now. "No punishment that can erase the memories or give us back the years you took. But I want the court to know what kind of person you are. I want the jury to hear it again. I want you to hear it." I turn my eyes toward him, and finally, finally, I let all the hatred surface.

"You're not sick. You're not confused. You're evil. And I hope you spend the rest of your life in a cell so small and dark it feels like the hell you put us through." A long, hollow silence follows. I fold the letter slowly, then lift my chin.

"I'm done."

Judge Carrington nods gently from the bench, her face unreadable but attentive. "Thank you, Selecia." I step down without waiting for permission. I can't stay on that stand another second. As I walk past the front row of seats, I catch Isadora's eyes. She looks proud. Shaken, but proud. And for the first time in a very long time, I let myself believe that maybe— just maybe—we're going to be okay.

CHAPTER 92: SENTENCING

The clock ticks louder than usual today. It's been three hours since the jury was excused, and each minute feels like a knife dragging slowly across my skin. I've read the same sentence in the Bible on my lap five times, but I still can't remember what it says. The words blur together like fog on glass. I close the book and press it against my stomach—against the life still growing inside me—hoping somehow it will anchor me.

Selecia sits next to me, hunched slightly forward, wringing her fingers. She hasn't spoken in a while. I can tell she's trying not to cry, not to tremble, but her lip keeps twitching.

"I keep thinking they're going to come in," I whisper. "And everything's going to change. One way or another."

She nods, but her voice catches when she speaks. "I don't even know what I want to hear anymore. I just want it to be over." The waiting room outside the courtroom is too quiet. Even the security guards seem subdued. Every time someone walks past the door, my heart launches into my throat, and I brace myself, only for them to keep walking. It's mental torture in slow motion.

I rub my hands along the bottom of my belly, where the fabric of my black maternity dress stretches tight. My ankles are sore, my back is throbbing, and my stomach keeps tightening with nerves that feel almost like early labor. I'm not ready. Not for anything, not for this baby, not for the verdict, not for what comes next. But I want him locked away. I need him locked away. Not just for me, but for her. For Selecia. For the baby.

"I'm scared," I finally admit.

Selecia doesn't flinch. "Me too." We sit like that for a while, shoulder to shoulder. Silent. The way we used to in the basement when the power was cut and we didn't dare move. Back then, silence meant safety. Now, it's agony.

The door creaks open, and my spine straightens. It's Lila Hawthorne, the prosecutor. Her face is unreadable, but the way she strolls, purposefully, tells me something's happened.

"They're ready," she says gently. I forget how to breathe.

"Take your time," she adds, seeing me clutch the edge of the bench. Selecia stands first and reaches out a hand. I grasp it and rise, my legs wobbly beneath the weight of everything, my body, my fear, the years of waiting. I squeeze her hand tightly, and we walk together down the hall toward the courtroom. Every step echoes. And with each one, I wonder if I'll be able to breathe again by the time we sit down.

The air is still, like it's holding its breath with us. I clutch Selecia's hand as we slide into the front row of the gallery. The weight of every eye in the room settles on us. Cameras aren't allowed inside, but I can still feel the invisible spotlight pressing down, like the world is watching anyway.

Blake sits at the defense table, stiff, pale, jaw clenched. He hasn't looked our way once. Mr. Price whispers something to him, but he doesn't nod. Doesn't blink. Just stares straight ahead. Coward.

I scan the jurors as they file in, each face solemn. Some won't make eye contact with us. One woman appears to have been crying. That tells me everything I need to know.

The bailiff clears his throat. "All rise." Everyone stands. My knees tremble beneath me, but I force myself up, anchoring on Selecia.

Judge Carrington enters and sits. "Be seated." The foreman, a gray-haired man with a blue tie and a shaky hand, rises slowly.

"Has the jury reached a verdict?" Judge Carrington asks.

"Yes, Your Honor." My heart pounds against my ribs. He passes the paper to the bailiff, who hands it to the judge. She reads it silently, then gives a slight nod.

"In the case of the Commonwealth versus Blake Winters," she begins, "on the charge of kidnapping in the first degree, how do you find the defendant?" The room feels like it freezes.

"Guilty."

I squeezed Selecia's hand so tightly that I think I might break her fingers.

"On the charge of aggravated kidnapping of a minor?"

"Guilty."

Selecia exhales. Not a sigh, more like a release of years she's been holding in.

"On the charge of attempted murder?"

"Guilty." I let out a gasp, and tears instantly rushed to my eyes.

"On the charge of aggravated sexual assault?"

"Guilty." My legs buckle slightly. I sit, stunned, one hand pressed over my mouth. I can't look away.

"On the charge of torture?"

"Guilty." Each word feels like justice carved in stone.

"And on the charge of domestic assault and battery?"

"Guilty." The list continues, charges stacked like bricks in the wall that will keep him behind bars forever. Each one met with the same answer. Guilty. When it's over, Judge Carrington takes a breath, glancing toward us before speaking.

"This court hereby sentences Blake Winters to the following:" I stop breathing.

"For the charge of first-degree kidnapping, the defendant is sentenced to 25 years. For the charge of aggravated kidnapping of a minor, 25 years, to be served consecutively. For attempted murder, 35 years. For aggravated sexual assault, life imprisonment. For torture, 30 years. For assault and battery, 10 years." There's a pause.

"All sentences are to be served consecutively, without the possibility of parole." I feel it before I register it, my shoulders crumpling, the sob rising in my chest. It's over. It's really over. The man who stole everything from us will never be free again.

The court murmurs with soft gasps and shifting bodies. Blake's shoulders don't move. He sits there, still, expressionless. I wonder if he's even listening. I wonder if he's finally realizing that this is real. He's never getting out—the gavel slams.

"Court is adjourned."

I lean into Selecia, sobbing into her shoulder, and she's crying too. We don't say anything. We don't have to. For the first time in years, we are no longer prisoners.

CHAPTER 93: UNWIND

The front door clicks softly behind us. The sound, so mundane, feels enormous tonight. For the first time in years, it's just a door. Not a prison gate. Not a ticking bomb. Not a fragile threshold separating survival from destruction. Just a door. And it's locked from the inside.

Selecia drops her bag and sinks to the couch without a word. Her head leans back, her eyes flutter shut. I do the same, curling onto the far end of the sectional, my belly heavy and aching, legs tingling from standing so long in court. It's quiet —no officers, no cameras, no lawyers—just us. Then, slowly, I exhale.

"We're really home," Selecia whispers.

Her voice is raw, like it hasn't caught up to her body yet. I glance at her. She's still wearing her formal outfit, the black blouse and dark jeans she picked with my mom the night before. Her sleeves are wrinkled. Her hair had fallen half out of the bun she had tried to keep in all day. She looks exhausted— but safe.

"Yeah," I murmur, curling my hand over the top of my stomach. "We really are."

Selecia opens her eyes and glances at me. "Do you think he's thinking about us right now?"

I shake my head slowly. "It doesn't matter anymore."

A long silence stretches between us, but this one feels earned. Unlike the suffocating silences we used to endure, this one is quiet like rest. Like calm. Selecia grabs the blanket draped over the back of the couch and pulls it across both of our legs without saying anything.

"You looked brave up there," she says after a moment, voice low. "Even when it hurt."

I try to smile. "You were brave, too. You told the truth, even when he tried to twist everything."

"He always did that, didn't he?" Her voice is sharp for a second, then softens. "It's weird. I thought I'd feel... better. Right away."

I look down. "Me too." We sit like that for a while longer until I hear soft footsteps from down the hall.

"Isadora?" Charlotte's voice is hesitant, barely above a whisper.

I sit up straighter. "In here, sweetheart." She rounds the corner and pauses just inside the living room, clutching a stuffed koala to her chest. Her eyes are wide, uncertain—but shining.

"I couldn't sleep," she says. I hold my arms open. She hesitates for just a second. Then she runs across the room and throws herself into my lap, nearly knocking the wind out of me. I wrap both arms around her, my hand instinctively cradling the side of her head. She smells like watermelon shampoo and home.

"I missed you so much," she says, her voice cracking. "So much."

My throat tightens. "I missed you, too. Every single day."

She leans back enough to look at me, her blue eyes rimmed red. "You're not going to leave again, right? You're not gonna disappear?"

"No," I whisper. "Never again. I promise." She clings tighter, her tiny arms wrapped around my belly, and I can feel Hope kicking gently beneath the pressure. Charlotte pulls back, eyes wide.

"Was that the baby?" she asks.

I laugh softly through the tears now streaking my cheeks. "Yeah. She's saying hi."

Charlotte presses her palm against my stomach, whispering, "Hi, baby. I'm your aunt." Selecia smiles softly across the room but says nothing, letting the moment breathe. I think of all the nights Charlotte cried for me without understanding why, and how every hug now has to count for the ones we missed.

From the hallway, I hear Mom's voice calling softly, "Tara's here."

Charlotte looks up. "Your best friend?"

I nod. "Want to come meet her?" She nods eagerly, hopping off my lap and grabbing my hand like we were never apart. I exchange a glance with Selecia—silent and full of meaning—and we follow Charlotte down the hallway toward the front of the house.

Tara stands just inside the foyer, twisting her hands together. Her eyes find mine, and I can tell she's been holding her breath since the moment she stepped into the house. There's a flicker of hesitation—like she doesn't know if she's supposed to comfort me or give me space—but I close the gap before she has to decide. I pull her into a hug.

She squeezes me tightly, exhaling all the tension she's been carrying since the trial started. "Izzy..." Her voice is barely above a whisper. "You made it through."

"I did." I don't say how close I came to unraveling. She pulls back to study me with soft eyes. Her gaze lingers on the curve of my belly, but she doesn't comment on it—she's seen me since the hospital, since those first quiet weeks back home when we were still adjusting to the world not spinning so violently.

"I kept thinking about you," she says. "During every update. Every headline. I wanted to be there every second."

"You were," I say gently. "Even when you couldn't be." Charlotte walks into the room, still holding her koala plush, and beams when she sees us on the couch. She climbs up beside me like she's done every night since I came home.

"I drew you and the baby again today," she says proudly. "I made you both crowns."

"You did?" I smile. "I can't wait to see it."

She hugs my arm tightly, resting her head against my shoulder. "I'm glad you're home, Izzy. You really promise you aren't going away again, right?"

I kiss the top of her head. "Never again." Tara watches the exchange quietly, her eyes glassy. She doesn't say anything, just brushes a tear off her cheek and smiles. After a few minutes, Charlotte hops down to show Selecia her new drawings, leaving the room quiet. Tara shifts her weight and leans back into the couch.

"Do you know what's next?" she asks.

I sigh. "That's the question." She gives me space to answer it.

"I'm going to have this baby," I say eventually. "Raise her the best I can. I want her to grow up never doubting she's safe or loved. I want to be… okay."

"You will be," Tara says softly.

"I'm scared I won't. That everything will follow me forever. Sometimes I can't breathe when I hear a door creak. I flinch when someone walks too fast behind me. I still dream about the dark."

Tara looks at me with steady eyes. "You survived. And now you're healing. That's more than enough right now." I rest my hands on my stomach, feeling Hope shift lightly inside.

"I've been thinking about speaking. Maybe not today, not even next month. But one day. I want to tell my story—not just to get it out, but to help someone else survive it too."

Tara nods without hesitation. "You should. And when you do, I'll be in the front row."

I smile at her, eyes burning. "Thank you." She squeezes my hand, and I don't pull away.

Later that night, the house had settled into silence as the night deepened. Charlotte's already in bed; her arms are tangled around her plush koala. Tara left an hour ago with promises to visit again soon, and now only Selecia and I remain in the dimly lit living room, curled on opposite ends of the couch. We don't speak at first.

The kind of silence we sit in isn't awkward—it's earned. After everything, neither of us rushes to fill the quiet. The TV hums low in the background, playing a rerun of some cooking show that neither of us is watching. My eyes are fixed on the shifting colors of the screen, but my mind is far away. Eventually, Selecia breaks the silence.

"Do you think it'll ever feel normal again?"

I turn my head slowly, meeting her gaze. "No. I don't think it'll go back to what we thought normal was. But I think we'll build something new. Something better."

She nods, her hands fidgeting in her lap. "I keep thinking about the way people looked at me in the courtroom, like I was fragile. Like I needed to be handled."

"They looked at me like that, too," I whisper. "It's weird.

I know we're strong. I know we survived. But sometimes I still feel like that girl in the basement."

"Me too." I glance at her, noticing how much older she looks now, older than fourteen. Not in a bad way. Just different. Wiser. Sharper around the edges.

"I meant what I said on the stand," she murmurs. "I pretended to be okay so you wouldn't have to worry. Even when it felt like I was breaking inside."

"I know," I say softly. "And I pretended to be strong so you wouldn't see me fall apart."

She smiles, a tired kind of smile that feels more real than anything we've worn in a long time. "We were both faking it."

"Yeah," I breathe. "But we made it out." She shifts closer, pulling the blanket from the back of the couch around both of us. I let her lean against my shoulder, the same way Charlotte had earlier.

"What do we do now?" she asks after a pause.

I think for a moment. "We go to sleep. We wake up. We keep going."

She's quiet for a while before whispering, "I want to go to school. Real school."

I glance down at her, surprised but proud. "You will."

"And I want to make friends who don't know me as the girl from the news. Just… Selecia."

My voice cracks slightly. "You'll have that too."

She shifts again, resting her head more fully against me. "And you? What do you want?" The question sits heavy on my chest. There are a million answers. Safety. Healing. Peace. But at this moment, I say only what I know is true.

"I want to be a good mom."

"You will be," she says without hesitation.

I blink away tears, staring at the flickering TV screen again. "And maybe I want ice cream."

Selecia lets out a breathy laugh. "You're definitely already a mom." We sit like that, quietly clinging to the threads of our new life—exhausted, scarred, but alive. The trial is over. Blake Winters is behind bars. And for the first time in nearly five years, tomorrow belongs to us.

CHAPTER 94: HOPE

The Arizona sun is still hanging low in the sky, casting long shadows across the parking lot as I lean into the side of the car, clutching the door handle with one hand and my swollen belly with the other. A sharp pain stabs low in my abdomen, wrapping around my back and locking every muscle in my body into a silent scream.

I groan, bracing myself as the contraction holds me hostage. Selecia is instantly by my side, her hands fluttering like frantic butterflies before she steadies herself and grabs my arm. "Isadora—hey—breathe, okay? Just breathe."

"I am—" I snap, then suck in a breath, guilt rushing through me as soon as the contraction eases.

"I'm sorry."

"It's okay," she says quickly, brushing hair from my damp forehead. "We're here. You're safe. The baby's okay." Tara is already running inside the hospital, waving down someone at the front desk. Another wave of pain comes. This one is more profound, more intense. My knees nearly buckle, but Selecia holds on tight, anchoring me as I pant through it.

The last few months flash before me in fragmented color: Blake's sentencing, the press outside the courthouse, the moments where it still didn't feel real. Now here I am. About to bring new life into the world. Hope. Her name is Hope Selene Rose. A nurse wheels out a chair, and I sink into it with a breathless cry. Tara is right behind her, talking fast.

"She's full-term—overdue by a few days—first baby—

contractions started twenty minutes ago."

The nurse nods and starts moving us through the automatic doors. "Okay, Mom, you're doing great. We've got you. Let's get you upstairs."

I flinch at the word "Mom." Not because I don't want it. But because it's real now. I'm going to be someone's mother. As the elevator doors slide shut, my fingers clench around the armrest. Selecia stands beside me, pale but determined.

"She's got this," she whispers to herself, more than to me. "We've got this."

The nurse checks my chart as we reach the maternity ward. "How far apart are the contractions now?"

"Two... maybe three minutes," I gasp. "They're powerful." We're wheeled into a room with pale walls and a wide window that overlooks the dry hills in the distance. I want to take it all in, this moment, this beginning, but my body has other plans. The next contraction crashes down on me, and I arch forward with a scream.

A second nurse appears with a hospital gown and assists me in changing. Tara is already filling out paperwork. Selecia stays close, holding my hand like it's the only thing anchoring either of us. And maybe it is.

"I'm scared," I whisper.

She squeezes my fingers. "You're not alone." Another contraction hits. And another.

Soon, the doctor enters—a middle-aged woman with a warm, calm voice. She checks me quickly, then looks up. "You're already at seven centimeters. It's time." Time. I close my eyes, letting the weight of that settle. The trial. The trauma. The darkness. All of it has led to this.

A child born not out of love... but in defiance of cruelty. A child I didn't ask for, but whom I love with a fierceness I can't explain. Selecia moves to my other side as they begin to set up the delivery area.

"We're gonna meet her soon," she says quietly. "Hope."

I nod through gritted teeth, tears streaming down my cheeks. Not from pain, but from everything else. Because for the first time in years… this pain means something good. And I can endure it. For her. For me. For us.

The room is awash in a soft amber glow, the lights dimmed as contractions come harder and faster. Sweat beads along my hairline, and my gown is soaked through at the back. I'm gripping the side of the bed with one hand and Selecia's fingers with the other. Then the door opens.

"Mom," I gasp as she walks in, breathless, her purse still slung over her shoulder.

"Isadora," she says, her eyes instantly filling with tears.

Her hands are on me before I can speak—one smoothing my hair back, the other cradling my face. "I'm here, baby. I'm right here."

And I lose it. All the pain, the fear, the pressure, it all swells up in my chest and bursts in a sob that shakes me to the core.

"I'm scared," I choke out.

"I know," she whispers. "But you're the strongest person I've ever known. And you're not doing this alone."

She presses her forehead to mine, then gently kisses it. Selecia doesn't move; she tightens her grip on my hand, grounding me with her presence like she has so many times before.

A nurse checks the monitor. "You're almost there. Nine and a half. Just a little longer."

I let my head fall back against the pillow. My thighs are

shaking, the pain radiating down my spine. My mom dabs my face with a cool cloth, and Selecia speaks softly, words I can't fully hear, but I feel them.

The doctor enters again, pulling on gloves. "Isadora, it's time. Next contraction, we're going to start pushing." Tara's still in the waiting room. I can't see her, but I know she's pacing, biting her thumbnail, probably muttering anxious prayers. The pain comes swiftly and cruelly. I cry out, gripping my mom's arm as my body tightens like a drawn bow.

"Push, honey," the doctor says gently. "Just like that. You've got her. She's almost here." I bear down with everything I have. My vision goes blurry, the world narrowing to the sound of my breath, the tension in my legs, the pounding in my ears. Then the pain subsides, briefly. I collapse against the pillow.

"You're doing amazing," my mom says, brushing tears from her cheeks. "I'm so proud of you." Another contraction. Another push. I scream, this time from the effort and not the fear. And then—

"I can see her head!" the doctor announces.

I sobbed again, my shoulders shaking. "Please, just get her out. Please—"

"One more, Isadora. One more push."

Selecia's voice cuts through the haze: "You can do it. She's almost here. Hope is almost here." I push—and then, relief. The unbearable tension releases, and I feel the shift as her body leaves mine. And suddenly, a cry, loud and sharp and real. My daughter. Hope Selene Rose.

"She's here," my mother breathes. And just like that, the entire world goes quiet except for that beautiful, broken wail. The doctor holds her up, coated and wriggling, her tiny arms flailing with life.

"Would you like to cut the cord?" the nurse asks gently, offering scissors to me. I nod through tears, my hand shaking as I do it, my fingers trembling so badly that the nurse guides my grip. The cord snaps with a soft snip, and they wrap her in a warm blanket. A moment later, they place her in my arms. Everything inside me stills. She's warm. Pink. Breathing. And real.

Her cries ease the second she touches my chest, her tiny body curling against mine as if she knows me. As if she's been waiting for this moment, too.

"Oh," I whisper, barely able to speak. "You're... perfect." My mom is crying beside me. Selecia is leaning over my shoulder, silent tears rolling down her cheeks.

"She's so small," Selecia says softly.

"She's Hope," I reply. And she is. Hope for healing. Hope for the future. Hope that everything Blake tried to take from me... he didn't win. I stroke her cheek with my finger, and she flinches, turning her head in a slow root. My breath catches. I glance at my mother.

"She's hungry."

My mom smiles through her tears. "She knows her mama." I nod slowly because I am her mama. I'm not just a survivor anymore. I'm someone's mother. And for the first time in years, I feel like I've finally stepped into the light.

CHAPTER 95: MIDNIGHT QUIET

The house is asleep. At least, most of it is. Outside the window, the streetlight hums softly, casting a gentle golden halo across the hardwood floor. A car passes slowly in the distance, tires crunching over gravel, headlights briefly sweeping the living room before disappearing again into the quiet.

I'm not sure what woke me first—Hope's soft fussing or the phantom pressure in my chest reminding me it was time to nurse. My body is still adjusting to all of this. I still sometimes wake up in a panic, thinking I'm in the basement, confused by the lightness of the sheets or the breeze from the open window. But tonight, I know exactly where I am. And who I'm with.

Cradled in my arms, Hope lets out a little cry, more of a whimper than a scream. I sway gently in the old rocking chair by the window; her small body curled against mine. She smells like lavender baby soap and formula powder. Her skin is impossibly soft, and when I look down at her face, her lashes fluttering as she settles again, I feel something rise in me that I still don't fully understand—love and pain wrapped up in the same breath. The clock reads 2:16 a.m.

Her feeding schedule is still unpredictable, though she's already sleeping longer than she used to. I shift her a little, guiding her to latch, and she sucks quietly. The silence feels full somehow, a sacred space. Like if I breathe too loudly, it'll shatter.

I glance toward the hallway, where the soft light from the nightlight spills onto the floor. Charlotte and Selecia are asleep in their shared room. I checked in before I came downstairs. Charlotte was curled up with her stuffed owl under one arm. Selecia was sprawled across the mattress, one arm dangling over the edge like she always does. I smile faintly, then wince a little at the pull in my abdomen—remnants of the healing.

There's a notebook on the side table beside me. I've been jotting down fragments of thoughts whenever I can—memories I don't want to forget, things I need to say someday when Hope is older. I haven't touched it in a few days. Tonight, though, I'm too tired to move. My muscles ache in ways I didn't expect. My back constantly hurts. My chest feels sore from the feeding. And sometimes... sometimes my heart still aches in quiet, haunting ways.

I rest my cheek lightly on the top of Hope's head. She's grown so much already. Her tiny fingers curl around the edge of my robe, and for a second, it takes my breath away. She doesn't even know the world she was born into, and yet she already feels like the center of mine.

"I'm trying," I whisper. "I don't know what I'm doing yet. But I'm trying."

CHAPTER 96: SELECIA STARTS HIGH SCHOOL

Selecia's POV

It's still dark outside when I wake up. The early morning haze hasn't cleared, and the sun barely peeks over the horizon, casting a sleepy blue over the town of Hadleigh. My alarm didn't even need to go off—I've been up for most of the night, staring at the ceiling.

Today is my first day of high school. I sit up slowly, heart pounding in my chest like it's trying to break free. My palms are damp, and my throat feels tight, like I've swallowed something sharp. My old therapist called it "anticipatory anxiety." I call it fear—real, raw fear.

My backpack is already packed, and my clothes are laid out neatly on the dresser: simple jeans, a lavender tee, and a hoodie that still smells like home. I tug it on like armor and head downstairs, where the kitchen lights are already on. Isadora stands over the stove, stirring oatmeal in a pot with one hand and bouncing Hope on her hip with the other. Hope's tiny fists reach for her hair, her sleepy giggles bubbling up like music, and for a moment, the scene is so typical it's almost jarring.

Isadora turns and smiles at me, but I can see the tension in her jaw. She's worried too. "Morning. You hungry?"

I shake my head. "Just... nervous."

"You're going to be okay," she says softly, setting Hope in her highchair and turning down the stove. "You've come so far, Selecia. I know today feels huge, but it's just the next step."

"I haven't been in a real school in years," I say quietly. "What if they ask questions? What if I forget how to be normal?"

She moves toward me and rests a hand on my shoulder. "Normal doesn't exist. You show up as yourself —brave, kind, and honest. That's more than enough." I nod, though my chest is tight. I wish I could believe her. The drive to school is quiet. Isadora parks out front, scanning the crowd of teenagers streaming into the brick building. My hands fidget in my lap.

"Do you want me to walk in with you?"

"No," I say quickly, then glance at her. "Thanks, though."

She gives me a reassuring smile. "You've got this. I'll be here when school lets out." I nod again and force the door open, stepping out into a sea of unfamiliar faces and cliques already forming on the steps. The building looks too big. Too loud. Too... normal. My feet move, but my head is screaming. What if someone recognizes me? What if they Google my name? Inside, I follow the posted signs to the office to get my schedule. The woman at the front desk hands it to me with a tight smile. "First day?" I nod.

"Welcome to Hadleigh High. Just let us know if you need anything."

The first few classes go by in a blur. Teachers introduce themselves. Students stare. I catch snippets of whispers when I walk in—quiet enough to seem polite, loud enough to sting. In English, I sit beside a girl named Liana. She smiles at me, actually smiles, and I brace myself for the question I know is coming.

"So... are you the girl from the news?" It's like getting punched in the stomach. I freeze, my heart pounding. My mouth opens, but nothing comes out.

She holds up her hands. "Sorry. That was rude. My mom told me you were coming. She's a social worker. She said you were, like... insanely strong." I blink at her.

"She also told me to shut up and just be your friend, so... here I am."

I let out a shaky laugh, and she grins wider. "Wanna sit with me at lunch?"

I nod, surprised by how much that tiny gesture matters. By the time last period rolls around, I feel like I've run a marathon with no water. My feet hurt. My brain is fried. But I made it. At dismissal, I spot Isadora's car and hurry toward it, my backpack bouncing against my spine. She opens the door before I get there.

"How was it?"

I slide into the passenger seat, exhaling hard, and give her the first genuine smile I've felt all day. "It was... okay. I made it."

She grins and squeezes my hand. "I knew you would." I don't say it out loud, but for the first time in a long time, I start to believe that maybe, just maybe, I belong in the world again.

CHAPTER 97:
FULL CIRCLE

Five months after Hope's birth. Three months since the trial ended.

The house is quiet, except for the soft rustling of a baby on a blanket. I stand in the doorway of the living room, a half-full bottle in my hand, watching Hope wiggle on her belly like she's gearing up for a race. Her arms flail. She grunts with determination. Her little fists dig into the blanket, and then, suddenly, she rolls. It happens so quickly that I almost miss it.

"Selecia!" I call, my voice cracking. "She did it!"

Selecia runs in from the kitchen, her socks sliding slightly on the hardwood floor. "What happened?"

"She rolled over!" We both drop to the floor, as if the carpet might disappear without warning. Hope is looking up at us now, beaming, as if she knows exactly how proud we are. Selecia grins and reaches out her finger. Hope grabs it instinctively.

"She's so proud of herself," Selecia whispers. I nod, my chest tightening. I try to hold on to the joy, to stay in this moment where my daughter is just a baby doing something beautiful. But the grief creeps in anyway. It always does. This milestone—her first roll—is something I imagined witnessing in a sunlit nursery, with baby books and lullabies. Not in a borrowed living room in a borrowed life. I blink the sting from my eyes and smile anyway.

"She's incredible," I say. Selecia doesn't respond, but I

see it in her face. She agrees. Later that week, I stepped out into the bright buzz of the grocery store. The air conditioning is too cold against my arms, and the fluorescent lights make everything look sterile. Hope sleeps in her wrap against my chest, warm and heavy and real.

I grip the shopping cart too hard as we make our way through the aisles. Every sound feels amplified. A man coughs near the freezer section, and I flinch—a cart squeaks. A child whines. I keep scanning—faces, exits, shadows. My heart hasn't slowed since we walked in. Hope stirs, her tiny head nuzzling deeper into my chest.

"You're okay," I murmur, fingers brushing the back of her head. "We're okay." I want to believe it. I want it to be true. But every step I take feels like walking through fog while holding a glass sculpture, one wrong move, and everything shatters again.

That night, the scent of lemon cleaner lingers in the air. I've wiped the kitchen counters twice, trying to keep the anxiety at bay. Dishes are drying neatly in the rack. I hear Hope fussing from the living room and wipe my hands on a towel before heading in. What I see stops me.

Selecia is lying on the floor beside Hope, her hair spread out like a halo, one of Hope's stuffed bunnies perched on her chest. Hope is on her belly again, babbling in protest as she tries another push-up.

"Almost there, Bean," Selecia coos gently. "Aunt Selecia's got front-row tickets." Hope lets out a squeal, and Selecia bursts into soft laughter. The sound is light, real. For a second, I don't see trauma or pain or shadows. I see two girls—one barely more than a child herself—bonding with a baby who has somehow managed to heal pieces of all of us. I lean against the doorframe, heart swelling and aching all at once. Selecia notices me watching. She doesn't flinch.

"She's gonna crawl any day now," she says, brushing Hope's hair back. "And when she does, I'm making her a trophy out of tinfoil."

"She loves you," I say, walking into the room. Selecia shrugs, trying to downplay it, but her eyes give her away.

"I love her too," she murmurs. "She's not just yours. She's... ours. Not his." I sink to the rug beside them. Hope flops onto her back and stares at us both with that wide-eyed wonder that only babies seem to possess.

"She's ours," I echo. And in that moment, surrounded by softness and laughter and the quiet hum of survival, I believe it.

CHAPTER 98: PURPOSE

Five Years Later

Five years have passed since the trial. Hope is five years old now, all curly blonde hair and bright, thoughtful eyes. She asks questions I'm not always ready to answer—like why I don't like elevators, or why I flinch when the mailman knocks too loudly. But she never asks where she came from. Not yet.

I stand in front of a high school auditorium in Hadleigh, the same town where everything started. The same town where it ended. Rows of students stare up at me, some bored, some curious, some clearly impacted already—clutching notebooks tighter, leaning forward, blinking back tears they don't understand.

I'm here as Detective Isadora Rose now. My badge is clipped to my belt, but I'm not here to investigate. I'm here to speak. To share the parts of my story that might keep one of these kids safe. Or strong. Or alive.

I breathe in through my nose, steadying myself. Behind me, the banner reads: Hadleigh High School - Empowerment Week: Real Stories from Real Survivors. I'm the final speaker. The lights are warm, and the room hums with quiet energy.

"My name is Isadora Rose," I begin, voice clear despite the tightening in my chest. "I was kidnapped when I was seventeen years old." A few gasps, a couple of widened eyes. I pause.

"I was held for nearly four years in a house less than thirty minutes from here. I was abused. Controlled. Starved. I was beaten into silence... until I learned to survive by pretending it didn't hurt anymore." The room is quiet. Even the ones who looked like they weren't paying attention now sit up straighter.

"I was not the only one taken. Another girl, a child, was brought into that home after me. Her name is Selecia. She was twelve years old. I had been alone for nearly two years when he brought her down to the basement and shackled her right beside me." My voice falters, but I don't let it break. This part always hurts.

"I made a promise to protect her. And I broke it, more than once. But we got out. We survived. And we're healing together." I pause again, eyes scanning the room. I see girls with tear-streaked cheeks, boys who won't look at me, a teacher dabbing at her eyes. And in the third row, a girl with her arms crossed tight across her chest, like she knows exactly what it's like to pretend you're fine when you're not.

"I'm here because I want you to know that survival is not the end of the story. Healing is messy. It's nonlinear. There are days I can't breathe in the middle of a crowded store. Nights, I wake up screaming. There are moments—watching my daughter sleep—when I feel an ache so deep, I think it might tear me apart. Because I'm so grateful she's here. And so angry that she came from something so violent." I inhale, deeper this time.

"But I'm also here to tell you, there is life after trauma. I became a victim advocate. I worked my way through school. I trained, applied, and was promoted to detective. I now specialize in cases involving missing and exploited children, because I know what it's like to wait for someone to care enough to look." A few students nod, wide-eyed. A boy in the back wipes his nose on his sleeve. The silence is heavy, but it's no longer uncomfortable, it's reverent.

"I was just a girl when I was taken. Now I'm a mother. A sister. A detective. A survivor. I do not belong to my pain anymore. And neither do you."

The applause starts slow but grows steady, a wave of claps that fills the air. I glance toward the teacher standing off to the side. She gives me a soft nod, mouthing, "Thank you." I take a step back from the mic, and then I see her. A little girl, no older than fifteen, was hovering near the edge of the stage. She looks like she wants to say something, but is terrified to move. I move as she steps closer.

"Hi," I say gently.

Her voice is a whisper. "Can I talk to you?"

"Of course."

She clutches her sleeve in one hand. "Sometimes… my stepdad says things that scare me. And he becomes furious if I talk back to him. My mom says he's just tired from work, but… I don't think that's true. I think he hurts her." I feel my heart splinter.

I lean closer, meeting her eyes. "Thank you for telling me. That was very brave."

She swallows hard, eyes glossy. "Is it bad if I don't feel safe?"

"No," I whisper. "It's not bad. It's honest. And I promise you, you're not alone." I glance toward the staff. A counselor is already approaching. Good.

"Would you be okay talking to her for a minute? She's really kind. And I'll stay nearby." The girl nods, her expression timid yet trusting. As the counselor takes her hand, I feel tears rise, not from sadness, but from purpose. Selecia is waiting for me in the back. We made it out. We're still here. We're still choosing life.

CHAPTER 99:
HEALING

The sunlight filters through the kitchen blinds in golden beams, casting stripes across the hardwood floor. It's a peaceful morning, the kind I never thought I'd experience again; soft, ordinary, safe.

Hope's giggles ring through the house as she races her plastic pony across the coffee table, her little legs swinging off the edge of the couch. She's five now—independent, clever, bright-eyed. Her hair's pulled up into a messy puffball of curls, and she's wearing her favorite pink dress with sparkly stars on it. She looks nothing like him.

Selecia stands at the stove, flipping pancakes like she's been doing it her whole life. She hums under her breath, her posture relaxed. She's nineteen now, confident in ways I never imagined back when we were just surviving. She's wearing an oversized hoodie and fuzzy socks, and for a second, it almost feels like we're just any other family.

I lean against the doorframe, coffee in hand, and take it all in. The warmth. The light. The normalcy.

From the living room, I hear Hope call out, "Mommy, look! She's doing a backflip!" referring to the pony. I laugh, my chest tightening in the best way. We've come so far. I sit at the kitchen table and glance toward the stack of mail. A pale blue envelope sits on top. I flip it over and see my name written in careful handwriting.

Inside is a folded letter from a teenage girl I spoke to at a school last month. Her words blur together through the sting of tears: *You made me feel seen. You made me feel like I wasn't broken.* She ends it with, *Thank you for surviving so you could help us survive, too.*

I place the letter on the table gently, then open my journal. The pages are nearly complete now—notes, thoughts, fragments of nightmares, and flickers of healing. Today I write:

We are still here. We survived. Not untouched but not destroyed either. Hope calls me Mommy. Selecia calls herself Auntie. And for the first time in years, I call this place home. Healing isn't a finish line. It's a rhythm. And we are learning the steps together.

A plate clinks down beside me. Selecia sits across from me, passing me a warm pancake with a smirk. "You're thinking too loud," she says.

I smile. "Just… grateful."

She shrugs, but her eyes soften. "You kept me alive, you know. Back then."

I shake my head. "No. You kept me alive. You reminded me who I was."

She looks down, then back up. "I'm proud to be Hope's aunt. And I'm proud of you." My eyes sting. I reach for her hand across the table, and for a long time, we sit there in quiet understanding.

That night, I tucked Hope into bed. She clutches her stuffed bunny and stares up at me. "Mommy… how did you know you wanted me?"

I brush her hair back. "Because I waited a very long time for you. And I will love you every day for the rest of my life."

She nods, satisfied. "Okay. Love you, Mama." As she falls asleep, I step outside into the crisp night air. The stars are out; clear, quiet, watchful. I breathe in deeply. For the first time in forever... I feel safe.

CHAPTER 100: THE ROAD AHEAD

The breeze carries the scent of fresh-cut grass and wildflowers as I walk up the steps of the community center. Hope skips ahead, holding a drawing she made—crayon hearts, a stick figure with wild curls, and the words I love my mommy scrawled across the bottom. It's taped to the podium, waiting for me inside.

Selecia trails behind us, phone in hand, her backpack slung over one shoulder. She's taller now. Braver, too. She's helping set up today's event—a survivor awareness night for teens and parents. Five years ago, we couldn't have imagined this moment. But here we are. I take the stage. The room quiets as I begin. My voice doesn't shake like it used to.

"I spent four years in captivity. I lost pieces of myself that I'm still finding again. But I also found strength I didn't know I had—and family I didn't expect to survive with. My daughter, Hope, was born from a time of darkness, but she is the light that gets me up every morning."

I pause, scanning the audience. "Recovery isn't a straight line. Some days are harder than others. But you are not alone. You are never alone. And healing is possible."

Afterward, a woman in the crowd hugs me with tears in her eyes. Her daughter clings to her side. A boy lingers after, asking shyly if I work with the police. I smile and nod. "Yes. I do." Because I'm not just a mother now. Not just a survivor. I'm a detective, specializing in child abductions. It took years of training, therapy, support, and persistence, but I made it. I use my past to find those still lost and bring them home. Later that night, we're all curled on the couch; Hope asleep on my chest, Selecia beside me, scrolling through college programs.

"Still thinking criminology?" I ask.

She nods. "Maybe psychology, too. You're kind of my inspiration."

I chuckle. "Kind of?"

"Don't get cocky." We laugh. Outside, the sky turns a deep indigo, stars flickering into view. Hope shifts in her sleep, one hand curled into my hoodie. There's no darkness here anymore. Only light. And love. And life is moving forward. The crash that nearly brought everything to an end gave way to something new. Something stronger. A future. And this time, we're in the driver's seat.

The End.

AUTHORS NOTE

Writing The Fatal Crash was one of the hardest and most healing things I've ever done.

This story was born out of a deep empathy for those who have endured the unthinkable. While fictional, it reflects real pain, real fear, and real hope. My heart goes out to every survivor, every person who has felt trapped, silenced, or broken. You are not alone. You are never alone.

I poured every ounce of my soul into this book—not just to tell a gripping story, but to honor those who have lived in silence. If this book resonated with you, I hope it reminded you that healing is possible, and your story matters.

Thank you for reading. Thank you for caring. And most of all— thank you for surviving.

Made in the USA
Columbia, SC
23 August 2025

61641370R00174